ABOUT THE AUTHOR

I0668975

Because Charlie Cochrane couldn't be trusted to do any of her jobs of choice – like managing a rugby team – she writes. Her mystery novels including the Edwardian era Cambridge Fellows series, and the contemporary Lindenshaw Mysteries. Multi-published, she has titles with Carina, Riptide, Lume and Bold Strokes, among others.

A member of the Romantic Novelists' Association, Mystery People and International Thriller Writers Inc, Charlie regularly appears at literary festivals and at reader and author conferences with The Deadly Dames.

THE CASE

OF THE

DEADLY

DECEPTION

Charlie Cochrane

WILLIAMS & WHITING

9781915887924

Williams & Whiting (Publishers)
15 Chestnut Grove, Hurstpierpoint,
West Sussex, BN6 9SS

Chapter One

April 1953

Dear Mr Bowe
*   You are invited to the next meeting of the Monday Evening Association. We assemble at seven thirty sharp, first and third Mondays of the month, in the offices of Herbert and Chapman, floor three, Clanfield House, Eagle Street, London. We appreciate that you are a busy man, so will understand if you can't join us on this occasion but we feel it vital you attend as soon as convenient.*
*   Yours sincerely,*
*   Lloyd Conway*
*   Chairman*
*   M.E.A.*

"Well, what do you make of that?" Toby Bowe, who'd thrust the letter into Alasdair Hamilton's hands almost as soon as he'd entered the latter's house—and then had waited with admirable patience for his fellow actor to peruse it—felt he could wait no longer. "It came this morning, forwarded from the studio, and I have no idea who Conway is or anything about this association he represents."

"I've never heard of him, either." Alasdair raised his eyebrow, the one which was heavily insured by Landseer Studios due to its notable capacity for expressing emotion. "Miss Marple was a member of a Tuesday Night Club, so perhaps these are fans of either Mrs Christie or detective fiction in general."

"I suppose that's possible, but they could have given a chap a clue as part of their invitation. What if I go there based on that premise, then find they're…I don't know…a group of artists who'd want me to pose *au naturel*?" Toby tapped the letter. "There's no address given for me to reply to, unless I send it via those offices."

"Hmm. It does smack somewhat of fishiness." Alasdair took the letter into his drawing room, where he stationed himself by the window to view it in a better light.

Toby suppressed a smile at the actions. Alasdair would no doubt not have given a thought to *himself* being seen in a better light, as well, nor to him presenting his best profile to the audience of one. He and Toby had been colleagues—and lovers—for long enough now not to have any element of vanity in their relationship. Yet what was done for the camera, or for the benefit of those in the stalls if the actor was on stage, could become habitual. And Alasdair did present a pleasing sight, standing with the missive in hand, the afternoon light catching his dark hair.

"So, what in the communication specifically smells of either fish, flesh or good red herring?" Toby asked as he settled himself into one of the comfortable fireside chairs.

"The name of the offices, for a start. *Herbert and Chapman*. Herbert Chapman."

"Oh, yes. The Arsenal and all that." Toby should have spotted the significance of the name. "If it's not a coincidence, it could be another indication of a love of detective fiction. An allusion to *The Arsenal Stadium Mystery*."

"I've not read that one. Should I?"

"Yes. It's quite fun. You'll have to imagine the men running around in shorts as the book isn't illustrated." Toby produced his cheeky grin, so beloved of newspaper and magazine photographers. "If Mr Conway and his merry band do enjoy reading of that type, perhaps that's the very reason they want me to attend one of their get-togethers."

"To talk about portraying Dr Watson on the screen or emulating his and Holmes's exploits off it?" Alasdair asked.

"Either or both. In each case they'd benefit from my inside knowledge." Landseer was unique in being the film studio that could boast of actors who were involved in detection onscreen and off.

"Then why not invite me to the meeting, as well?" Alasdair couldn't hide his disappointment at not being asked.

"Perhaps they have done and your invitation has been delayed in the post? They wouldn't invite us both via one letter, surely, as they can't—please God—be aware of the exact relationship between us."

"True. Or perhaps they are exclusively fans of Watson rather than Holmes. Let's check if Eagle Street exists, anyway." Alasdair went to his bookcase, selected the A to Z, then perched himself with it on the arm of Toby's chair. "Well, the road's here. Just north of Lincoln's Inn. Not an area I know."

"Indeed." Toby took the letter back, although studying it for further clues seemed a vain pursuit. "I think I'll get the Landseer people on this. *They'll* surely know if this Conway chap or his group have a reputation, say for inveigling film stars into their clutches then performing terrible things upon them. If Landseer advise me to go ahead, they might also provide a bodyguard, to prevent the clothes from being ripped off my muscular frame."

"Twit. The *Monday Evening Association* is unlikely to turn out to be populated by your adoring female public. Aren't they called something like *The Toby Bowe Appreciation Society*?"

"They are indeed and a more splendid bunch of women you could not wish to meet. I think you're right in saying this has to be a different kind of organisation, though: adoring male public, perhaps, given that Lloyd is a chap's name." Toby folded the invitation and tucked it in the pocket of his jacket. "I'll reply to him once Landseer give the go ahead. Perhaps I'm being over cautious, purely from

3

the lack of information. Whoever this group is, facing them can't be as dangerous as squaring up to a Junkers with a trigger-happy pilot."

Alasdair took Toby's hand. "One can only hope. And if they *are* genuine fans, too coy to advertise the fact, it would be a shame to disappoint them. Common decency must always be observed towards those who ultimately pay our wages."

"Let alone always observing the avoidance of adverse publicity." Toby chuckled.

"Were you joking about needing a bodyguard?" Alasdair asked.

"Only partly. It wouldn't surprise me if Sir Ian, should he get wind of this, insists I'm properly looked after. Some burly chap to act as chauffeur and be in the offing in case of trouble." Sir Ian Sheringham, head of the studio, wouldn't want one of his most valuable properties to be put into a potentially tricky situation. "Are you volunteering to disguise yourself for the part?"

"No thank you, much as I'm intrigued by the whole business. It's simply that I have someone in mind for such a role, should it be required."

"Are you going to tell me who?"

"You'll have to guess. Clue one, your godfather mentioned him a while back as being a useful person to have in one's corner if trouble was brewing. He'd helped him out with a case, I believe."

Toby furrowed his brow. "That doesn't narrow down the field much. He's often running across people, helpful or otherwise." Matthew Firestone, being one of the police force's most reliable—and successful—officers met plenty of folk and had many tales about them to regale his friends with.

4

"Then consider clue two. He's pally with the brother of one of Matthew's other godsons. I think I've got that right."

"Right or not, it doesn't help much, either. Matthew has stood at the font so many times he might as well be ordained. Another clue please, Sherlock. At the risk of me having to play an astonished Watson at how obvious the answer is."

Alasdair, who was evidently enjoying this greatly said, "Third and last clue. He has a connection to a certain person you're portraying in our upcoming release."

"Jonty Stewart? Oh, of course. We're talking about his great nephew, aren't we?"

"Correct, my dear Watson. Jonny Stewart, which is rather confusing name wise but at least memorable because of the similarity to Jonty. Except in your case obviously not memorable at all." Alasdair snorted.

Toby now recalled the conversation with Matthew clearly, but didn't want to admit that he hadn't been paying attention throughout, because there'd been a rather handsome waiter in the offing who'd been making eyes at him. It had taken all of Toby's concentration to ensure he gave no hint of response to the saucy chap, not least because he had all he needed—romance wise—currently sitting on the arm of his chair.

"Why do you have Jonny in mind, as opposed to anybody that Landseer could suggest?" Toby asked.

"It feels neat and tidy, with the Stewart connection." Alasdair liked things neat and tidy. "It might even be useful publicity if this thing somehow becomes public. Young Jonny carrying the family torch."

"Quite." They weren't portraying Holmes and Watson in this latest offering but the entirely real Jonty Stewart and Orlando Coppersmith. "You really do think there's something odd about this, don't you?"

5

"Yes. I couldn't tell you exactly why—a pricking of my thumbs, maybe—but it's like when we'd scrambled, and were flying in an apparently clear sky yet knew there were bandits about."

A shiver shot down Toby's spine. He remembered that feeling in every detail and hoped he'd never experience such a sensation again.

***

Those at Landseer studios who seemed to know everything there was to know—about anything—were tasked with looking at the letter and gave Toby his answer very promptly, or so he reported to Alasdair. There was apparently nothing in the communication from Conway that rang any corporate alarm bells, so if he wanted to attend the *Monday Evening Association* meeting on April the twentieth, he could.

"They say they don't recognise the name or address as being linked to any of their unpleasant correspondents. You know, like the ones who take umbrage at the way Landseer portrays Holmes and Watson, particularly your Sherlock getting his end away with whichever minx Fiona is playing." Toby grinned over his teacup.

They were both at the studios, grabbing a cuppa before a meeting about all the activities surrounding the launch of their new film. Fiona Marsden would be attending, too, she being the key third part of the Landseer star acting triumvirate. The fact that she'd recently begun a romance with Jonty Stewart's nephew, the present holder of the family title, wouldn't hurt publicise the new film, either.

"A chaste kiss in the final five minutes counts as getting one's end away, does it?" Alasdair said, with a snort.

"In the fans' eyes, yes, according to the complaints received. Although these folk are no doubt right in saying

6

that Sherlock never went so far with a woman. Nor man neither, I'd guess."

"He wasn't a real person, you know."

"*I* know that. Although I'm not sure everyone else does." Toby took a drink. "Apparently, 221b Baker Street receives post from people hither and yon wanting the great detective to solve their problems. Those letters can't all have been sent as a bit of a joke."

Good point. "And will Sir Ian allow you to go into the Eagle Street lions' den alone?"

"Absolutely not." Toby explained—much to Alasdair's satisfaction—that Sir Ian, had happened to drop into the department concerned when they'd been making their enquiries. "As a result of which, he's just sent me a note. He's worried about potential risks to yours truly and said that he'd need to organise somebody to go with me. I said you might have the very chap."

"Excellent. I'll ring up to Sir Ian's office, right now, and suggest Jonny. I've got two numbers for the latter, office and home, garnered from his great uncle Jonty."

"Have you? How sensible." Toby nodded approval. "What did the Cambridge connections think of the idea?"

"They gave it their whole-hearted approval. I also discovered more about the mystery he helped Matthew with. Remember that story about Ivor Gregg the actor going missing? Jonny and a pal of his were involved with getting that sorted."

"Well done him." Toby raised his teacup to make a toast. "I did wonder if Sir Ian was going to suggest *you* as my wingman but either he doesn't want to risk both of our handsome faces being bashed about or he's avoiding us being seen together too often when not on studio business."

"The second, I'd say." There was an increasing risk of people becoming suspicious, especially when none of the fledgling romances he and Toby were apparently involved in actually took flight. "Talking of which, I wonder which young ladies they'll hang on our arms for the premiere?"

"I'm due a rising starlet, although I have hinted that a bluestocking from Girton might be more fun and a novelty for the press coverage. I'm sure Jonty or Orlando have a suitable contact."

Alasdair raised his non-insured eyebrow. "That would be a novelty. It's a while since I was paired with a lesser daughter of minor nobility so I guess my partner will be along those lines. I do feel sorry for these women."

The machinations of the Landseer publicity offices, which provided the daughters of captains of industry or other eligible ladies as the actors' "dates" for events, had proved successful so far but surely there was a limit to how long they could get away with it?

"Quite. Hopes dashed and all that." If Toby was going to add to that remark, he was prevented by the arrival of his dresser, who wanted to nab him for five minutes, if she could, regarding one of the costumes for their next film, *The Heart That Wears the Crown*. With a grin and a, "No peace for the wicked," Toby let himself be taken off.

Alasdair could profitably use the time to ring through to Sir Ian, which he did without delay.

"Sir Ian? Do you have a moment?"

"I do, Alasdair. You just caught me before I go into a meeting about *Naughty Nelly*. Someone's having kittens about the title. And the script."

Naughty Nelly: there was a production that had already caused a problem or two, including losing its leading man to a fatal accident two days into shooting at the start of February. The role had been recast but production proper had yet to recommence. Alasdair hoped that the royal connection both films shared wouldn't prove an ill omen.

8

"Then I won't delay you. I only wanted to suggest a suitable bodyguard—if that's not too strong a term—for Toby, when he goes off to this strange meeting he's been invited to."

"Not too strong a term at all," Sir Ian said. "Do you have as strong a smell of rat as I do?"

"Absolutely. So does Toby, although not as foul-smelling an odour as ours. I couldn't tell you why, Sir Ian, and I haven't been quite so frank about it with him but I'm not at all happy about this invitation. If I can't go with him, which would no doubt be too great a risk on other fronts, then I want to do all I can to protect him, albeit vicariously."

"Agreed on both counts. You'll be in public view alongside each other often enough in the next few weeks, so if it's not official Landseer business or to do with your detecting work, I'd rather being seen together didn't happen." Sir Ian rarely put his foot down in such a way: the *Naughty Nelly* business must be getting to him. "It's a shame these two Cambridge chaps you're portraying are too long in the tooth to do the honours on the bodyguard front."

"Quite. Although the person I want to propose is of the same family—the Stewarts—and according to our constabulary friend Matthew Firestone, a good man in a tight corner."

"Another Stewart? They're getting everywhere, given Fiona's latest *amour*." Sir Ian chuckled. "Still, that would all hang together nicely with the new film, should it come to public attention. Can I leave you to organise that with him, please?"

"Of course."

"Now, while I have you. It may appear that I've been slightly tardy regarding your and Toby's companions for the premiere of *Death Stalks the College*, but I haven't. In fact, it was all set up a while ago, at the suggestion of your two Cambridge contacts."

"That sounds intriguing." Maybe Toby would be getting his blue stocking companion.

"We certainly thought so when we heard their idea. It also fits nicely with the film, given that the two ladies concerned both helped you clear up that recent case with the Victorian corpse in the vaults. Names being…" the sound of papers being rummaged through came down the line, "Mrs Bessy Cutting and Miss Geraldine Topley. The publicity department are going to make a splash about it over the next few days but we've had to hold fire because Miss Topley had a fall and we weren't sure if she'd have to pull out of the event and we'd need to call on one of the usual suspects. Luckily, she's fully recovered so can attend. I hope that gets your approval."

"It does indeed. Much better than having another young woman disappointed at the lack of follow up from either of us."

"Exactly. The public will love them being there, of course, suggesting as it does that one of *them* might end up on your arm on a similar occasion in future."

"That could be a suitable strategy for all such events." And an answer to the thorny issue of why their companions tended to be for one evening only. "You could hold a ballot or a raffle—a shilling to enter and all proceeds to the Royal British Legion."

"That's brilliant, Alasdair. I'll jot the idea down right now or else I'll forget. Can you let Toby know about the arrangements? You can fight over who gets Bessy and who gets Geraldine." Sir Ian chuckled.

"I will do so at the first opportunity. Good luck with *Nelly*."

"I'll need it. All the content is a matter of historical fact, of course, but the censor may cut up rough. We never have that problem with your films, and long may that continue.

10

Ave Imperator, morituri te salutant." With which comment, Sir Ian ended the call, leaving Alasdair to wonder at just how bad the upcoming meeting would be and how near the knuckle the script of *Naughty Nelly* was. Not anything that could be lodged against *The Heart That Wears the Crown*, even though it was frankly a piece of opportunism. One that had benefitted from Nelly's problems, because the delay in production had meant slack capacity in various departments which had allowed the Cambridge film to be whizzed out in record time and without the risk of it looking like a quota quickie. In turn, the coronation film could then be moved forward and got out in a timely fashion.

The Heart That Wears the Crown had a long history. The film had first been mooted in the early years of Landseer studios, some twenty years previously, in anticipation of the day when the then Prince of Wales would succeed to the throne and the screen representation of a coronation would chime with the real one being held in June. The general disquiet caused by both King Edward's abdication, and his choice of partner, had led to the film project being shelved indefinitely. Now, the country suddenly found itself with a young, beautiful queen, whose upcoming coronation was an occasion likely to shine as brightly as the diamonds in her crown amidst the lingering post-war austerity. So, the Landseer script was quietly dusted off and reworked into its present format, as suiting the trio of stars.

Assuming nothing awful happens to Toby at his meeting.

Alasdair decided to ring Jonny immediately, because if the man was unavailable, or didn't wish to take up the commission, then *he'd* have to go back to Sir Ian cap in hand to report his failure. Fortune must have been smiling on the endeavour, though, because Alasdair not only caught Jonny at work, he professed himself delighted to help, particularly when told that Matthew Firestone had recommended him. "It all sounds very mysterious, though, Mr Hamilton."

"Call me Alasdair, please. And yes, too mysterious for anyone's liking. We might be being over-cautious but as your great uncle Jonty may have told you, we do our own bits of sleuthing, in a small way, and it's possible we've made an enemy or two as we've done so." Which idea had only come into Alasdair's head that moment. Not that he could think of any specific enemies offhand, but those they'd helped to convict would have friends and relatives who might seek revenge.

"If there's any rough stuff, I'll be prepared. Should Toby and I meet beforehand to make a plan of campaign?"

"Sounds a splendid idea. I'll get him to give you a call this evening, if that's convenient. You can sort out the details between you both."

"Aye, aye, captain. I'm looking forward to it."

"Cheeky scamp," Alasdair said, with a grin. It sounded like Jonny and Toby would get on like a house on fire, the pair of little rascals. Surely between them they'd be able to cope with anything Mr Conway's meeting had to throw their way.

And *he'd* have to sit on his hands, to ensure he resisted all temptation to lurk in the Eagle Street area on Monday evening, just in case another pair of hands—or fists—were needed.

Chapter Two

Monday evening at the appointed time, Toby stood outside Clanfield House scratching his head. "What do you make of this?"

Jonny Stewart eyed the board which listed the occupants of the building, then he too scratched his head. "There's no firm called *Herbert and Chapman* on there."

"Correct. No floor three listed, either."

"It's definitely the right building. Perhaps the name plate fell off the board." Jonny shrugged. "Strange start to the evening, though."

"Quite." The temptation to simply turn tail had been growing in Toby since the point the heavens opened, halfway through his taxi journey, when he'd realised he'd forgotten his umbrella. He'd reminded himself that wasn't the spirit which had helped win the war and steeled himself to get wet. The clouds, however, while at present threatening, had temporarily finished dumping their contents on London. Toby peered through the glass of the door. "I think there's someone we could ask inside. After you."

Jonny led the way into the foyer, where a rather bored looking man sat at a desk. He rose and gave a desultory salute. "Can I help you, gentlemen?"

"We're here for a meeting. Offices of *Herbert and Chapman*, on the third floor, only the name plates outside don't help." Jonny held his hat rather like a schoolboy might when visiting a sweet shop and enquiring after the availability of bulls-eyes.

"Oh, them." The porter rolled his eyes, then peered at Toby. "Are you that actor?"

"I'm *an* actor, yes."

"We get plenty of them here. Visiting the theatrical agents on floor two or dropping into where you're going. I could name names, but I won't." He pointed to the stairs. "Anyway, it's up three flights and turn to your left. There's one of the crew there already, although not his nibs."

"Mr Conway?" Toby asked.

"That's the one. And here he is."

Toby turned, to see a well turned-out, middle-aged gentleman—with an air somehow suggestive of a solicitor working in a small town—coming through the door.

"Mr Bowe! Such a delight to meet you in person." Conway thrust out his hand. "You're taller than you appear on the screen."

"Thank you. People usually say that it's the other way round." Toby gave him his most practiced *dealing with the public* smile. "This is Jonny Stewart, by the way. I'm afraid the powers that be at Landseer didn't want me trotting off into the unknown without accompaniment, especially when we're so close to a premiere."

"Oh. How do you do?" Conway, after a brief look of puzzlement, annoyance, or both, shook Jonny's hand. "Yes, we should have expected you wouldn't come alone. You're welcome, Mr Stewart."

"It's a pleasure to be here." Jonny flashed a grin as charming as his great uncle's. "Although we're not entirely sure what this is about."

Conway waved his hand, airily. "Oh, you'll soon find out. Come along. Thank you, Fred."

"Delighted, Mr Conway," the doorman replied, in tones that conveyed anything but pleasure.

Toby and Jonny followed their host up the stairs, to a dimly lit corridor on what—by counting—must have been the third floor. To the left was a door bearing the words *Messrs Herbert and Chapman*, through the glass panel of which a light shone.

14

"I have to confess that this made me smile." Toby indicated the name. "Touch of 'Come on the Arsenal!'"

"Billy Chapman's my cousin and he lets us use their premises for our meetings." Conway smiled. "He gets plenty of football jokes thrown at him, given his partner's name, which is galling because he can't stand the game."

"I bet that annoys him." One apparent peculiarity appeared to have a mundane explanation.

"So, you came." Toby jumped as a female voice sounded behind him. He spun round to face a pretty, dark haired woman, perhaps in her mid-thirties, who was wearing black slacks, a red jumper and a tentative smile. "Sorry to have startled you, Mr Bowe. I'd been off powdering my nose. I'm Moira. And this is…?"

"Jonny Stewart." Toby waved a hand at his companion. "I can't be allowed out on my own, according to the studio."

"Are you that vulnerable? Lucky the RAF didn't think the same." Moira grinned, then turned to Jonny. "Stewart as in one of the main characters in Mr Bowe's upcoming film?"

Jonny bowed. "The very same. We have a habit of poking our noses in, the family Stewart, so I'm keeping with tradition."

"Ignore him," Toby said. "He's also here to provide moral support as I had no idea what kind of meeting I was agreeing to attend."

"Ah, yes, sorry. I should have been a bit more explicit in my letter but it's rather difficult. Still, all will be clear soon." Conway opened the office door and ushered them into a large, well-appointed room. Several other doors led off from it, including a couple labelled with the names of the principals, although at least three people must have worked in the main room, given the number of desks and the elegantly printed desktop signs that gave their names. Mr J

Salt, Miss L Fraser, Miss R Young. Were there any Arsenal connected surnames there? Toby might have to consult his football mad nephew. Nevertheless, indications were that *Herbert and Chapman* was a genuine firm, although what business they were involved in wasn't clear.

"I know it's never easy," Moira said, "meeting a group of strangers with whom you have little in common, although I suppose you're used to it in your business, Mr Bowe."

"Please call me Toby. My mother would never forgive me standing on ceremony."

"Well, we mustn't disappoint her. Now, you'll have to excuse me while I go and make refreshments. Would coffee be acceptable to you both?"

"Splendid, thank you," Toby replied.

"Rather. Need a hand?" Jonny asked.

"That would be very kind." Moira inclined her head. "Until I grow another pair of hands, it'll always be a juggling act." She and Jonny set off for some inner sanctum, while Toby made a further assessment of his surroundings. A ring of comfy looking chairs, interspersed with the odd small table, suggested they were expecting seven people to be in attendance.

"Will we want another one for Jonny, Mr Conway?" Toby indicated the seating arrangements.

"No need. I always set an extra place. In case of waifs and strays." Conway chuckled, making the large, hairy mole on the side of his cheek bounce up and down in a manner reminiscent of Alasdair's eyebrow. "Please call me Lloyd. As you say, no standing on ceremony."

Toby jerked his thumb over his shoulder, towards the front of the building. "I hope your waifs and strays aren't as confused as we were when we arrived. There's no name plate out there for *Herbert and Chapman*, nor any reference to this floor."

16

"The other office on this level is at present unoccupied, I believe. As for Billy's business, it's of a delicate nature—they handle the kind of cases that other firms might be loath to take, so they exercise as much discretion as possible and also keep publicity to a minimum. They get plenty of custom by word of mouth."

Again, a reasonable explanation, although one that didn't quite answer the question. "While it's just the two of us here, you said in your letter it was vital I attended one of your meetings. Why was that?"

Any answer Lloyd was about to provide was forestalled by a man bursting through the door. "Am I late?" he asked. "This blasted watch keeps losing time."

"No, you're fine, Richard," Lloyd said. "A tad early, if anything."

"Excellent. Shall I go and offer Moira my services with the old coffee cups?"

"Three would be a crowd and it's a small kitchen. She's got an extremely charming young man helping her out. Mr Bowe's bodyguard." Lloyd grinned, slyly.

"Jonny would be amused to hear himself called that, although in essence it's true. They're very protective of their personnel, are Landseer." Toby thrust out his hand. "Pleased to meet you, Richard."

"The feeling's mutual." Richard cast a little-boy-lost glance at the door Moira had gone through. "I'd better take a seat, then."

"Excuse me while I just…" Lloyd headed for one of the desks, where he began to go through some papers.

Toby, who'd been feeling increasingly wrong-footed since the moment he and Jonny hadn't been able to find the name plates, wished he'd been the one to offer his help with the refreshments, rather than being left to twiddle his thumbs. He plonked himself in a chair and studied the newcomer for a moment. Richard possessed an air redolent of his having come straight from a rival studio, where he'd been working on a film—black and white, definitely—and perhaps starring John Mills doing something heroic in a spitfire five hundred feet above Kent. Albeit there were plenty of men with a similar air about them, still carrying it from the world war or from the Korean. Then you had to count those for whom national service had left a stamp upon their character, so perhaps Richard wasn't so unusual. In terms of his age, which Toby would estimate as early forties, he'd would surely have seen active service yet the vague air of artificiality about the man proved intriguing.

Why not ask him? "What do you do, Richard?"

"Eh? Oh, my job, you mean? Nothing glamorous. I'm an actuary."

"That sounds frightfully clever. Numbers, isn't it?" And proof that Toby's deduction had been completely wrong.

"Yes. Using them to assess risk and the like. It keeps me out of mischief." Richard gave an unexpected—and charming—grin.

"What does?" A deep voice sounded from the door, as another man, of a similar age to the others, entered the room.

"Playing with numbers. Good evening, Jeff."

"Bonjour, Richard." Jeff made a bow in his direction and then in Toby's. "Bonjour, esteemed guest."

"Pleased to meet you, Jeff." Toby returned the bow. Here was another slightly theatrical character: if Lloyd and Moira hadn't appeared to be normal—meaning not putting on an act—Toby would have believed he'd walked into something resembling a play rehearsal. Still, perhaps Richard and Jeff were simply nervous, which could make people behave in a peculiar way.

Before the conversation could continue, Jonny backed into the room bearing a tray laden with steaming cups. "Here we are," he said, "although I can't take any credit for this, other than acting as a pack mule."

Another round of introductions followed, then a distribution of coffee and biscuits, with Lloyd returning from whatever he was doing and people settling into their seats to drink. Toby still felt perplexed, even if Jonny—who'd clearly hit it off with Moira—looked completely at home, as if he'd been coming to these meetings for ages. Maybe when Toby had got a biscuit or two inside him he'd feel a bit more upbeat, the therapeutic qualities of a custard cream being well known.

"I think we're all here, so we can crack on," Lloyd said, glancing around the circle and pausing briefly when he came to the vacant chair. "Mr Bowe deserves an explanation about what we do."

At last. "As I keep saying, call me Toby, please. I'm not royalty."

"Toby. Let me start by saying that we're not anything obvious, such as a set of film buffs with a particular interest in Landseer, nor a group of people who spend all their time trying to explain away the contradictions in the Sherlock Holmes books."

"You must be a mind reader, Lloyd, because that's two of the options I'd considered." Toby took a bite of biscuit, aware that his quip had produced an oddly discomforted reaction in the group.

"None of us have that particular facility, alas. We do, however, each have special qualities. Skills, one might say, that slightly sets each of us apart..." Lloyd waved his non-cup holding hand to take in the whole group. "That's our connection and why we meet, because nobody else understands. I'm sure you, as an actor, appreciate that no-one could, for example, comprehend the challenges concerned with making a film unless they were in the industry."

"That's very true. I suppose it's like those who served in a certain undercover capacity during the war. Beyond the comprehension of those who weren't at the heart of it." Toby hadn't just used the analogy to show his agreement: he was hoping the reference might bring a reaction, a shared experience of such work within this group would make sense of what had been said. No reaction came, apart from nods, although perhaps his drawing a bow at a venture hadn't been such a clever idea. Folk who were involved in undercover work would have been adept at keeping it undercover.

"I feel I should clarify what Lloyd means," Moira said, earning herself an annoyed glance from him, "when he says that we're all a bit different to the norm. I know that every person is unique in both personality and abilities—I could never produce the magical effect on the screen that Miss Marsden seems to have—but our uniqueness is...well, unique."

Toby and Jonny shared a bewildered look, before the latter asked, "You'll have to be more explicit. Are we talking about being scarily clever, like my famous great uncle and his pals?"

"Good lord, no!" Richard said, probably more fervently than he'd intended to, given his subsequent embarrassed expression. "Nothing as handy as being highly intelligent. In fact, the skills we've got are practically useless." That didn't quite go with being an actuary, although that might be English self-deprecation in action.

"They're not useless skills." Moira gave him an encouraging smile. "We just haven't yet found the best application for them. There's nothing we could have used them for during the war, Toby. Not like the combination of hand, eye and sheer nerve that would have helped make you such a good pilot. Didn't I read somewhere that an ex-Luftwaffe officer said you'd developed a reputation among them?"

"I believe so. I don't think that was the studio publicity machine making hay. I have to say it's my parents who should take the credit for supplying me with the qualities you've mentioned and I'd add a healthy dollop of luck to that listed. Better men—better pilots—than I was didn't have the success or make it through. Perhaps it was the twelve-sided threepence my mother sewed into my uniform that acted as a lucky charm." Toby took a sip of what was surprisingly good coffee. Maybe Moira's special skill was being a dab hand in the catering department, although that would hardly be unique, even in Britain.

"But you've been able to use your abilities to serve your country twice over, Toby," Richard said. "Defending the skies and then raising spirits post-war. I have my facility with numbers, which *did* prove useful when I was in logistics, because planning's vital to the war effort, but I wish there'd been some way to use my other skill."

"Which was…?" Jonny prompted, evidently fed up with not being given any detail.

Richard sat up ramrod straight, then glanced at Lloyd, who nodded. "I always know how long the sermon will be as soon as the vicar begins to speak."

Jonny's chuckle—quickly suppressed and apologised for—mirrored Toby's first reaction, although his acting ability meant he'd been quicker about hiding it. "I'm afraid I must be being rather dim. Could you explain that, please?"

"Of course, Jonny. As I said, I can predict the length of a sermon, irrespective of who's preaching. I'm accurate to the nearest tenth of a second, possibly to the nearest hundredth, although nobody in the congregation generally has a watch precise enough to test any of those decimal places." Richard gave Moira, who was sitting on his right, a little smile.

"A hundredth of a second?" Jonny whistled. "That's the most impressive thing I've heard in ages."

The pair of them sounded entirely serious, as though Richard was reporting an innings he'd played at Lord's and Jonny was truly enraptured by the account.

"Thank you. Not everyone is as appreciative of my skill. There are conspiracies. My friends here have heard all about them, so if they'll indulge me for a moment while I recount them again…"

"Go ahead. I never tire of hearing about them," Jeff said. "You won't believe this, Toby and Jonny, but fellow members of the congregation try to catch me out."

Toby, grateful that he'd had so many opportunities to practice dissembling when in public with Alasdair, put on a fascinated expression while he tried to work out what was going on. Richard didn't appear deranged, nor did the other three, who seemed to believe every word he said. It was especially true of Moira, who was gazing appreciatively at the man's handsome profile, wrapped up in a story that was becoming increasingly bizarre. Maybe Toby was asleep and dreaming and would soon wake to discover it was still Monday morning.

Richard was pressing on. "People employ the deeply underhand stuff often found in an Anglican church full of ladies and gentlemen old enough to know better. Even the rector's in on it, starting off at a lick from the pulpit then slowing down, in an attempt to wrong foot me."

"Isn't it awful?" Moira said. "So cruel. Especially from people who call themselves Christian."

"They can be the very worst," Jonny said, shaking his head. "Some of the least Christ-like people I know are

Christians." That could have been his great uncle talking. "Do you turn the other cheek, Richard?"

"I'm afraid that's something I've struggled with. I have too often been tempted to get my own back, thereby rendering any attempt to nobble me completely worthless. You see, I don't base my prediction on anything logical like the preacher's prior form, nor the bulk of his notes. I just know, in the same was as *you* know that it's daybreak when the sun comes up. I'm always right, no matter what people do to prevent it." Richard eyed his audience. "Last winter, I was coming down with a touch of the flu and, being groggy, I accidentally said the predicted time out loud when the vicar mounted the steps to the pulpit. I was *so* loud that he heard. He began by speaking as slowly and deliberately as possible, to extend the length of his talk—everyone knew what was up, of course, so they were smirking and whispering. I began timing him, which I don't do routinely, because it grew boring after the seventeen time of being right."

"This is wonderful," Jonny said. "I mean, it's inexplicable, but it's an oddity I appreciate."

Alasdair deserved a special thank you for having suggested Jonny as a companion for the evening: the young man was taking everything in his stride. If Toby had been on his own, there was a good chance he'd have been making an excuse and leaving at this point.

Instead, it was time he chipped into the conversation. "That's a low blow for a vicar to make. Can I ask how they knew you could predict the sermon time, in the first place? You don't sound like you're the type who would go around boasting."

"I'm not, Toby. I'd rather nobody at all knew what I can do, outside of this room. The thing is, I got rather drunk at the harvest supper of 1949 and told the vicar's wife. Of course, after that it all spread like wildfire."

That detail sounded accurate. "So, what happened with the case of the ecclesiastical nobbling? Which, incidentally, sounds like something Alasdair and I might tackle in one of our Holmes and Watson films."

"It would make a good film, if a rather comedic one, especially as the vicar was hoist on his own petard," Richard replied, clearly delighted at Toby's interest. "He still had at least two pages of notes to get through with only one second left on the clock, at which point the church boiler exploded. Brought a premature end to his game and prompted an evacuation of the building. I emerged victorious with an old lady on each arm, whom I helped to safety."

"The hero of the hour. Does the vicar ever try the opposite?" Jonny asked. "Galloping through his notes to beat the time you've set?"

"Oh, yes. Just the once, about a month after the boiler incident. This time it was the curate, who was preaching at evensong, and had the gall to ask me before the service how long I thought he'd be in the pulpit for." Richard's eyebrows were almost as eloquent as Alasdair's at expressing his disdain.

"How would he know you weren't lying with the answer you gave him?" Toby asked, then had to remind himself that there was little point in making such a cross-examination, as surely none of this could be true.

"Because he knows I wouldn't tell a lie in church. Even if I wanted to, I couldn't because people see right through me. I had my chance during the war to use my facility with numbers to…well to do more interesting things than logistics but I had to decline the offer. I simply don't dissemble very well, and my face would have given me away if questioned about it. Anyway, I told the curate the

24

predicted time and he went off with a smug grin, so I was expecting trouble. When he started off preaching, he went at a hell of a lick—if he'd carried on like that, he'd have been well inside what I'd forecast." Richard paused, milking his audience's interest. "But then he had a coughing fit. Swallowed a fly or something and almost choked. By the time he was given a glass of water and recovered sufficiently to continue, my forecast turned out to be bang on." The smug grin plastered across Richard's face suddenly disappeared. "I sound horribly like a show off. I'm not."

"I don't think any of us are," Lloyd said, soothingly. "We can't help what skills we've been given—it's how we use them that counts. Thanks for being brave and going first."

"I think it was less being brave than being sensible. Getting the trauma out of the way." Richard sat back, arms crossed.

Lloyd turned to Jeff. "Would you like to enlighten Toby and Jonny about your special gift?"

"I'd be delighted. I can't claim anything as spectacular as old Richard here and I feel rather embarrassed because it does benefit me personally, unlike his skill which reaps no rewards." Jeff had laid down his cup and, seemingly alongside it, his over-hearty persona. He sounded deadly serious. "I always get a seat on a tram, or the underground, or whatever. No matter how busy it is."

Jonny must have been better prepared for this strange revelation, saying, "That sounds handy."

"It's been very useful. Picture this: it's the rush hour and along comes the bus. There's no sign of a spare place to park your backside—excuse the crudity, Moira—but as soon as I get on, an empty place appears and down I sit." Jeff raised his hand. "Now, before you think I'm being a touch selfish, that's a debate I've had with myself since it first happened. Am I somehow taking advantage, when I shouldn't be? So, obviously, I make a point of giving the seat I've found to somebody who really needs it, like an older person or a lady. I wouldn't want them standing when I'm perfectly capable of doing so."

Toby couldn't resist asking the obvious, despite the doubt it cast on the account. "Are you sure it's not simply a run of exceptional luck, Jeff? Like the run of luck I'm certain I experienced when we scrambled all those times and I came home unharmed."

"You might think so." Jeff glanced uneasily at Lloyd. "But it's gone on too long, too consistently, and the details are too intricate. For example, I have to con myself in advance that I'm actually going to keep the seat if I get one. It never seems to work out if I'm determined to give it away to the woman next to me on the station platform who seems to be in an interesting condition. In that instance I don't get a seat at all. It's very complicated."

Complicated or self-delusional? And why the shifty glance?

"Tell Toby about the crash," Moira said.

"Oh, yes. That happened quite early on in this palaver and was one of those strange events that had me wondering if there was more to what was happening than luck. It was long before I met Lloyd and he explained everything, of course." Jeff gave the man concerned a nod. "So, back in 1944 I was home on sick leave, getting over a nasty break to my lower leg. Don't ever attempt a ship's ladder in a force eight gale off Sheerness. Anyhow, I was recovering well and only had a week left before I needed to be re-embarking, so I set off up west for a meal and a show. For some reason all the buses were heaving with passengers, but I got on one and, of course, a seat was waiting for me because someone hopped off at the last moment. I didn't feel too guilty at

26

first, because I was still a bit ginger about the old tibia and its recovery. Then the heavens opened and I remembered two old gents who'd been at the bus stop with me and I thought of how they'd be getting drenched, as a result of which I felt dreadful. I had my greatcoat on so would have been fine and that pair could have been left catching their deaths."

This was quite a story, but was it real? This account also had a certain cinematic quality, as might have been depicted in an arty black and white film from an avant-garde director and the level of detail appeared over-egged. "Did the bus crash?"

"Yes. A lorry was coming in the other direction, had to brake suddenly, lost control on the wet road and ploughed into us. I only learned the details afterwards, because all my attention was on thinking about my old men and I have almost no memory of the accident itself. I woke up in hospital, concussed and bruised but otherwise fine. When I discovered that the conductress and one passenger had been killed and several people injured, my first thought was to be grateful that I'd got the seat and not one of my old codgers. I knew it was all meant to be."

"Which just proves how valuable your ability was." Moira gave Jeff a smile.

Toby would agree—if the tale was real—but nothing yet had addressed the question of why he'd been invited to hear these confessions. At present, assuming he hadn't been picked on by a bunch of semi-lunatics, the only idea he'd come up with centred on that theatricality of what he'd heard. Did those present want to suggest to Landseer that they make a film about the group's alleged powers, a madcap farce that would make *Henry Himself*, the studio's biggest earning comedic hit, seem positively staid?

27

Maybe it was the other part of Toby's life they were interested in, the increasingly well-known penchant for amateur detection. If they had something that needed investigating, like a missing group member—hence the extra chair—or some funds that had gone astray, they might want to call on his skills and this was simply providing what they felt would be relevant background.

"Moira, your turn, I believe," Lloyd said.

"Well, if I must…" Moira rolled her eyes, in a way that Fiona could have emulated with aplomb. "I always have the correct money to pay for things."

"Well, *that's* more than useful." Jonny beamed.

"Thank you, Jonny, although if you're expecting it'll be my round in the pub, later, then I'm afraid you're mistaken." Moira gave him as charming a smile as Fiona could have produced, and who could blame her? Given his handsome face and impeccable manners, Jonny could easily find himself a role in films, if he got bored with whatever he did to earn a living. "It's not as straightforward as it might appear, so I'd better explain."

Jonny raised a hand. "Before you do that, please can I apologise about my remark. I'd hate to have you think that I was wanting to take advantage of your largesse."

"I don't think that at all. Although it's true that I generally hate people knowing about what happens, because someone would want to make gain from it." Moira shook her head. "The chaps here, as you call them, never do."

Funny that Moira wanted to keep her supposed ability secret because of worry about being taken advantage of but hadn't mentioned keeping it secret because people would think her strange.

"That's because we're gentlemen all," Lloyd said. "You don't have access to infinite resources, do you, Moira?"

"I do not. And if there's no change in my pocket to start with it won't miraculously appear there just because you want me to buy you a pint of Guinness. For example, having the correct money couldn't happen in the specific instance of going to the pub tonight because my pockets are empty at present. If I go and put some coppers in there now, in anticipation of a specific event, nothing will happen, I'm afraid."

Toby took a deep breath. Funny how these so-called abilities were hedged about with conditions that rendered them incapable of objective testing.

Moira continued. "To clarify, if I *do* have small change, it always turns out to be the correct amount I need, whether the bill comes to one and eleven or three and sixpence halfpenny. As a once off, though, because afterwards my pockets are empty."

"Are you always in profit or do you make a loss?" Jonny asked, again giving the impression that he was discussing something mundane.

"It varies. If I start out with five bob and I need to pay seven and six, then I'm up. If I've got three half crowns to start with but the bill's two and eleven, then that's suddenly how much I've got and I'm money down." Moira shrugged. "I used to keep a running account, but I soon found that the ups and downs just about balance. I'm never going to make it onto the rich list, but I won't go stony broke, either."

This was all becoming too much for Toby. "Hold on," he said. "Young Jonny seems to be on top of all of this, but I'm feeling completely baffled. I'm struggling to take it in."

Moira patted his arm maternally, despite the fact they must have been a similar age. "Of course it is, Toby. All of us here have struggled to comprehend what's going on but then we've each had times in our lives we thought we were the only ones who could do these strange things. It's wonderful to discover we're not alone."

Alasdair was going to love hearing about this. Toby could imagine both of his lover's eyebrows tapping out a morse code-like series of messages conveying disbelief and concern. He doubted Alasdair would let him come to another meeting, though, even if he wanted to and irrespective of whether he had an entire rugby scrum of bodyguards to watch over him.

Time for action. "Lloyd, before you explain to me what your special ability is, please could you tell me why I've been invited here?"

"Isn't it obvious, Toby?" Lloyd said.

"It clearly can't be, or he wouldn't have asked," Jeff cut in, with a hard edge to his voice suggesting he was also losing patience.

Lloyd shot him a withering look. "Thank you, Jeff. Toby, you've no doubt got the general gist of our little group. We've all got unique abilities. Mine, which is relevant to my answer, I assure you, is that I can detect people who possess these special gifts. Richard was the first I met, and we've added to our number steadily." Another glance at the empty chair before pressing on. "Therefore, I knew as soon as I met Jonny downstairs that he's unlucky enough not to possess any exceptional skill. You, however…"

Toby shook his head. "I'm sorry to disappoint you, but my special power is simply helping to get seats filled in the cinema and that's hardly unique to me."

"Are you sure?" Lloyd, eyes narrowed, scrutinised him.

"Absolutely positive. I think if there was anything else I was able to do I'd know by now. Unless it helped me be a better pilot, in which case it hardly seems to fit the bill as you've explained it to me."

"Unless you've not yet had to employ whatever your skill is," Richard said.

"Well, I suppose that's possible." Although Toby didn't believe a word of it. He'd also noticed Lloyd's brief look of annoyance when Richard made the suggestion. "I'm sorry not to be able to join your club," he lied, "but thank you for inviting me along. I wish you every success for the future."

"Hear hear." Jonny rose from his chair. "It's been a pleasure to meet you all."

"You don't have to go, either of you," Moira said. "You can be our guests for the evening. I'll make more coffee."

Toby, who'd already edged towards the door, raised his hand. "We couldn't impose any further on your wonderful hospitality. You'll no doubt have business to discuss that might be awkward to complete in the presence of outsiders and we've been honoured enough to have been given your confidences. I promise that nothing we've heard today will go further." Except into one particular set of ears.

"You're a gentleman, sir. As are you, Jonny." Jeff left his chair, came over and shook both their hands. "You're welcome to drop into any of our meetings, as far as I'm concerned. Either or both of you."

"Thank you." Toby nudged Jonny's arm and they quickly made their escape.

Once safely outside, the doorman having greeted them with a cheery, "Off early? Don't blame you!" as they went past, Toby said, "Well, what do you make of all that?"

Jonny puffed out his cheeks. "I don't know. Got a load of thoughts buzzing around my head and wouldn't mind discussing them with a third party. Are you going to brief Alasdair on what's transpired?"

"Naturally." Toby eyed Jonny sidelong as they headed to find a taxi. "As soon as is feasible."

31

"If it's any help, can I say that the aged great uncle Jonty not only gave me some sound advice concerning the Ivor Gregg disappearance I was involved in clearing up but also about my friendship with my pal Roger. It was regarding the nature of our relationship with each other, advice which I swiftly acted on and I'm jolly glad I did. Hopefully that might illustrate that you're in sympathetic company. Him and Professor Coppersmith, Roger and I…" Jonny gave him a shy grin.

Toby came to an abrupt halt. "Well, I'm blowed. Does everyone know?"

"Don't worry, Uncle Jonty hasn't mentioned anything about you and Alasdair, him being a discreet old bird. But any man like myself would have the chance of noticing the way you look at each other when you're Holmes and Watsoning, even if the average person doesn't. If I've got that deduction hopelessly wrong, then please pretend I said nothing, or give me a stiff right to the jaw: either is acceptable. If I'm correct, can you take what I've said as a long way round of stating that if you were intending to pop across and see Alasdair now, please can I tag along? I promise to make myself scarce when required."

Toby chuckled. "Perhaps Lloyd was wrong when he said you didn't have one of these daft powers the rest allegedly have. You seem to have read my mind about where I'm due to head next." He shot out his arm to hail a cab which had conveniently come around the corner. "We'll go there right away."

Chapter Three

When Alasdair opened his front door soon after hearing Toby's distinctive tattoo on the knocker, he was surprised to find a young man, who must have been Jonny Stewart, standing on the doorstep as well.

"This is Jonny, but you'll have deduced that already, Sherlock," Toby said as he bustled into the hallway. "He's proved invaluable tonight and hopefully will carry on the good work when it comes to the briefing we need to give you. It's been quite an evening."

"One that seems to have ended earlier than expected?" Alasdair ushered them into his sitting room.

"We left before the meeting ended," Jonny explained. "Actually, I don't suppose it was even halfway through."

There was clearly an extraordinary tale to relate. "You must be in need of a refreshment. I've an excellent bottle of hock in the refrigerator, although it's a case of fend for ourselves, as Morgan's having an evening off."

"Let me go and organise three glasses and a corkscrew," Toby offered. "I'll leave Jonny to make the speech he made earlier which persuaded me to bring him along. I warn you, it's long-winded."

"It won't be, this time," Jonny said to Toby's back as the actor left the room. "You know about the Ivor Gregg stuff but you may not know the exact relationship between me and my pal Roger with whom I worked on the case. The aged great-uncle provided pearls of wisdom on that front, he and his mathematical professor being exceptionally well placed to understand the personal situation. As I believe you and Toby also are, which is why he let me tag along, given that I'm not going to go blabbing about why, for example, he seems to be so at home in your house."

If that wasn't the long-winded version, Alasdair dreaded to think what the young man had said to Toby. "Pleased to hear about the lack of blabbing. Discretion must always be our watch word."

"Quite. I wish all men in our position would be as sensible." Jonny ran his hand through his blond locks. "This *Monday Evening Association* malarkey is going to need a touch of discretion, too, although not in the same way."

"It certainly is." Toby backed through the door with an opened bottle in one hand and three glasses expertly held in the other. "While I pour, do you want to provide a factual outline of what happened, from the moment the doorman made that rather waspish aside when we were on the way in, up until the one he made when we were on the way out? I propose there be no comment or speculation from any of us until Alasdair's been brought up to date."

"Am I allowed to pose any questions?" Alasdair asked.

"Only for clarification purposes. It's been an experience, old bean, and one I'm still trying to process, so reliving the last few hours will help me get my thoughts a bit clearer. Here." Toby handed Alasdair a glass of hock. "Yours is on the way, Jonny."

"Thanks. Well, here goes…" Jonny started the tale with the pair of them on the pavement, unsure they were in the right place, then took in the doorman, the arrival of Lloyd and volunteering to help Moira with coffee, at which point Toby took over.

Alasdair listened with growing incredulity. If he hadn't been able to read Toby like a book, he'd have suspected that he was having his leg pulled, especially when they got to the bit with Moira and the spare change in her pocket. But it was clear Toby was in deadly earnest and that the evening had unsettled him.

"And there you have it," Toby said, when he'd reached the part where he and Jonny were back on the pavement again. "With *Gentleman Jeff* assuring us we had a standing invitation to come back as far as he was concerned, while Lloyd had a face like a wet Wednesday."

Jonny nodded. "There's an atmosphere between those two and I suspect Lloyd didn't like his place as leader being usurped. I rather pumped Moira while we were doing our Lyons Corner House stuff with the coffees. She implied the club was a bit of a support group for people with a shared experience, although she didn't let on anything about this unique powers nonsense. She did say that Lloyd's the driving force behind it all. And at no point did I get the impression that she's dotty. Feet firmly on the ground, I'd say, so either I'm a poor judge of character, which is possible, or she's as good at acting as you two."

"That's the feeling I got about Richard and Jeff, as well," Toby said. "Richard said something about not being able to dissemble but I sensed that was false modesty."

"But that's not the impression you got about this Lloyd chap?" Alasdair asked.

"No. He's…" Toby shrugged. "Intense. You should have seen his face at the point when he insisted I had some special ability and I insisted I didn't. He wasn't surprised or disappointed, more like angry at being made out to be in the wrong."

"So, if he was the only one of the group who came across as odd, then how do you explain all this stuff about sermons and seats and all the rest? Do you really believe these things happen outside of a comic book or a Marx brothers' film?" Alasdair didn't.

"Of course not, Alasdair. It's the discrepancy that's so intriguing." Toby twirled his glass, studying the golden liquid as though it might contain the answer to the mystery.

"We've all of us experienced things that defy rational explanation, and there are stories a-plenty from wartime that folk swear are true, like the *comrade in white* from the Great War. These stories didn't have the same ring to them, if that makes sense."

"It does to me," Jonny said. "Great uncle Jonty explains away some strange coincidences as being due to his Mama sitting on her cloud manipulating events on earth to her satisfaction. When she's not checking that the angels are wearing enough layers against the cold. He's had some strange events in his life, too. You know what happened with him and Orlando in 1919?"

Alasdair nodded. "A story that beggars belief, except we know it's factual."

"Exactly. I may be wrong but, like Toby, I don't think this was a case of angelic intervention."

"So," Toby said, "the only explanation I've come up with so far is that these powers aren't real but *they* might believe they are, especially if Lloyd's so insistent that he's right about them."

"That might be so," Jonny said. "If Jeff has convinced himself he'll get a seat on a bus, then every time he does so, that's more justification of his belief. On the occasions he doesn't, he simply puts it down to one of those exceptions he talked about, so the exception is never made to test the rule. He says he's conned himself into saying he'll keep the seat so he can give it away or some such rubbish. He also said at one point *if* I get a seat, rather than *when*, which I suspect was a slight giveaway. Anyway, as self-delusions go, it's one that's pretty harmless, I'd have said."

As Jonny spoke, Alasdair studied him, Jonty having warned him that his great-nephew liked to present himself as being like one of Bertie's feckless pals from a Jeeves and Wooster story, hiding the fact he wasn't at all lacking in

36

brains. What Alasdair had seen so far bore out that assessment.

"I'd accept the *deluding himself* theory," Toby said. "If the story of Jeff's accident is true—and that's one of the few things which *could* be checked—it's possible the experience might have…let's say it affected his perceptions of reality. Maybe that's when his belief first arose."

"That's an excellent point." Alasdair stroked his chin. Toby would have heard the upcoming confession before and perhaps had it in mind when he'd spoken. "When I began operational flying during the war, I'd usually come back from a sortie to find out that some poor sod, maybe a pilot who was much better in the air than I was, hadn't made it home. The first few times that happened, I tied myself in knots asking why, but one of the more experienced chaps soon took me under his wing and put me right. He said that in the end you just have to accept that's the way it is: a particular German bullet had someone else's name on it and not yours. I know at least one other pilot who couldn't accept that and drove himself half mad trying to come up with a logical explanation."

"Wartime can play awful tricks on a mind under pressure." Toby gave him a sympathetic smile. "So, we can rationalise Jeff's story. What about Richard? There's a significant point of difference to Jeff, because the latter doesn't appear to have confessed to anyone except the Monday evening crew. Whereas Richard says he let his story slip to the vicar's wife, as a result of which people try to catch him out with his predictions. That's harder to account for."

Jonny, who'd drained his glass, waggled it, rather like a prop. "Not if you look at it from a completely different angle. What if, rather than being delusional, he's putting on

37

a show, probably to impress Moira, whom he fancies like billy-oh."

"Does he? I missed that." Toby rose, to fetch the wine bottle. "I must have been too wrapped up in trying to work out why they wanted me there."

"One up to the Stewarts for spotting it, and the fact that she seems to like him, too. If he was another of Lloyd's mistakes, he might have been so overcome with passion on his first visit that he had to make up a story, plumped for the sermon thing and then was stuck with it. A tale he had to embroider, hence all the details about the boiler blowing up and the choking episode. Thanks." Jonny held out his glass to be refilled.

"That makes sense in view of what you've related," Alasdair said. "It would be very difficult to check up on his story unless you visited his parish and even then Richard might pretend that the vicar had sworn all the congregation to secrecy because he didn't want to bring attention to their church."

"There was certainly an air of artificiality—for want of a better word—about him," Toby observed. "As there was with Jeff at first, although that might have been nerves. People often put on a show when they're finding their feet with strangers. And what about the lovely Moira herself?"

Jonny shrugged. "She strikes me as being least easy to explain away."

"Do you think she's pretending for Richard's sake," Alasdair asked, "or wouldn't that work chronologically if he's trying to impress her?"

"It might work if she's doing it for Jeff's sake. She gets invited by Lloyd, who's got it wrong again. First meeting she attends, Jeff's there, she goes swoony, makes up some nonsense, etc etc." Toby placed the empty bottle back on the tray then took his seat once more. "Again, who's to prove or disprove the exact change thing, because she also put a proviso on it about not being able to plan it in advance. Richard's the only person who seemed loophole less."

"Perhaps he's not been able to come up with a suitable one," Jonny suggested.

"What about this Lloyd chap?" Alasdair asked. "He says he knows when people have a special ability. Is that all a front to get a certain group of people together for some underhand reason? Did he strike you as nefarious?"

"Not at first. He came across as business-like, explained the *Herbert and Chapman* name stuff in a reasonable way and generally appeared sympathetic and caring towards his little crew. It was only when I insisted that he was wrong about my so-called powers that he put on a face like thunder." Toby studied his glass again. "He suggested that maybe I hadn't had to use them yet. No, I correct myself, because it was Richard who said that and Lloyd shot him a dirty look. Perhaps that's *his* loophole and he didn't appreciate having his thunder stolen." Toby launched into a northern accent. "You do have powers, Mr Bowe, but you're not aware of them yet because they've not come into use. Give it time, tha knows."

Alasdair snorted. "Your devoted Yorkshire fans would be less than devoted if they heard your attempt at their brogue. Does Lloyd really talk like that?"

"He does," Jonny confirmed. "Without the 'tha knows' or any such expressions from East of the Pennines. I'd agree with Toby's assessment of him whole-heartedly. The man's got a temper, or a chip on his shoulder, or both. I saw the way he looked at us when we left and that was pure daggers. Incidentally, the business with the name plate still puzzles me. Or business with the lack of nameplate, to be precise."

"Lloyd did come up with an explanation for that while you were canoodling with Moira in the kitchen. I should have mentioned it already, sorry." Toby wrinkled his nose. "He said the firm doesn't publicise its location because they handle delicate business for their clients and wish to maintain discretion for them. Whether he means they deal in high class divorce cases or something much more shady, along the lines of entrapment, I don't know. The offices gave the impression it was both a genuine firm and a busy one."

"That impression's correct," Alasdair said. "I couldn't just sit here contributing nothing, so I've been doing a bit of digging the last few days. As part of which I had the good sense to mention the company name to Morgan. He'd heard of the firm, through one of his pals at his gentleman's gentleman club and remembered the name because of the Arsenal connotation. *Herbert and Chapman* appear to operate as a combination of solicitors and private investigators, and they do handle a wide range of cases. From a tricky divorce to those that are both unpleasant and controversial. The eldest son of a peer of the realm gets caught doing something unmentionable to little boys and they're the people to go to in order to have the best chance of either getting him off or having it hushed up. That's not a theoretical example, by the way. They're rather good at creating a plausible scenario to suggest that the accused is an innocent victim."

Toby shuddered. "How vile. I feel dirty all over now, just from sitting in the office."

"There's more. Remember Charles Carstone, the actor?" Alasdair asked.

"The chap whom Landseer brought in to play Charles the Second in *Naughty Nelly*?" Toby nodded. "Jonny, this fellow tripped and fell under a train at somewhere like Bank on the Central Line, when he was on his way home. Killed pretty well instantly."

"Chancery Lane, although the rest is correct," Alasdair said. "There was speculation about whether it was more than a mere trip, but the inquest—going on witness testimony—concluded it was accidental. No evidence that he was pushed or that he'd thrown himself under the wheels."

"In fact," Toby cut in, "he had a good Samaritan nearby who grabbed him, almost effected a rescue and then had themselves to be hauled back before there was a double tragedy. Of course, Carstone was an actor and, like us, would know how to make a supposed stumble look realistic. If he had a life insurance policy, it would be nullified in the case of suicide, which is incentive enough to put on an act."

Alasdair nodded. "Keep that possibility of a faked stumble in mind, because Carstone was apparently one of *Herbert and Chapman's* clients. Possibly a less savoury one, which was kept under wraps."

Jonny puffed out his cheeks. "Landseer doing its cover-up work again?"

"I doubt it," Toby replied. "Sir Ian may wink at our relationship, but he'd draw the line at interfering with children, if that's what this Carstone was accused of, so he can't have known."

"It can't have got as far as a police charge, either," Alasdair pointed out, "or that fact would surely have come out at the inquest. So, possibly he feared something emerging and took his own life. Or we're jumping to the wrong conclusion."

"Irrespective of that, Morgan *has* done well turfing up all this information." Toby gave an appreciative bob of the head. "I wonder if Moira and the rest know what goes on in those offices during the day?"

"They might not, given the less savoury aspects are not common knowledge. Except to those like Morgan who know everything about everything." Alasdair grinned.

"I hope the club members don't realise," Jonny said, "because I liked all of them. Except for him in charge, of course."

"Ditto. Here's another thing, Alasdair," Toby said. "There was one more chair in the little circle than necessary for the number of backsides present. Lloyd gave a vague impression he might have been expecting someone else."

Jonny nodded. "He definitely eyed that empty chair a couple of times. As though perhaps somebody had been invited on the off chance, like you were Toby, but had yet to show."

"Or had attended in the past but had stopped," Alasdair suggested. "And for whom they always leave an empty chair in the hope that he or she will reappear one day?" A nice missing person's case would be gratifying to stick one's nose into.

"That's possible." Toby frowned. "Do you think that Lloyd's invitation was merely a ruse and they actually wanted us to investigate something, like a member of the group who's mysteriously gone missing?"

"That would make more sense than this taradiddle about who can do what, but why not ask you outright?" Alasdair pointed out.

Toby shrugged. "Perhaps they were testing me out, making sure I was as nice and reliable in real life as I always am on the screen. Or perhaps they'd meant to ask me to help, but because I had Jonny alongside and they were unsure of his role in things, they were waiting for the next time to come clean. I have a standing invitation to attend whenever I want, so they might be hoping I reappear."

"Perhaps. Although that's a risk, given that you upped sticks and left early. Why not say something while you were still at the door, if it seemed their last chance?"

"Maybe they were reluctant because it wasn't all the group who wanted to avail themselves of your services," Jonny said. "What if it was Moira or Jeff, or any combination of three, who had the idea of searching for their lost member but didn't know how to go about it. Then Lloyd tells them that Toby Bowe, actor and amateur sleuth, has powers like they do and has been invited along to a meeting. They see this as their chance."

"Why not start with the police if you want to find a missing person? Not meaning to be argumentative, Jonny, just testing your theory." Alasdair rose. "Time to open another bottle of hock, or would you prefer port?"

"Whichever lubricates my brain cells best, if my ideas are to be under such rigorous scrutiny." Jonny held out his glass as Alasdair came to collect it. "What if they went to the police and got sent off with a flea in their ears, given that the missing person was a grown man or woman with no dependants. Or they *had* dependants, but they were the sort that one couldn't blame them for wanting to get away from. Perhaps it's as simple as the police having more important cases to deal with at the time."

"There are other reasons why people don't go to the police. They have things they want to keep hidden and would rather not take the risk of bringing themselves to official notice in any way. Ah, excellent." Toby admired the glass of port Alasdair had given him. "An excellent colour: this will be a treat."

"I hope so." Alasdair slipped into his favourite chair once more. "I'll accept your arguments and follow up with another question for the pair of you. Why do you think it's the others, not Lloyd, who want someone found?"

"Two things. The objective fact that the open invitation for us to attend another meeting came from Jeff, not Lloyd, and the subjective fact that I really didn't like the latter

43

whereas I liked the others." Jonny rolled his eyes. "Instinctive, I know, and the sort of sloppy thinking that Professor Coppersmith probably slaps his students' legs for."

"Instinctive reactions aren't to be dismissed," Toby said, "if they support an idea rather than become the idea itself. People talk about feminine intuition or a man having a hunch but I'm sure it comes down to our brains working behind the scenes, analysing what we see and hear and coming to a conclusion. We've both, independently, decided there's something unpleasant about Lloyd."

Jonny nodded. "Well, if we're allowing hunches, my other conclusion from tonight is that there's something going on below the surface of that group and, while I'm not forming any definite ideas as to what that is, I'm itching to know more. I'd be happy to return to the fray in a fortnight and see what transpires. Although I suppose if it's *your* investigational expertise they want to tap into, then that may not get us any further forward."

"Would you go back, Toby?" Alasdair asked. "Not on your own, I hasten to add, because having listened to what you've said I'm still concerned they could be a bunch of lunatics. Sir Ian would be having kittens if he were here. What will you tell him, by the way? He'll be wanting a report."

"To take your questions in order, I don't know. Like Jonny, I want to know more, but I'd rather tackle Moira or Jeff on their own, or else I don't think we'll get any further forward." Toby caressed his glass, clearly still processing the events of the last few hours. "Yes, I would take a wingman with me, not simply for protection but because two eyes are better than one. Jonny picked up things I didn't and vice versa. As for Sir Ian…I think I'll drop him a note telling as much of the truth as I can. An outline of the

44

evening, my gratitude to Jonny, our feeling that this might be about a case and a promise to keep him updated."

Alasdair nodded slowly. That seemed a reasonable strategy. "Sir Ian has eyes and ears working for him everywhere—as does the Landseer publicity department—so the story might even ring a bell."

"People who bother actors for reason unknown and now it's Landseer's turn?" Jonny asked.

"Who knows? It's a strange world, as Matthew Firestone could tell you. Can I ask if Jonny is short for Jonathan, by the way?" Alasdair added.

"It is. Named after the aged great-uncle, but we had to have a different shortened version to avoid confusion." Jonny chuckled, handsome face alight with glee. "Awkward when one of us is in trouble and we get the full *Jonathan*, because who's being picked out? We tend to assume both of us are being referred to, as that's always possible."

"That sounds like Toby, here. Always getting into mischief."

"Alasdair, now that I've met you both, I can see exactly why you were cast as my notable relative and his partner for this film you're about to release." Jonny looked from Alasdair to Toby and back again. "There's only a general physical likeness, but personality wise it's an excellent fit and that enhances the resemblance."

"You can thank Landseer for coming up with such an excellent idea," Toby said. "The film project not only gave us paid employment, it helped us get involved in a long-dormant case. I dare say you've heard all about that."

"I have. The body in the crypt." Jonny, face suddenly serious, laid down his glass. "I do hope that violent death isn't what we're dealing with here. People who've gone missing—whether of their own volition or not—and who can be found and returned to the arms of their loved ones is one thing. Cold-blooded murder is another."

***

"Jonny's a nice lad," Toby said, when they'd returned to the sitting room after taking leave of their guest. "Both bright and perceptive. These traits clearly run in the family."

"He's discreet, too, although not so much that I didn't notice his amused little smile when he left. The one that smacked of, 'I'll make myself scarce so you can get up to whatever you want to get up to.'"

"I wonder if he's off home to his pal Roger so they can get up to whatever *they* want." Toby stretched and yawned. "It's a shame we can't take advantage of the opportunity he's given us."

"Quite. We'll have no problem turning up tomorrow with a face full of stubble, but if the pair of us are both yawning and looking more than a touch worse for wear, it would hardly help the Landseer cause. Let alone the risk it presents of accurate conclusions being drawn about what we'd been up to."

The next morning would see them attending a charity event hosted by a shaving cream manufacturer, which involved various actors—who would not be allowed to have shave beforehand—being rendered smooth-skinned. Alasdair wasn't clear how it could help promote their new film but if the Landseer publicity department was certain it would, then its knowledge must be bowed to. There'd be other nights they could spend together.

"A kiss or two before I depart?" Toby pulled Alasdair towards him. "As a sort of deposit against future favours to be claimed?"

"I think that would be more than acceptable."

When they broke the clinch, a touch tousled, Toby reached up to ruffle Alasdair's hair some more. "You'll have to slather on the Brylcreem, tomorrow. You won't necessarily have any of the support team to wrestle these locks into control."

"I wouldn't bet on that. We'll be on parade, Toby, so we could well find ourselves being preened and prettified. Costume all ours, though, so make sure you're as dapper as a male mannequin."

"I've a new blazer for the occasion. I'll be dazzling."

"You always are, sweetheart."

Chapter Four

On Thursday, the Landseer regulars were once more assembled at the studio to discuss a revised shooting schedule and other practical matters for *The Heart That Wears the Crown*. When Toby arrived, he handed the receptionist an envelope addressed to Sir Ian, and asked for it to be despatched to the great man's office as soon as convenient. It contained an outline of events so far, one which would hopefully not occasion too much alarm. In return, the receptionist handed Toby a letter which had arrived in the Wednesday afternoon post.

"We knew you'd be here today so didn't redirect it," she said, with a smile befitting the matronly, no-nonsense woman that she was.

"Thank you, Brenda." Toby studied the handwriting on the envelope but it didn't appear familiar.

"It's already been opened and checked, as I believe Sir Ian has insisted on at present?" Brenda had evidently been told why the envelope was unsealed but not the reason behind it and appeared to be fishing for an explanation.

Toby wasn't going to provide it. "One can't be too careful these days. Both our fans and our detractors can get a little over-excited." He extracted the letter, read it, then carefully pocketed the thing. "Are Miss Marsden or Mr Hamilton here yet?"

"Mr Hamilton, yes."

"Thank you." Toby headed off for the room where they'd be assembling, in the hope that he'd catch Alasdair before they needed to make a start on the business of the morning. He should see this latest communication as a matter of urgency.

When Toby reached his destination, he found Alasdair, cup in hand, chatting to Alexander Rattigan, their usual director.

"Toby!" Alexander gave him a wave. "Can I pour you a coffee?"

"Please. May I borrow Alasdair for a second, though? I've had a letter I want him to take a gander at."

"Of course. Is this to do with your mysterious group? Alasdair was outlining your adventures." Alexander handed Toby a steaming coffee. "It's like something out of one of our scripts."

"That's what it felt like on Monday evening." Toby waved the letter. "Come and see this, Alasdair." He took his fellow actor off to one side. "There have been developments."

Dear Mr Bowe

I believe that we owe both you and Mr Stewart an explanation. When you left our meeting you must have borne a very strange impression of us.

Toby sniffed as they read the content together. "That's putting it mildly."

The thing is, whatever Lloyd thought he was doing that evening, it wasn't my intention, nor Richard or Jeff's. We got rather too involved with who reckons they can do what and rather forgot the effect that could have on someone who wasn't expecting to hear it.

"She appears to have read the situation well," Alasdair observed. "I wonder if the word *reckons* has any significance."

"Implication that at least one person was making up what they were saying or that the group has its doubts about the veracity of the stories? You could be right."

We'd rather explain in person, if we may, assuming we can find a convenient place and time. Perhaps Mr Stewart

49

would like to be present, as well, and we'd also extend that invitation to Mr Hamilton, who appears to be your partner in solving crime.

"Just try and stop me being there," Alasdair said. "I've a feeling there are plenty of revelations left in this business and I'd rather witness them in person."

"Quite rightly. There's plenty of nuance missed when you hear something reported as opposed to getting it straight from the horse's mouth, no matter how well the report is made. Or how effective the accent," Toby added, with a cackle.

I'll understand completely if you'd rather not meet any of us again but if you could find the time to do so I believe you'd find it both interesting and...I'm struggling to find the word I want. Vitally important, if not to you then to our country, or so we believe. You can contact me at the telephone number given above, during working hours.

Alasdair pointed at the number. "Whitehall exchange. She does move in exalted circles. I wonder if this is connected to her work?"

"Meaning she has to go around the houses because of she can't openly discuss it? Possibly."

Please don't mention any of this to Lloyd, should you have any further correspondence with him. Again, I'd rather explain everything in person. Richard and Jeff are aware that I'm writing to you and would like to be part of any future meeting.

Sincerely

Moira Matthews

"Well, well. Are you going to ring her?"

Toby snorted. "Are you going to kiss Fiona in this new film?" He lowered his voice. "I know our diaries are full in the forthcoming weeks with the premieres and all the other stuff that accompanies them but we've got a couple of evenings set aside for *moi et toi, seulement*, so if you'd be happy to divert one of those to this other cause…"

"Of course. We'll still have the night that follows said evening," Alasdair whispered.

Before Toby could reply, the arrival of Fiona signalled that they had to return to business. Concentrating on the matter in hand, given the tempting thought of a night spent in Alasdair's bed, would require every ounce of professionalism.

When they broke for lunch, the postboy brought Toby a reply from Sir Ian. It thanked him for the update and gave him carte blanche to proceed as he and Alasdair saw fit, so long as they exercised common sense and didn't put themselves into danger. As far as Toby was concerned, that carte blanche meant he didn't at present have to give a further update regarding this latest communication, nor on what they intended to do about it. They would take Jonny along to provide another set of fists.

After Toby had eaten enough lunch to keep him going through the afternoon, he made his excuses to the supporting actors he was sharing his table with and went off to find a telephone somewhere quiet. Why not try to catch Moira as soon as he could? The publicity department, whose members were already briefed about the *Monday Evening Association*, would be the ideal spot.

He managed to get through straight away on what must have been a direct line. "Miss Matthews?"

"Yes? Oh, is that Mr Bowe?"

"It is indeed. Thank you for your note. I confess myself most intrigued by it."

"That's what I intended. We—Richard and Jeff and I—were so worried that we'd sent you running for the hills, never to be seen again. It must have been a lot to take in and things aren't quite as they appear." She paused. "Could you

51

bear to meet us in person again? Lloyd won't be there if that makes it easier."

"That proposed meeting is what I'm calling about. I have a few dates that both Alasdair and I could make. I hope they'd work for Jonny, because he also has a bit of a pedigree in solving crimes, as you put it." That was a slight exaggeration, although Toby and Alasdair's investigational career—if it could be called by such a name—had started with doing a friend a favour and looking into what had become of someone who'd apparently vanished.

"I hope he can attend, too. We'd like him to understand the truth, as well, and not be left thinking we're a bunch of lunatics who should all be in Colney Hatch. I also put together some dates on the off chance that you'd be in contact. How does next Monday suit?"

"That's on my list of available dates. Did you have a venue in mind or should we book somewhere?"

"A couple of times we've used a private room at *The Swan with Two Necks*, which is off Ealing Broadway, if that's not too far. It's a classy sort of place."

"Then that sounds perfect. Seven o'clock too early as a rendezvous time?"

"I was going to suggest something similar. I'm sure you've no need of beauty sleep but I have to take all I can get." Which couldn't have been fishing for compliments, because before Toby could reply, Moira said, "We'll see you then," and hung up.

Toby picked up the scrap of paper where he'd been jotting down the details of the venue and time. How had this Swan place—it surely had to be a pub, given the name—ended up as Moira's regular venue?

When he returned to the studio dining room, Alasdair was still there, drinking coffee and apparently perusing a script at a table on his own.

"Appointment made," Toby said, as he plonked himself into the seat opposite his partner.

"I assumed you'd gone to ring Moira, so I lurked here reading and trying to look like I wanted to be alone."

"Good idea, Greta Garbo. Or did she say she wanted to be left alone?" Toby pushed the paper across the table. "Place and time. It's apparently a posh pub and according to Moira we can get a private room. She's used it before and whether it was for her and the other two or on different business, I didn't ask. I suspect she'll be a lot more forthcoming without *himself* being present. She made a point of assuring me Lloyd won't be there. 'If that helps' or some such words. I hope Jonny can also be there on Monday, so that if the evening ends up in a straight fight, we won't be outnumbered. I don't want to square up to Moira, though, because I bet she'd get me in a half-Nelson before I drew breath."

"Daft beggar. Will you ring Jonny and inform him or will I?"

"If you could, that would be helpful. After this afternoon's session, I have to go straight to a soiree with my actual fan club. I'm getting the make-up department to spruce me up beforehand, so that I don't let the team down." Toby smoothed back his hair, which he felt had got a touch dishevelled in his rushing around. "Although you've a similar event to attend, haven't you? Young Jonny might have to wait until tomorrow."

"I'll squeeze him in somehow." Alasdair grinned. "I have to pull my weight in this business."

"You always do." Toby drained his cup. "And now, for a stirring tale of secret royal romance, or whatever the publicity department will describe it as."

Alasdair sniffed. "It's rather a treat making this film. Slightly different to recent offerings but still fitting nicely into the Bowe-Hamilton-Marsden oeuvre."

"As well as being a convenient way to cash in on upcoming events. Rumours of some time on location in a thinly disguised Italy, too, unless they can make Cromer or wherever double convincingly for somewhere that most definitely isn't England."

"Yes. We can't make the connection *that* obvious, although nobody could take offence at the concept. It's an as yet unmarried king being crowned, it's set both in a past age and in one of those strange, somewhere-in-the-middle-of-Europe type of countries that only exist between the pages of a book or in a screenplay." Alasdair shook his head. "And even Fiona in her pomp might not be as glamorous as our Queen."

"Her Majesty certainly has a film star's charisma. Hm." Toby pursed his lips. "Italy. Doesn't Orlando have a drop of Italian blood in him? Some ancestral Coppersmith who obliged a noblewoman in the bed department and got amply rewarded for it, if I'm not mistaken."

"He does. The obliging chap was an actual copper smith, too, I believe. I don't suppose that connection is part of a plan to make this next film dovetail with the Cambridge one, but it might be useful for the publicity wallahs to milk, if they can play up the family history and bowdlerise the services provided." Alasdair shrugged. "Perhaps we'll have another Coppersmith and Stewart film next in line, rather than a Holmes and Watson."

"Who knows? Whatever carries on paying the wages." Toby rose from the table. "We should report for duty. Although thinking of Watson makes me also remember Holmes asking him to take his service revolver on their potentially dangerous assignments. I hope we won't find ourselves needing something similar next week."

Chapter Five

The weekend promised a flurry of activity. Toby and Alasdair managed to snatch an evening together on Friday before the debut of *Death Stalks the College* the next day, and then had yet another charity event scheduled for them on Sunday.

When Saturday came, Alasdair found himself relishing the premiere more than he had any previous opening night, helped enormously by not having the strain of a fake girlfriend on either his or Toby's arm. Bessy and Geraldine soon turned out to be ideal dates, both dressed up to the nines and clearly loving every moment from the very time they were deposited by a Landseer limousine at the pre-party venue. They proved intelligent, witty, interested in everything that was going on, and not given to any flirting. Alasdair felt he could relax and enjoy himself, almost in the way he might had Toby been allowed to be his escort for the night.

"I have to confess that my daughter has threatened never to speak to me again," Bessy said, as she cradled a glass of champagne. "Not only for being Landseer's guests but for the whole package. Dresses and hairdressing and all."

Geraldine chuckled. "I insisted the young lass who did my make-up didn't obscure all my wrinkles, or how else would people know it was me if they saw my picture in the newspaper? By the way, is Dr Stewart going to be here this evening?"

"Alas, not." Toby sighed. "There's a clash in their diaries with a major event at St Bride's. He and Professor Coppersmith will be chatting up prospective benefactors for the college, so a mere cinematic release has to play second fiddle. We're having another bash in Cambridge on Wednesday, where the film will make its East Country

56

premiere and they'll be attending that one as guests of honour. We get to dine in St Bride's beforehand, which will be rather exciting."

"Two premieres means twice the fun and twice the publicity." Geraldine gave a knowing chuckle. "So, Alasdair, have you two got a case in progress at present?"

"We might and we might not. All will hopefully be clear by Monday night. If the matter involves any connection to the environs of the *Old Manor*, we'll know whose help to call on." Alasdair attempted a tricky manoeuvre of his eyebrow, suitable to not-quite-flirting with an elderly lady.

"Are you allowed to give us any details or is it all hush-hush?" Geraldine asked.

"It's all jolly peculiar," Toby said. "You're two eminently sensible ladies. What would you think if someone you met—in fact, more than one person—told you that they possessed strange powers? We're not talking about being able to fly, like Superman, or even the athletic prowess of William Wilson, who's my nephew's favourite character in his boys' periodicals. I'd like to give an example of the powers they claim, but wouldn't want to use a real one, as we're not sure yet what we're dealing with. Sorry to be so vague."

"You're forgiven. It all sounds intriguing, doesn't it, Geraldine?" Bessy gave her friend an understanding look, as though they dealt with this kind of thing all the time. Maybe the life of a typical Sussex village contained more strange goings-on than Alasdair gave it credit for.

"It does," Geraldine said. "Could you suggest something similar in nature to what these people claim to be able to do?"

Toby frowned. "Well, let's say that I claimed I could read people's minds but only when they were in the queue for the Odeon cinema. And then I forgot what they were thinking when I left unless I wrote it down while still in the queue. The actual claims are equally peculiar and specific, with some provisos about situations in which they don't work."

"Hm." Bessy narrowed her eyes. "If the person telling me was aged under seven, I'd say they were indulging in make believe and that they might well truly think they could do these things. The borders of reality and imagination aren't clear cut when you're small. Were they aged over seven, though, I'd think they were deliberately making things up to get attention. Are these people desperate to attract folk's notice or be lauded?"

"Yes, no and don't know." Toby shrugged. "Sorry, that's quite a hopeless answer but it's the best I can do at present. The individuals give the impression that they don't want people at large knowing what they're capable of, but each clearly values being amongst what they regard as their peers. They were a most pleasant bunch. The chap, Lloyd, who leads the group appears a different kettle of fish."

"How interesting," Geraldine said, dark eyes shining like black pearls.

"Indeed. I couldn't read him. It wouldn't surprise me if he wants to expand his little group for some reason, like self-aggrandisement. I could be slandering the man, though, because my impression is mainly based on the fact that I didn't like him."

"What did you think of him, Alasdair?" Geraldine asked.

"Not as yet. That's why Monday evening will be key, when both dogs get to see the rabbits, although not Lloyd, though." Alasdair frowned. "This man even had the audacity to suggest that Toby himself possessed one of these bizarre powers. Which he insists he hasn't, and *he* should know."

Geraldine sniffed. "Your Lloyd reminds me of several people I've known through the years, all of whom have wanted to be as big a fish as they can in whatever small pond they find themselves swimming in. They start to form a clique and either browbeat or inveigle people into joining it. I don't suppose he likes anyone challenging him?"

"You suppose correctly." Before Toby could provide any further insight, an announcement came that they had to be on the move. A red carpet, a throng of fans and a showing of the new film awaited.

***

Death Stalks the College proved to be a rip-roaring success with the first night audience, inducing the obligatory sighs, gasps and chuckles in all the right places. Alasdair thought he'd rarely seen Toby look so handsome onscreen, while Fiona positively glowed, no doubt due to the influence of her—at the time of filming—fledgling romance. He'd spotted one of the more discerning critics in the audience and the chap had given Alasdair a thumbs-up, so unless he was being two-faced, they should have at least one positive review in the morning papers. Not that a lacklustre write-up was likely to put off any of their most ardent fans.

"That was lovely," Bessy said, when they met up again for a drink afterwards, the actors having had to go off in the interim, to take their bows and accept the applause. "You've got all Dr Stewart's mannerisms to a 't', Toby. Am I right in saying I spotted him and the professor in the background in the scene where you were taking Miss Marsden punting?"

"You were spot on. Dr Panesar was there, too," Toby replied. "That handsome Indian gentleman with the magnificent white beard."

"*I* noticed him and I wish he'd been featured throughout. Quite heart-fluttering for we mature ladies." Geraldine fanned herself with her hand. "Will you be calling on our Cambridge friends to help with your new mystery? Assuming that it turns out to be something in need of solution."

"Only if we feel they have specialist knowledge to offer us," Alasdair said. "They tell us they have case of their own, even now and we wouldn't want to impose on their time."

"I see." Geraldine snorted. "Or is it a case of not wanting to share the fun?"

Toby laughed so hard he nearly spilled his drink. "You read us like a script, Geraldine. There is something satisfying about working a problem through by oneself."

"Ah." Bessy shared a look with her friend. "If that's so, are we allowed to make another contribution or has our chance gone?"

"Feel free, given that we asked you," Alasdair said. "I'm guessing you wouldn't count amongst those Toby wouldn't want involved, as you're not amateur sleuths."

Toby nodded enthusiastically. "He's right. Unless you *are* detectives and are hiding the fact from us, of course."

Bessy raised her fingers, like a girl guide making a vow. "I promise we're not, although I can understand how people get smitten with the activity, because while you were up on the stage, doing your waving and smiling, Geraldine and I were having a chat about your people and their peculiar claims. We've got another possible explanation or two about what might be going on. Only it might be a touch far-fetched."

"It's *not* far-fetched. That's Bessy hiding her light under a bushel," Geraldine said. "She was reminded of her aunt, in the aftermath of the Great War. Go on and tell them." She gave Bessy a nudge.

"I don't think I'm going to be able to explain my thoughts very well but here they are. Before I get onto Aunt Beatrice, let me tell you why I thought of her. You say the next bit." Bessy returned the nudge.

"We were discussing those folk who want to brag about their war exploits," Geraldine said. "We all know people who exaggerate real events to the extent they become a blatant lie, so I wondered if this applied here."

"You mean there could be a grain of truth in the stories?" Alasdair glanced at Toby, who raised an eyebrow and then shrugged. "Odd things did go on during the war—bizarre experiments and the like—that we heard rumours about, didn't they, Toby?"

"Absolutely," Toby agreed. "Things we may never get to know the truth behind. One of the group did say they hadn't been able to use their skills during wartime but that might have been a deliberate bluff. I consistently got a feeling of both artificiality and the need to be of use."

"That might chime with the rest of our thinking." Bessy waved her hand. "We'd been discussing people who brag when the lights started to dim. Suddenly we were whisked off to Cambridge and the days of my childhood. It was quite magical. We'd got to the middle of the film and there was a scene in which Miss Marsden was offering her help to Alasdair—as Dr Coppersmith—and I immediately thought of my Aunt Beatrice. A handsome woman of great character."

"Tell them how you described it to me," Geraldine encouraged her.

Bessy, blushing, said, "She flashed onto the screen of my mind as vividly as Miss Marsden in the film."

"Doesn't she have a lovely way with words?" Geraldine glowed with pride at her friend.

"She certainly does." Toby lowered his voice. "You mustn't repeat what I'm about to say or I shall get into awful trouble, but you've been much more interesting companions for the evening than any we've had before."

Now both women blushed. "You'd better not tell your husband, or he'll be getting jealous, Bessy," Geraldine said.

"He says I should enjoy every moment. It's not like I'll get the chance again. Are we allowed to ask what your next film is?" Bessy added.

"It's called *The Heart That Wears the Crown*." Alasdair grinned. "It's an old project that was put on the shelf and it's been brought back into life for obvious reasons. The film won't be ready for the big day itself, which is probably as well, because that would be slightly tasteless. Better to bring it out nearer Christmas and revive memories of the actual event."

Geraldine nodded. "I'm pleased we're here for this film and not the next. Much as I admire her majesty, I fear I'll be tired of all things coronation related by the time we get there. My cousin is involved in the planning and he keeps telling me about it in boring detail. Let's get back to Aunt Beatrice before I let drop any secrets I shouldn't."

"And before this champagne gets to my head." Bessy took a deep breath. "That scene I was talking about. I'm afraid that I didn't really concentrate at that point, but the action appeared to be all romance, so I don't think I'd miss much."

"Don't say that in front of our devotees. You'd be lynched." Alasdair put that judgement as another point on the plus side of the scale for their companions. As far as he and Toby were concerned, those romantic scenes were always the weakest in the films but the audience in general really did love them.

Bessy chuckled. "We'd best get back to my aunt. She was active on the home front back in 1916, doing what you'd call men's work and being very successful at it. You can imagine her frustration when the troops returned and she soon found herself out of a job. She had the skills and the brains—an unusual amount of both, you might say, for a woman of her humble background—but now she had to return to having no outlet for them. She spent a couple of years casting around, quite frustrated, desperate to be of more use than working in a shop or whatever was supposedly more fitting for us poor females."

"It's a travesty." Geraldine said. "Such a waste, not only for her but for all the women in that position. It makes my blood boil. Sorry, Bessy, I've got on my high horse again."

"You're entitled to. Anyway, Aunt Beatrice was fortunate, because she eventually found a sympathetic male ear to pour her troubles into. Eric was a charming, well-to-do chap who you might have expected to propose, but instead he suggested that she study medicine and he'd subsidise her studies. She took him up on the offer and has never regretted that decision."

"What a wonderful story," Toby said, "although I'm not sure that I see how it relates to our mysterious group."

"You will in a moment," Geraldine promised. "Remember that she wasn't alone in feeling such frustration, whether after the great war or this last one. The distaff side of the equation often finds itself back on the scrapheap again, having to be content with the kitchen stove and the nappy bucket, no matter how much brain or talent they have. And men go back to a boring office job when they've been involved in much more exciting activities."

"That's an excellent point," Alasdair said. "Toby and I were fortunate post-war, swopping one satisfying career for another. I'm not saying making films is anywhere near as necessary to Britain as us scrambling when the German planes came over, but it's equally interesting and fulfilling."

Toby nodded. "We were fortunate on another count. We can talk pretty freely about what we did, not that we like to much, because it sounds big-headed. Others, however, are still bound by the Official Secrets Act—they couldn't talk about what they did while the war was still on and they can't now."

"Yes," Geraldine said. "I bet if you asked Dr Stewart and Professor Coppersmith what they were doing at the start of the great war, you'd be putting them on the spot. I only know they were involved in something secret because my father mentioned it, because he'd done something similar. I don't know about our Cambridge friends, but it rankled with my father that he had no recognition, either official or from friends and family, about what an input he'd had to the war effort."

"I'm feeling a bit confused now," Alasdair confessed. "Are you suggesting that these people we spoke about ended the war feeling their service hadn't been recognised or frustrated that the contribution they'd made had been swopped for nothing more fulfilling than operating filing cabinets?"

Bessy flicked back a lock of hair which had come astray, despite the ministrations of the Landseer make-up department and the ton of lacquer they'd no doubt applied. "A bit of both, we'd say. They want to recreate the feeling of being of some worth. Sorry if our ideas are only a ragbag of loose ends."

"Loose ends or not, we'll bear them in mind when we see these people," Alasdair said. "We might be able to link some small remark to one of your theories."

The arrival of Sir Ian, and the subsequent round of introductions, put paid to any further discussion. As he chatted up Bessy and Geraldine—there was no other way to describe Sir Ian's style—and garnered their opinion of the new film, Alasdair tried to fix these new ideas in his mind before they got muddled and lost among the champagne and chit-chat.

Were the *Monday Evening Association* members trying to find a purpose in life—perhaps reflected in Moira's suggestion that they'd be serving their country—or were they merely a bunch of braggarts? Or was there another explanation that the combined brains of himself, Toby, Jonny and the two ladies hadn't yet figured out? Loose ends? There seemed to be a whole ball of them that appeared to be getting more difficult to tie together rather than easier.

Chapter Six

On the way home, a tired but clearly happy Toby confessed that the Bessy and Geraldine strategy had been a stroke of genius.

"The best opening night I've ever attended," he said.

"I'd agree. Everyone was clearly taken with our guests." Alasdair settled himself into the opposite corner of the Landseer limousine from Toby. Despite having their usual chauffeur, one who understood that he wouldn't be dropping one man off at his house and then taking the other elsewhere, he and Toby wouldn't be sitting too close to each other. Easy enough for somebody on the pavement to peer in.

"Even Sir Ian seemed charmed by them and they're not his usual type." Toby chuckled. "I have to say I hadn't anticipated that they'd be such a help regarding the business of Lloyd's gang. So many ideas."

"Yes. Quite a lot for us to contemplate there, although perhaps best not to reach any conclusions until we've seen Moira and her merry men. Assuming they *are* merry?"

Toby shrugged. "I think they have the potential to be. We'll see what they're like away from the influence of he whose club it is. Getting back to tonight, do you think that the 'win an evening with the stars' ballot idea will be used for future functions?"

"Possibly, although it can't guarantee we'd end up with such charming and interesting guests as we had tonight."

"True." Toby glanced over at the glass dividing passengers from driver, no doubt checking that the communication window was shut. There was probably no need to be so cautious within earshot of this chauffeur but some habits were ingrained. "However, the scheme does carry the clear implication that such an evening is a one off.

It wouldn't surprise me if the publicity department made use of it in other ways."

"Such as?"

"Saying that such a ballot isn't just about rewarding faithful fans. Making an implication that part of the rationale was because our real-life girlfriends were too shy to appear in public and had only agreed to us having companions for events if they were selected at random and could pose no threat."

"But wouldn't that lead to a frenzy of speculation to identify these girlfriends?"

"I suppose so." Toby doodled in the condensation on the window: a love heart, which he swiftly rubbed out. "The solving of one problem raises another. Such is life."

Alasdair patted his arm. "On the positive side, Landseer could, of course, fix any supposedly random ballot to ensure we were paired with someone able to keep up a decent conversation and more mature women would always be welcome. Less risk of flirting."

"Really? Didn't you see Sir Ian putting on the style with Bessy? I hope she doesn't report that back, or her husband Bob will be up here like a shot demanding an explanation." The mere idea seemed to have raised Toby's spirits. "How would you be able to wangle all of those details about ages or interests onto an entry form for a supposedly unbiased draw, without it looking suspicious, though?"

Alasdair considered the question. "The age would be easy. People would have to give their date of birth to ensure that they were of a suitable age. Nobody under twenty-one allowed to enter."

"That would work. What about the other bit. How do we make sure they're not vapid?"

"I'd suggest getting them to write a little paragraph about themselves, but that would blow apart the story that it's a random ballot. Perhaps the Landseer people would have a better idea."

"They *do* usually come up with something." Toby stifled a yawn. "Excuse me. Too much excitement. We need to keep chatting to keep me awake. This random-but-not-random ballot. Would it only be open to females or would we include chaps of a more mature nature? I rather fancy the idea of having a Chelsea pensioner as companion if it's the premiere for one of our war films."

That was a rather appealing idea. However… "I can imagine the publicity value in that, but there is a drawback. If we're seen with a chap at our sides, might that imply what we wouldn't want implying?"

"Well, we've ridden our luck almost to the point it's exhausted. How much longer will we be able to keep up the confirmed bachelor or secret girlfriend ruses before someone smells a rat? It'll be fine once we've made it through to being grey haired and are seen to be beyond the matching and hatching phase but until then…"

Alasdair shuddered. "Let's not think about that now."

"Getting older or getting caught?"

"Either. Both. Let's just bask in the glow of an evening that went well. We don't get enough occasions to be alone together, especially at the moment."

"Then we'll sit in silence and pretend that all is well and will continue to be well." Toby broke into a glorious smile, the warmth of which cheered Alasdair all the way home.

The minute they entered his hallway and shut the door to the world outside, Alasdair drew Toby into a kiss-laden clinch.

"That was just what the doctor ordered," Toby said, as they came up for air. "I've been thinking about that happening all the journey."

"Glad to be of service." Alasdair edged them towards his sitting room, where a nicely banked fire and a comfy sofa awaited. "Nightcap?"

"No thank you. It would send me to sleep and that would be a waste of our time." Toby drew him onto the sofa. "I sometimes feel like a grass widow or a woman patiently waiting at home while her man's off fighting. Not that I ever have felt like a woman, so I should have said grass widower, but you get the drift."

"I do. Which is a word I can never use in a church with the love of my life beside me, more's the pity." Alasdair stroked the ring finger of Toby's left hand. "Although we're slightly better off than a wife or sweetheart stuck on the home front, because do see each other regularly through Landseer and even our times of getting to share a bed together are hardly separated by months. We're more fortunate than most men in our situation."

"Are we? Wouldn't we be better off having faces that aren't instantly recognisable?"

"I don't think so. Don't think I haven't given the same issue some thought over the last few years." Alasdair circled Toby's ring finger with his. "I concluded that the pros outweigh the cons. We're in an industry that's generally more sympathetic to our situation than others might be. Imagine if we'd stayed in the forces."

"I'd rather not imagine it, if you don't mind." Toby nestled closer. "You're probably right. I got to spend the premiere with you and while we couldn't quite sit in the stalls and hold hands, we could enjoy the experience together without looking over our shoulders every two minutes."

"Exactly. And while we haven't quite worked out how to emulate our distinguished Cambridge friends in their well-nigh perfect domestic set-up, it's not like we can only ever meet in a cheap hotel or a sordid club. No marriages of convenience leading to wives at home wondering why we're more attentive to each other than to them."

Alasdair turned Toby's face so they could share another kiss, at the conclusion of which, Toby said, "What on earth were you thinking about when you should had a hundred percent of your attention on kissing me? Don't deny it."

"Sorry. It was talking about sneaking off behind one's wife's back that must have made me think of your *Monday Evening* mob. I mean, what if the whole business is as mundane as Moira being mistress to both Jeff and Richard and the club providing the only opportunity for them to spend time together without rousing suspicion?"

"It can't be the only time they spend together—nor can suspicion be the only thing roused—if she's their mistress, unless they utilise that little kitchen as a makeshift knocking shop."

"Knocking shop?" Alasdair was going to jiggle his insured eyebrow but felt too tired to bother. "Such a delightful choice of words, and ones you definitely wouldn't read in a Landseer script. However—in the admittedly unlikely event that this scenario is accurate—a man and a woman would have more opportunity to sleep together than we would. Moira pops on a wedding ring, she and Jeff head down to Chichester on the two-fifteen and enter a hotel together. He's allegedly away on business, so somewhere further from home might be better, but you get the idea. They present themselves as Mr and Mrs Jessop, say they're on honeymoon, and spend most of the next few days in their room, risking only a few sniggers from the chambermaid and the other staff who know what they're up to. We can't do that, alas."

"Our Cambridge pals have managed it, because Jonty told me all about it. They used to take a two-bedroom suite and be very careful about making sure both beds had evidence of occupation." Toby sighed. "Apparently it was easier either side of the first world war because men would often share bedrooms platonically. Evidence *Three Men in a Boat, Red House Mystery,* and all that."

"I wonder how much the platonic sharing wasn't platonic? *Red House Mystery* is a case in point."

"Quite. Still, if our faces were less well known and we could get on the two-fifteen to Chichester and find some little hotel, I'd want a better alias than Jessop. Something with a bit of style. Like Whitford-Cholmondeley."

"Really? That sounds like a stop on the Ilfracombe to Barnstaple line and sticks out like a sore thumb, rather than having the ordinariness of Jessop or Hutchings." How had this conversation got so far off track? "Anyway, man cannot live by sex alone, nor woman neither, so even if said knocking were happening elsewhere with Moira and her merry men—or man—they might want simply to spend time together outside of a bed, as I mentioned us doing."

"True" Toby sat up, clearly warming to the theme. "In which case, all the strange tales of strange powers would act not so much to impress the others but to make a smokescreen for Lloyd, who mistakenly approached one of them in the first place and they played along. Knowing such a club would itself be a smokescreen for Mrs Jeff or Mr Moira. Hold on, though. We're getting ahead of ourselves, as usual. This new theory introduces as many questions as it solves. Did they know each other beforehand and take advantage of the club or is that where they met in the first place? All being asked by Lloyd, who made an error as he did with me."

"The latter may be more likely. It could also explain the tension you said was in the air, if Lloyd didn't realise that love would blossom over the confessions and coffee cups

71

and that his nice gang of special people has turned into…"
Alasdair cast around for any other words than *knocking
shop*, but Toby beat him to it.

"A knocking shop. Let's take that as the primary
possibility, because it's more plausible than them knowing
each other beforehand for said rogering purposes and
somehow inveigling Lloyd into having them all as
members." Toby chortled at the *double entendre*.

"Stop it with the smut. We have our upcoming meeting
with these people and at this rate my entire repertoire of
acting skills won't help me keep a straight face."

"You'll manage. Anyway, I hope that's as sordid as any
of this gets. I keep thinking about some of *Herbert and
Chapman's* clients and praying that Lloyd's gang aren't the
kind who prey on children and that their meetings aren't
simply creating a respectable front. My invitation being part
of the veneer of propriety, them knowing I wouldn't join
their membership."

"That's a labyrinthine piece of thinking. Not outside of
the bounds of possibility. *I* keep thinking about Charles
Carstone and why he was their client. He was supposed to
be in a genuinely happy marriage, which makes a divorce
case less likely."

"Therefore, your mind veers towards something illegal
for which he hadn't yet been charged and Messrs H and C
being commissioned for that eventuality. Only he either
slipped or jumped before things came into the open?"

"Something like that. Anyway, before we get carried
away, none of these theories explain why Moira has asked
us to meet them again or how anything could be said to
apply to serving our country. Now, we said that man cannot
live by sex alone."

"To be accurate, *you* said that." Toby's eyes twinkled.

"I stand corrected. *I* said that. However, this man can't live without his ration of it. We've been doing an awful lot of talking and thinking—all of which is to the good—but time's winged chariot and all that. I have a nice, big bed available in my big, warm bedroom. If you'd do me the honour of occupying part of it, there'd be no happier man."

"Of course I—hold on." Toby slapped Alasdair's leg. "Didn't you use that line to Fiona in one of our early films? Only you were offering her a place at the kitchen table as opposed to one in your bed, to get it past the censor, although we all knew what your character meant."

"I assure you it wasn't intentional. I thought the words sounded familiar as they sprang to my lips but by then it was too late."

"Hmm. Well, sir, I don't want to be wooed with second hand lines. You need to come up with something better than that."

"Let me see…" Alasdair ran his spare hand—the one that wasn't holding Toby—through his hair. "I shan't do the whole 'If I could write the beauty of your eyes' bit because that's obviously been used before and so has, 'I wish I didn't love you so much.' Anyway, the latter is inaccurate. What about, Toby Bowe, will you come to bed with me and let me leave you raddled?"

"I will." Toby extricated himself from Alasdair's grip, rose from the sofa and then grabbed him by the hand. "Come on old man. To quote another our films, the game's afoot. And it's in other parts of the anatomy, as well."

73

Chapter Seven

By the time Monday evening came, Toby had pretty well recovered from the excesses of Alasdair's bed and was ready to get his mind away from his nether regions and into the right place for investigation. Alasdair had driven over, picked him up and they'd headed west to a car park just around the corner from *The Swan with Two Necks*. Here Jonny was waiting, having made his way there straight from work.

"All hail!" Jonny waved and came over as they got out of the car. "The game's afoot and all that, only—in honour of Professor Coppersmith—I'm quoting *Henry the Fifth* and not Sherlock."

"He'd be glad to hear it," Alasdair said, while Toby suppressed a grin in remembrance of the phrase being quoted on Saturday night and the events which had followed.

"Ready for the fray?" Jonny asked.

"As ready as I'll ever be." Toby rolled his eyes. "It seemed such a good idea last week but all today I've had a building sense of dread that this will prove a damp squib or a mare's nest."

"Oh, ye of little faith." Jonny grabbed them both by the arm and set off at a brisk pace for the pub.

From the moment the three went through the door, and at the briefest glance around, *The Swan with Two Necks* appeared to live up to the reputation Moira had given it. As Fred Astaire might have sung, it simply reeked of class. It wasn't simply a matter of the clientele, who from their smartness of dress wouldn't have looked out of place in an exclusive London club, but the building itself. This proved elegant, with well-maintained décor and a bar that could have stepped out of a West End hotel: if Toby had felt slightly discombobulated by his experience the previous week at Clarence House on Eagle Street, then Alasdair must be experiencing the same sensation now, given his facial expression.

"Anyone else detect the faint whiff of theatricality here that Toby picked up last Monday at Clanfield House? Like I'm in a John Mills film." Jonny whispered, as they stood in the doorway scanning the room for Moira.

"I'll answer that when we're not being scrutinised," Alasdair said.

They'd certainly caught folk's attention and been given the once over by most of those present, although whether that was because they were newcomers or that two of their faces were remarkably well-known, Toby couldn't tell.

As they neared the bar, the man serving behind it grinned. "You must be Moira's guests. I'll let her know."

He'd got as far as opening the counter when the woman concerned emerged from a door to what must be the back room. "I thought I heard my name and decided to save you a job, Malcolm," she told the barman with an easy familiarity that suggested she was a regular habitue of the place. "Here are my three Daniels, come to the lions' den."

"I thought of us more as the Three Musketeers." Jonny held his hand out to shake hers. "Daniel might be more like it, though."

"I hope we're not actually Meshach, Shadrach and Abednego," Toby said, taking his turn at handshaking and trying to prevent his recollection of the conversation concerning Watson's service revolver from appearing on his face. "My mother has written me a note to say I'm to be excused fiery furnaces. This is Alasdair."

"Delighted to meet you." Another batch of handshaking. "I must assure you all—and Toby's mother—that none of you are really in danger." Moira's bright smile disappeared,

75

to be replaced with an expression of concern. "You're not actually worried about this evening, are you? The lions' den comment was no more than a joke, to break the ice."

Alasdair flashed his most charming smile. "The unknown is always rather disconcerting, and this situation is awash with unknowns."

Moira sighed. "Yes. I do feel I have to keep apologising for all the intrigue but, you see, this business is rather complicated and not solely my story to tell. While meeting last week was useful, it also complicated matters. However, I promise you won't leave here in the same state of confusion and ignorance that you must have done then."

"Is that because Lloyd isn't here?" Jonny asked, sweetening the direct question with a chuckle.

"You might say so. *The Monday Evening Association* is rather his baby and he'd be mortified to think we were meeting without him, especially with Toby being present. You see, he'd begun to think of you as his *coup de theatre*." Moira shrugged, apologetically.

"But this isn't his club, is it?" Alasdair said. "Despite three members expected to attend. I mean, just because Toby and I are present doesn't make it a Landseer event."

"I'd wish you good luck if you tried telling Lloyd that." Moira made a moue of displeasure. "He'd be afraid we were making a breakaway group, with our film star agreeing to attend, despite your leaving in such a marked—if charming—manner last week."

"Moira," Toby said, "can I reiterate that I don't possess and never have possessed any unusual powers. I don't accept the assertion that I may have something lying dormant that has not yet been revealed to me."

Moira studied him briefly before saying, "I believe you. Lloyd isn't as infallible as he thinks he is. Ah, here are the boys."

Richard and Jeff came over and a fresh round of greetings and introductions were effected. Richard still resembled a second-string actor from a war film, although in this setting it didn't stick out so much. Eighty per cent of the clientele could have been extras in a bar scene where John Mills was taking a heartrending farewell of his light of love. Jeff also seemed to have toned down the heartiness since their previous meeting, which suggested it might have formed some kind of defence mechanism against Lloyd. Drinks were ordered, which the barman said he'd bring to the back room, into which the company now repaired.

"Does Alasdair know what happened at the meeting a week ago?" Jeff asked, as they settled around an unlaid table in what turned out to be surprisingly comfy chairs.

"Yes, he's had a briefing from both of us," Toby said. "Service habits die hard, so a full report after action feels a formality."

Alasdair nodded. "And once we started practicing some amateur investigating, it proved jolly useful to have kept up the habit."

"It's a natural consequence of a curious mind, too," Jonny said. "I was too young to serve and didn't have that discipline drummed into me during National Service, but if anything unusual happens to me, I want to discuss it with either a friend or one of my highly inquisitive family."

"So, you see, poor Alasdair's had his ear bent from both sides." Toby paused to scan those present and emphasise his upcoming point. "Not that he was much the wiser than we were at the end of it. I confess I'd never have called myself a coward but I couldn't wait to be away from those offices last week and Jonny here felt the same. It needed glasses of both hock and port to restore our equilibrium and if it wasn't for that aforementioned natural curiosity, I'm not sure we'd be here tonight. What is this all about?"

"An apology for a start," Jeff said. "We didn't mean to drive you to drink but Lloyd gets rather over-excited."

Toby felt his hackles rise at yet another apology but no answer to his question. "It wasn't simply him, it was your stories about sermons and bus seats and the like, none of which I was prepared for." He took a deep breath. "Can we cut to the key part of the script, as 'twere? What is all this about?"

The entrance of the barman with a tray of drinks—poorly timed, as far as Toby was concerned—lessened the tension. Once the door was closed again, Moira asked, "Did you notice the empty chair in the circle at the meeting last Monday?"

"We couldn't miss the thing," Jonny said. "Lloyd kept glancing at it, for one thing."

Moira nodded, cradling her gin and tonic but not yet drinking from the glass. "He did indeed. You see, there used to be a fifth member of our group, Alexandra Cummings, but she's not attended for the last couple of months. Lloyd lives in hope that she'll turn up again and always sets her a place, though."

"And you want to find out what's happened to her?" Alasdair asked.

"Yes," Moira and Jeff chimed in unison, while Richard said, "Absolutely."

"Then you need to give us as much information as possible. Including why you're so worried about her." Alasdair produced a leatherbound notepad and elegant propelling pencil, with which to take notes: clearly he wanted to create the best impression.

"Let's start with the order of events." Jeff laid down his beer.

"Let's not," Toby said. "I'm sorry, everyone, but much as I'm interested in helping find this lady, we don't simply need information on *her*. Before I agree to take on any commission, I want to know exactly what's going on concerning your special powers, because I know I don't have one and frankly I doubt you all do. If you don't want to answer, then we can simply decide if we want to leave, without any rancour on either side." He hadn't meant to be quite so frank at this early stage of the evening, but his patience was running low. He glanced at Alasdair and Jonny, who both nodded.

To Toby's surprise, Moira broke into a grin. "I knew you wouldn't be as gullible as Lloyd. No, we don't have any powers, beyond the ability to tell a good tale."

"Not good enough, though, in your case," Jeff said. "If we promise to be totally frank, will you promise to help us keep up the pretence with Lloyd or others, if need be? It might be vitally important."

"I'm more than pleased to agree to that. It's a weight off my shoulders, not having to wonder why such apparently well-balanced and intelligent people were spouting bizarre stuff about sermons and change and whatever. Happy with that, lads?" Toby asked the other two.

Jonny nodded again, while Alasdair said, "Absolutely. If pretence is needed, we've the relevant experience."

Best to press on while those present assumed that Alasdair was only referring to their acting and didn't think any deeper. "Then tell us how we can help. Jeff, shall we start with your order of events, as you put it?"

"Alexandra was already a member of the group when I joined, last October. She and Lloyd had met a couple of times before then, so I was the third member. Then Moira came along a fortnight later and Richard's the baby of the group at about four months' attendance."

Richard snorted. "That makes me sound as though I'm still being pushed in my nanny's perambulator. Alexandra was such a pleasant girl—rather I should say she was a pleasant young woman. Very welcoming to all of us and someone who stood no nonsense from Lloyd. If he started to get visions of grandeur she'd prick his balloon of pomposity with some quip."

"Did he resent having said balloon burst?" Alasdair asked.

"Seemingly not. She did it in the most charming fashion, you see, although even if she hadn't, he might not have been upset by it." Moira shrugged. "I dare say he'd have reacted differently if she'd been an Alexander. My assessment is that Lloyd's deferential to women but doesn't like men standing up to him. Would that be right?"

"Absolutely," Jeff said. "Richard and I have been on the wrong end of a withering look or two."

Good to know that Toby and Jonny's reading of the tension at the previous meeting appeared to be accurate. "Any reason he likes to be top dog?"

"We-ell," Moira said, pinching her bottom lip between her thumb and forefinger, "strictly between us six, he didn't have that high powered a job during the war and it's clear he resents the fact."

That accorded with one of the theories aired at the premiere: they'd have to let Bessy and Geraldine know of their success.

"About these visions of grandeur Lloyd has." Alasdair tapped his notepad, where he'd evidently jotted down the fact. "Can you be more specific?"

"Only in that he wants us to use our powers—" Richard cast an uncomfortable glance at Toby as he said the word, "—our *supposed* powers, for a greater purpose. He's convinced we've been blessed with what we can do for a reason and, according to him, we simply have to discover what that reason is."

Jonny raised his hand. "I suspect I'm being rather dim, but I'm not clear about how you were recruited to this group and why you put on such a show to maintain your membership rather than run away, like we did. Not to mention Lloyd thinking he can find a 'greater purpose' for sermon predicting or bus seat grabbing. They're hardly the weapons for stopping the Russians invading."

"There's no accounting for the workings of Lloyd's mind, I'm afraid," Jeff said. "As for joining the group, I already vaguely knew Alexandra from work. For a while, she was one of the secretaries to a department we worked alongside. On one occasion, several of us went out for lunch together—someone's birthday, I think—and she told me she'd joined a new group. One which had changed her life. She regarded the *Monday Evening Association* as a place where like minds could meet and be a support to each other. She said she'd been lonely, because she was an only child and her parents lived miles away. I thought no more of it until I was in Oxford Street a week later and saw her chatting to Lloyd. She introduced us, he gave me the once over, and the next week I got an invitation—via the internal post at work—to join them. I went along and got a hell of a surprise when they started talking about powers, but I wanted to stay so I had to come up with something on the spur of the moment. If I'd had more time to think about it, I'd have made a better fist of things, but they seemed to believe the bus seat story. They probably *wanted* to believe, and I *was* in a bus crash during the war, so I could salt the story with a fair degree of truth."

"What made you want to stay with the group?" Toby enquired.

When Jeff hesitated to answer—and went red in the process—Moira leaped in. "Because Alexandra was such a nice girl that any red-blooded male would have wanted to spend time with her, especially if he could impress her. Hence Jeff cementing his place in the group."

"What was Alexandra's supposed power?" Alasdair asked.

"She could predict the weather." Jeff was evidently happier talking about this. "Not by reading charts and barometers or whatever, but by instinct."

"Now that *would* be distinctly useful. Assuming it were true, which I guess it isn't," Toby said.

"She was certain it was," Jeff asserted, "and the odd occasions I heard her do her party trick, she was pretty spot on. However, as I understand it from a chap who explained it to me years ago, British weather gets into set patterns. If you simply say that tomorrow's weather will be the same as today's, you'll be right something like seventy five percent of the time."

Toby sniffed. "I suppose there must have been an exception to her so-called powers, as with Moira and her empty pockets."

"There was." Jeff nodded. "You see, her ability allegedly couldn't work if people didn't believe she could do it. You won't be surprised to hear that."

"I don't think we are." Toby shared a knowing glance with his two colleagues. "Well, that's how you came into things, Jeff. What about you two?"

"I joined next, so I'll take up the story," Moira said. "I've known Jeff on and off since the time of the blitz, from running across each other in our work back then. More recently, I bumped into him at a party and he told me about this odd meeting he'd been to a few days previously. I was intrigued, so we planned for me to go along, with my 'spare change' story prepared in advance. As it turned out, we both decided to keep attending, but that's another part of the story that I'll hold fire on for the moment."

Jeff's taking the initiative on bringing along a new member would go towards explaining the tension between him and Lloyd, if the former felt his prerogative of issuing invitations had been usurped. The story also begged several questions about what work Moira and Jeff had been doing and how ships came into it, unless his account of his war service had also been so much hot air.

"You felt that coming to the meetings wasn't a waste of your time, then?" Alasdair asked, perhaps wondering if he'd get a hint at whether Moira's decision to stay involved fancying Jeff.

"Absolutely not. We felt we were doing something useful again."

Did that chime with what Bessy had said about a post-war return to work proving a let down?

Before Toby could formulate an appropriate question, Richard put down his empty glass and said, "That just leaves me. I met Lloyd in December, at an old boys reunion of all things. I vaguely remembered him from my time at school although we were never really pals. We had the usual chat about where we worked now and the like: the next thing I knew, he was inviting me to this *Monday Evening Association*. My experience at my first meeting was as bewildering as yours must have been, Toby. I wanted to stay, because I enjoyed everyone's company so had to concoct a story off the cuff. When I was younger, we used to hold sweepstakes on the length of the vicar's sermon, so that inspired me."

Enjoyed everyone's company? Toby would guess it was Moira's in particular, rather than Alexandra's.

"Thanks for making all that clear," Jonny said. "Is this a good time to get a second round of drinks in? My treat, on behalf of all those Stewarts who love a good mystery."

83

The ordering of drinks and visits to the toilet allowed everyone a chance to take stock. Toby and Alasdair's paths crossed as they headed to and from the lavatory respectively.

"Happier now we have an explanation?" Alasdair asked.

"Absolutely. Although I don't think we're anywhere near the *full* story. No wonder I was reminded of *Henry Himself* when I first met them. As labyrinthine a set of circumstances as in that film, only in this case it's for real. At least, I hope it is. I couldn't bear it if they're still pretending."

Alasdair's insured eyebrow beautifully communicated his sympathy with the notion.

Once they'd reassembled, Jeff took a draught of beer and said, "Back to Alexandra. The first Monday meeting in March, she didn't turn up. We delayed our start but decided something must have happened at the last moment and she hadn't been able to get word to us. A fortnight later she didn't attend again and none of us had heard from her in the interim. She'd changed her job in the interim, so I couldn't even catch her at work and nobody in the office seems to know where she's employed now. Or if they do know, they aren't telling. We asked Lloyd if he'd tried to make contact, but he simply said that of course he had and changed the subject. It was clearly a sore point with him, although that spare chair still appears every time we meet, as though he's expecting her to return. Perhaps he does know more about it than he's saying."

"Or wants to pretend that she's likely to come back," Moira said, "maybe knowing damn well that she won't or can't."

"Do you think that Lloyd has got something to do with her non-appearance?" Jonny asked.

"Possibly." Moira spread her hands. "We just don't know what's happened to her, which is why we wanted to talk to you. I know you're busy but I also know you like to dabble—that's not meant to be insulting, it simply seems the best word—in detection. Would you have time to look into it? Even if you find Alexandra and she simply says, 'I hate the whole boiling and don't want to speak to any of them ever again.' It's not simply a matter of knowing why she went—we'd like to be sure that she's safe."

Now they seemed to be coming to the crux.

"Why should she be in any danger?" Alasdair asked. "She might, for example, have had an argument with Lloyd and decided she'd had enough. In that case he might not want to admit what had happened, especially if he'd been at fault. From what I've heard, he doesn't strike me as a man who likes to be in the wrong."

"That's all true, but there's more," Richard said. "I saw her, at the end of January having a row with somebody outside *Fortnum and Masons*. A younger chap—by which I mean more her age than mine—and they were at it hammer and tongs. He grabbed her arm at one point, and she shrugged him off. I was about to intervene when she stomped away. It may have nothing to do with anything, of course, but I wanted you to know because some chaps are horribly violent towards women, and awful crimes do get committed. Young women are never seen again, because…well, we're all adults and we know the kind of things that happen to them."

Alasdair, who'd been wearing a look of concentration for the last few minutes, a look which increasingly suggested he was trying to hide his exasperation, laid down his drink. "As you say, that's all true, although why on earth do you think that applies in this case? There are plenty of reasons people go off. Maybe she's moved back in with her parents to get away from an ex-boyfriend—perhaps the one she argued with—and she's not bothered enough to let any of you know the fact. Unless you've got something concrete to offer us, then I'm afraid it's likely to be a waste of our time. Even if she were a victim of one of these vile men who often strike at random, we'd have less chance of pinning him down than the police would. If you truly believe she's in danger, go to them."

"But you're the men who helped catch *The Grey Assassin*." Richard's face resembled that of a kicked puppy.

"We are," Toby said, "but there were clues a-plenty to go on, in that case, including the bodies of the victims. We'd look pretty stupid going to our police contacts if all we have to say is that Alexandra has stopped coming to your club. We can't work miracles."

After an awkward pause, Jeff asked, "Do you know anything about the firm whose offices we meet at?"

"As we understand it, *Herbert and Chapman* aren't your usual solicitors. They handle all kinds of cases, some of which other companies might not wish to touch." Which suggested a point for Toby to raise. "They also have an investigational arm, which begs the question of why you've not used them."

"Use Lloyd's chums?" Moira snorted. "They'd snitch straight back to him. Given that we're allowed to use their offices for free, despite their reputation for confidentiality, Lloyd must be in a privileged position with them."

"From what we've heard, that's nothing to boast of," Alasdair said, his uninsured eyebrow registering disdain. "I have it on good authority that the firm also deals with the kind of cases that a decent person might balk at. If the eldest son of a lord was caught interfering with young boys, *Herbert and Chapman* would try to get the case hushed up or, if that failed, arrange the defence."

"How sickening," Richard said, face drawn.

Moira sniffed disdainfully. "Nothing about them surprises me. I've seen what goes in their bins sometimes."

"We should insist on a change of venue." Jeff grimaced. "You may think I'm overreacting but I'd rather not be in the same room that's been trodden by anyone who's done such things. I had a pal at school it had happened to. Disgusting stuff. I wish we didn't have to discuss it."

"Why did you ask, then?" Jonny said.

"This is where things become more complicated than a case of a missing woman, although the two might be related. It's also where the issue becomes more important than one person's life." Jeff glanced at Moira.

She nodded. "Well put. Alexandra worked at *Herbert and Chapman* for a short while, after she moved on from Jeff's place of work, but she left them very abruptly. That was just before her final Monday evening meeting, which is when she told us she'd changed jobs again, although not all the details about why."

"She was positively glowing at the prospect," Richard said. "Sorry, Moira. I shouldn't have interrupted your flow."

"Not to worry." Moira gave him a tight-lipped smile. "Having heard your information, Alasdair, I think we have a possible explanation, which might make her leaving there less sinister-feeling. You see, we think it—and her disappearance—might be linked to something that she accidentally heard in the office."

Toby hoped this would be the nub of the matter at last. "Go on."

"At the last meeting of February, I was making coffee and Alexandra was helping. She seemed a little out of sorts so I asked what was wrong. She said she'd been in the office the week before and picked up one of the telephones to make a call but must have got a crossed line." Moira glanced at the door, perhaps making sure it was firmly closed. "Two people were discussing the coronation. How it would make a huge statement to disrupt the event in some way."

"Disrupt the coronation?" Alasdair sounded rightly horrified. "That sounds treasonable."

"Exactly what she thought. Alexandra recognised one of the voices as being someone who worked in her office, although she wouldn't tell me his name. I'm guessing, from the fact she referred to him as 'the b…' and changed that to 'the bloke I work with' that it was one of the bosses. The other person she didn't recognise, although he was keen to make this disruption as violent as possible: small acts weren't worth the effort, apparently. The one from Alexandra's office was egging him on." Moira sighed. "That's all she could report, because they must have realised they were being overheard and clammed up. She put the phone down and made herself scarce. The next week she was told by a friend about a better opportunity, so she gave notice and off she went. We've been worried that what she heard was a genuine threat, rather than just hot air coming from someone who wanted to puff up their importance."

"You think this is serious enough to lead her into hiding, possibly because she feels in danger?" Alasdair suggested. "Or is your thinking that somebody's decided they had to get her out of the way because she knew too much?"

Richard grimaced. "We've considered both of those."

"Does Lloyd know anything about this business?" Jonny asked. "You mentioned a greater purpose he had in mind, so I wondered if this was it. Part of his plans for you using your—admittedly—non-existent powers to combat the threat."

"If it is," Richard said, "he's not mentioned anything to us and every fortnight that passes is a fortnight closer to the big day. Him being so pally with Billy Chapman, there's a chance he might be in on the plot."

"That's another one of the reasons we've continued to stick with the group," Moira explained. "On the off chance that he might let something slip or that Alexandra might return and we can ask her directly."

Toby raised his hand. "I have to ask this, so please don't take it amiss. Given that all three of you concocted a story about things you could do that were actually all my eye and Betty Martin, is it possible that Alexandra's story is equally poppycock?"

"That's something else we've considered," Richard said. "Moira swears that when they had their chat over the kettle, Alexandra looked and sounded both upset and scared at what had happened."

Moira nodded. "She'd have had to be as accomplished an actress as Miss Marsden, if it was all pretend. I got no impression that she simply wanted to be the centre of attention by crying wolf, if that makes sense"

"It does," Toby replied. "Do you have anything else you can tell us to aid us in finding her?"

"Hold on a minute," Jonny said, drumming the table. "I know that my illustrious actor pals here are dab hands at amateur investigation, but this has turned into a bigger business than they should be dealing with alone. Surely you need the proper authorities involved. Did Alexandra go to the police? If not, why haven't you? If she overheard a possible plot before she left your group that means it's been in development for over two months and time becomes more of the essence with each passing hour if we want to foil it."

"Jonny's right," Alasdair said. "We could be entering the territory of anarchists throwing bombs at the coronation procession or something equally vile, in which case one or

89

all of you need head off to the nearest police station and report what you know. It's a matter of weeks away. June the second, not October or November."

"They'll laugh us to scorn." Jeff ran his hands through his hair. "I hate being the centre of attention at the best of times and the thought of reporting this fills me with horror, despite understanding full well that it's my public duty. All we can do is tell the police is a second-hand account of what somebody told us they heard and said person isn't around to corroborate any of the facts. That's a key part of why we'd like to speak to Alexandra again, and urgently. To get enough information for the police to think it sufficiently vital to investigate. Despite what Moira said about her plausibility, Alexandra could have made up the story, or embroidered it, in the same way that I heavily embroidered the tale of my bus crash and then we'd be wasting the police's time. Or maybe the authorities would try to get more information from Lloyd and he'd start talking about the powers nonsense: the next thing you know they'll assume we're a bunch of lunatics and lock *us* up."

"If they won't take your story seriously," Toby said, "then leave it with us. We'll talk directly to Matthew Firestone, our connection at Scotland Yard. If *we* think the situation worth considering, he'll approach it with the right degree of gravitas."

"He might also take Alexandra's disappearance more seriously, too, given the sequence of events leading up to it," Alasdair pointed out. "She becomes a possible key witness."

"I agree," Jonny said. "The case is completely altered, begging the question of whether you can afford *not* to go and tell them. I'm thinking of the welfare of another young woman, a royal one. If anything happened at the coronation, could you ever forgive yourselves?"

"You're quite right, Jonny." Moira looked suitably shamefaced. "We should be girding our loins and not being cowards."

"Exactly. I'm assuming that Toby and Alasdair feel the same as I do, that time is of the essence, so *I'll* be speaking to Superintendent Firestone tomorrow if nobody else volunteers. I'd rather be thought silly and find myself being sent off with a flea in my ear for wasting his time than risk some poor soul being hurt because I didn't speak up."

"You are quite right," Richard said, with a sigh. "It's all such a mess, you see. We've mulled it over time and again—to act or not to act, you might say—so when Lloyd said he was going to invite Toby to a meeting, we thought that our prayers had been answered. Not only because of his talents in detection, but the fact that Alexandra was…is still, I hope…a great devotee of him and Alasdair. A member of both your fan clubs, apparently, so we were hoping that fact in itself may help to gather more information about her than we've managed to get our hands on. If you have connections to your devotees, of course."

"We do indeed," Alasdair said, "and it's a shame we didn't know about Alexandra a month ago, as we've been at their respective gatherings within the past few weeks. We might have been able to pick up some information on where she is."

"She might even have been present at those meetings," Toby pointed out, "and I'm afraid I haven't got a return engagement booked for a while."

"Same in my case," Alasdair said.

"Still, we know the chairwomen of our appreciation societies rather well and could easily bend their ears. I'd anticipate that they'd love being able to help, if we keep the matter as nothing more than trying to help you locate her and we leave the other aspects for the moment."

"You don't happen to have a picture of her?" Alasdair asked. "Not that either of us have photographic memories, but we might recall the face. You never know."

Jeff shook his head. "Alas, we don't."

"We could give you a description," Richard suggested, "although I'm not sure it will help that much. She was Moira's height, had mousy hair and brown eyes, was very pretty and soft spoken. Late twenties at a guess and always neatly turned out. She gave me the impression she'd quite like to be in films herself. Touch of Lorelei, perhaps."

"She didn't look like Marilyn Monroe, though," Moira said, clearly thinking of the musical film the lovely Marilyn and the equally stunning Jane Russell had in production. Was there a touch of asperity about Alexandra's appearance?

Toby cracked on with his response. "I'm afraid that could apply to several of those ladies who attend my fan club's meetings, and because we have no reason to each other's do's, we wouldn't know if anyone had been at both unless they mentioned it, which they didn't."

"Still, assuming Alexandra Cummings isn't an alias then we might be able to come up with a contact address at the very least." Alasdair paused, clearly choosing his words carefully. "I think—and don't take this amiss—that given all we've discussed, it would be as well for one or all of us to continue acting as go-betweens. If she has a reason not to get in touch with you which overrides your need to speak to her, then we can pose the relevant questions about what she overheard."

"I think we understand the wisdom of that." Moira glanced at the other two, who nodded in agreement. "Our priorities should be primarily to establish that she's well and, if she did hear a threat being made, then we discover as much detail as we can, to pass on to the relevant people."

"In that case, while Jonny gets on to Superintendent Firestone tomorrow," Alasdair said, "we'll talk to the delightful and eminently sensible ladies who run our appreciation societies."

"I think there's another person we should speak to, as well," Toby proposed. "We may not be in close contact with anyone directly involved in organising the big event, but we know somebody who is. She's got a formidable brain on her, to boot. She'll know what to do."

Chapter Eight

"Well, what about that?" Toby said, as soon as they were all three in Alasdair's car en route to his house for a council of war. "What we've learned tonight casts quite a different complexion on the whole thing."

"More reassuring on some counts and infinitely more worrying on others, however, I'd say." Alasdair, as careful a driver as he'd been as daring a pilot, kept his eyes on the road.

"While I admire the honesty that three displayed," Jonny piped up from the back seat, "I'm more than a little aggrieved at their spinelessness. I don't mind ringing Matthew with the news but they could easily have done it themselves. Their hanging fire is hardly the spirit that made Britain great."

"Quite." Alasdair snorted. "Although, to be fair, I suppose we all three take working with the police for granted. Being able to have an honest conversation with the officers concerned and freely airing our ideas with them, for example. It isn't as easy for other folk."

"It's also possible they've had bad experiences in the past that have affected them. Six of the best for apple scrumping, maybe. My father has always said that visiting my school in his parental role made him feel like a seven year old again and he was often worried he'd be getting the cane once more." Toby twisted round to address Jonny. "I think you should ring Matthew as soon as we're home, rather than leaving it until tomorrow."

"Gladly, although isn't the hour a tad late?"

Toby chuckled. "He's quite used to it, poor chap, and the lateness of the hour will emphasise the importance of the information we've to impart. He knows full well that we wouldn't disturb his rest for anything trivial."

As it turned out, Matthew wasn't at home. His wife answered the call, or so Jonny reported as he re-entered Alasdair's sitting room after his abortive attempt at making contact. "He's out with colleagues celebrating someone's retirement. She offered to take a message but I felt that was unwise. I mean, I'm sure she's trustworthy, but I want to speak to him directly or else the importance will get watered down somewhat as it passes through various hands. I said I'll try to ring him at Scotland Yard in the morning, and asked her to pass on my regards and hopes that he's passed a pleasant evening and will be in a fit state to take my message on the morrow."

"Cheeky young scamp." Toby sniggered. "I hope he appreciates the spirit in which the wishes were made."

"If I doubted that I wouldn't have said it. Perhaps it's for the best he wasn't there, though. Gives me the chance to sleep on things." Jonny slipped into one of Alasdair's eminently comfortable chairs. "If I let my subconscious mind work on the matter, it might produce a more cohesive story, although at least I won't have to deal with mentioning the so-called special powers, because that would have stymied all credibility. No wonder there was a whiff of theatricality at that meeting last Monday, eh Toby?"

"Exactly. Ah, what a good man you are, Morgan." Toby beamed as Alasdair's valet appeared with a tray of bottles, to offer a nightcap, and a plate of small, delicious looking savouries. "You spoil us."

"It sounds as though you have a case, sirs, so your brains will need feeding and lubricating."

Once Morgan had ensured everyone had been tended to and had returned to his own domain once more, Alasdair said, "Talking of theatricality, could anyone else detect a whiff of it about that pub tonight? I'd describe it as feeling authentic, only somehow out of place."

Toby nodded. "Yes, I felt the same. Geographically it was awry—in that it should have been in the centre of London, perhaps—and the same applied chronologically. It wouldn't have felt amiss back in 1941 if it had been next to an air force base and formed an unofficial mess for the crews."

"Precisely. But I've no idea why the landlord should achieve that feeling, unless they're trying to recreate an atmosphere for people who miss the camaraderie of those times and who live in the local area."

"Which suggests that one or more of Moira and her pals could be local, Alasdair," Jonny said. "I don't recall any of them saying where they lived, although given their track record anything they told us on the two occasions we've seen them is up for scrutiny. It may purely be the pub's atmosphere they go for, especially if somebody's recommended it as a place for like-minded souls."

"The 'like-minded souls' aspect keeps raising its head and begs another question or two." Alasdair twirled his glass carefully, admiring the colours. "Despite everything that came out tonight, I'm not entirely eliminating the possibility that Alexandra made up the story regarding her powers and also perhaps the tale of what she overheard. Or the possibility that Moira et al have exaggerated the importance of what she—reportedly—said she heard because it makes *them* feel important. Or helps them to impress each other. Richard is rather smitten with Moira, isn't he?"

"Absolutely hooked, I'd say." Toby nodded. "Although it's gratifying to think that almost every theory we batted about with Jonny or the ladies concerning why this bunch pretended to have their powers had some element of truth in it, including the romance one."

Alasdair sniggered. "Except for your knocking shop idea. I don't think that came too close."

"I'd say it did in spirit if not in degree of the romance involved, which seems barely to have got past the admiring at a distance stage. *I* also have some lingering queries. Awfully coincidental that Lloyd invited me to their meeting, don't you think, if Moira et al, as you deem them, wanted us to go into sleuthing mode?"

"Actors whom the missing girl was crazy about, to boot?" Alasdair rolled his eyes. "Yes. I know coincidences are an everyday thing, but this one does seem a bit far-fetched."

"Maybe they all dropped hints, to plant the idea in Lloyd's mind. *That Mr Bowe reminds me awfully of you, Lloyd. I wonder why.*" Jonny's impersonation of Moira had captured the intonation perfectly, although the accompanying fluttering of the eyelids didn't fit her style. Still, his theory was a good one. "Do you think Lloyd has any idea he's being conned? I mean, he must have thought his ship had come in, with each new invitee producing an account of their strange power, just as he'd predicted they'd possess. Until you threw a spanner in the works by being the first to suggest he'd got it wrong, of course."

"I'd imagine he's totally oblivious. Probably thinks I'm hiding what I can do because Landseer wouldn't want word getting out." Toby shrugged. "What next, then? We'll get on with the fan club connection, you talk to Matthew, young Jonny, and then what? Surely there's more we can be doing. As Richard rightly said, every fortnight that passes gets us closer to the big event and cuts down the time available to deal with anyone who wants to disrupt it."

"Agreed," Alasdair said. "Our job doesn't end at either locating Alexandra or briefing the police. The more information we can garner, the less time Matthew and his men will waste on potential dead ends. Having said that, it wouldn't surprise me if—when you report in tomorrow—

you discover that all we're doing is adding to something the police already know and, please God, what we provide will be the key piece of information that helps *them* throw a spanner in the works. That's the best case, of course. The worst is that this is all news to them and all hell breaks loose."

"Do you know," Jonny said, rather shamefaced, "it hadn't occurred to me that the authorities might already know about this. Just goes to show how much more experienced you are in this business than I am and how much broader your thinking is. The notion also raises the possibility that Alexandra went to the police herself, is regarded as a key witness and the authorities have put her into hiding somewhere. That would explain all the lack of contact."

Toby leaned forward to give Jonny and avuncular tap on the knee. "As your aged and learned relative—and his equally learned partner—would agree, you mustn't rule out any possibility prematurely, not make any assumptions. It's taken us a while to realise that every idea needs considering before discarding and even then you sometimes have to hoik it back out of the mental wastepaper basket. Your key witness idea has a lot going for it. Alasdair, you're looking rather pensive."

"Sorry. I was thinking it would be worth picking Morgan's brain further, him being the one who supplied the information on *Herbert and Chapman* in the first place. You don't need to watch your p's and q's with him, by the way." Alasdair gave Jonny a knowing twitch of the eyebrow. "He knows all about our domestic situation and doesn't bat an eyelid."

"I'd already guessed that." Jonny smoothed back his hair, maybe automatically: Morgan, despite being perhaps ten years his senior, was still an attractive man. "A sympathetic soul?"

"In more ways than one, I believe, although he never says anything. I've always suspected him of harbouring a close pal or two at that club of his." Alasdair grinned.

"Close pal as in the kind of pals Roger and I are?"

"Quite. Although what he does in his own time is no business of mine, so long as it doesn't bring disgrace on Landseer. He understands who ultimately ensures his wages are paid." Alasdair rose, then rang the bell.

Morgan entered the room swiftly, with a nod and a willing, "May I be of assistance?"

"Indeed, although not in the supplying food and drink category. That rather squalid firm of solicitors I picked your brains about. *Herbert and Chapman*. Any further information to impart?" If he'd been talking to anyone else but Morgan, Alasdair might have used the question, "Have you any dirt to dish?" but the manservant—who'd never stoop so low as to be involved in mere gossip—wouldn't have approved.

"It's relevant to the case we've taken up this evening," Toby said, "which might simply involve finding a missing person but equally might be about foiling a plot. The woman we've been asked to locate may have overheard a conversation she wasn't supposed to, concerning a threat to national security. With that in mind, we're particularly interested in anything or anyone to do with the firm who or which might touch on anarchist activity."

"Anarchist?" Morgan's eyebrow proved almost as eloquent as his master's. "The chap who told me about them did describe the whole boiling as an unpatriotic bunch, not to be trusted."

"Any idea what that opinion was based on?" Alasdair asked.

"I believe—if I'm not mixing them up with another firm—that at least one of the principals was involved with Mosley. A supporter of the British Union of Fascists if not one of the actual Blackshirts."

Alasdair shared a satisfied glance with both his guests. That was the first possible bit of corroborative evidence for what Alexandra had confessed she'd overheard, albeit a circumstantial piece. Fascists were no doubt still operating in Britain and they might well believe that some of those attending the coronation would be valid targets for furthering their vile aims. The heads of state from some of the countries within the Commonwealth of Nations, for instance.

"My friend has never approved of such men and their beliefs," Morgan added.

"No sensible British man or woman would," Jonny said. "Especially in light of the stories which emerged from Germany at the end of the war. Do you have a name for said stinker?"

"Not that I can recall offhand. I may have jotted it down, if I can go and check?"

"Certainly." As Morgan headed towards his domain, Alasdair grinned. "We make progress, gentlemen."

"We do indeed. No wonder they don't have a name plate for their offices." Jonny eyed the door, as though willing Morgan to return with a whole list of names and examples of nefarious activities. "I'm delighted to be handing the police a Mosley supporter to strengthen our case. Although wouldn't they be ultra-patriotic, at least on the face of it?"

"To her majesty, perhaps," Toby said, "although they may take a dim view of certain foreign heads of state, especially when they're in a position of power but not the correct colour of skin—in their view—so to be. Anyway, when did logic ever apply to people with extreme views?

They probably tweak what they believe to justify whatever action they want to take. My father used to call them thugs looking for an outlet for their thuggery."

"I won't repeat what my father says about them." Jonny, twirling his glass, seemed to be more at ease now, having something more concrete to report to Firestone. "The old chap's description of Hitler would never have got past the censor and into one of your films."

Before Jonny could divulge said colourful description, Morgan returned, apologetically confessing that his notes hadn't included names, nor indeed anything he hadn't already divulged. "However, the chap who gave me all the information is no longer in service—in fact, he hasn't been for years, so he's one of the emeritus members at the club, as it were. He runs his own pub and possesses the good sense, for our purposes, to have the establishment on the telephone. Shall I see if I can catch him now and pick his brains?"

"Please do," Alasdair said, with a wave in the general direction of his own phone. "The more information we can garner tonight, the better."

Morgan nodded. "Mr Bowe, you mentioned a threat to security. Might I have some further detail on that, if you have it? Not that I'll reveal anything to my friend: it would merely be useful to have some context before entering into the discussion with him."

"I have no doubts that we can rely on your discretion. All we know is that it's possible they—a vaguely defined 'they' but connected to *Herbert and Chapman*—might be targeting the coronation, although in what way we have no idea." Toby spread his hands. "In fact, what we have is as thin as cigarette paper."

"I quite understand. Time will be of the essence, then." Morgan edged towards the door.

"If you could ask him if he knows anything about Charles Carstone, as well?" Alasdair suggested. "Probably nothing to do with this other business, but he keeps coming to mind."

"Same here," Toby said. "I'd love to know exactly why he needed their services."

"I'll try my best, sirs." Morgan disappeared into the hallway.

"Shall I close the door?" Jonny asked, tipping his head towards where it had been left slightly ajar when the manservant left.

Alasdair nodded. "Please do. He has his own methods, I'm sure, and as much as I'd be intrigued to hear them in action, a man must be allowed his degree of secrecy."

"Tell me all about your next film, if you're allowed to," Jonny said. "Then we won't be tempted to try and listen in to his half of the conversation."

"Excellent idea." Toby launched into an account of their latest project and how it had been revived from its dormant original.

Alasdair had barely started giving his opinion on the dialogue—which was better than usual, he felt—when Morgan re-entered the room, wearing a satisfied smile.

"There's no point in asking if you caught your friend nor if he had things of interest to tell you," Alasdair said.

The satisfied smile turned sheepish. "Is it that obvious, sir?"

"A silent film star couldn't have portrayed events so beautifully." Alasdair indicated a seat. "Please join us for a nightcap: you've clearly earned it."

"That would be most welcome. I shan't pretend I won't feel the benefit of it. One feels tainted by association, even if it's at several removes. Thank you." Morgan accepted the glass Toby had thrust in his direction and took a sip from it.

"I told Dennis—my contact—that you were on the trail of someone who used to work for *Herbert and Chapman*, which is why I'd asked about the company previously. He was glad to help and answered as many of my questions as he could. He'd had all the information from his son, who'd worked there for a short while before he was so disgusted at all the goings on that he found fresh employ. But before we discuss those, let me deal with Charles Carstone. Apparently, he feared he would be named as a correspondent in not one but two divorce cases and he wanted advice. Probably on whether he could avoid being dragged into the mire."

"Is that all?" Jonny asked. "We're not living in Victorian times. I know some folk still find it scandalous, but surely not in show-business."

"He was a Catholic," Toby said, quietly. "Quite a devout one, irrespective of his extra-curricular activities. I know because we chatted at a Landseer do one day and he spoke about how ironic it would be to have a Catholic called Charles playing a king of the same name who flirted— probably for political ends—with Catholicism. If the women he was involved with were of the same denomination it wouldn't sit well with the studio."

"Wasn't he married, as well? Sir Ian wouldn't like having such a flagrant adulterer on his books. Even if he were depicting a flagrant adulterer," Alasdair added. "Thanks, Morgan. It seems like we barked up the wrong tree where he's concerned. Back to the goings on."

"Yes, sir. It seems gossip among the employees was that both principals in the firm had been involved in Mosley's mob and they're said to have maintained similar sympathies up to the present day, although they clearly keep them under wraps."

"Matthew Firestone needs to know this," Toby said, "although I'd hope that it isn't news to everyone at Scotland Yard and that a quiet eye is already being kept on such folk. Did Dennis have anything to say about this mob's activities as opposed to their point of view?"

"Oh yes, sir, although nothing that would ring too many alarm bells unless you have the other piece of the jigsaw to attach it to."

"Then take a seat and tell all, please. Toby will organise some refreshment: the worker has earned his reward." Alasdair waited until Morgan was settled once more, with a plate of savouries, before asking, "Do you know when Dennis's son was working there? I'm just wondering if he overlapped with our missing woman."

"This would be the back end of last year and the start of this. I did ask if Dennis had heard tell of any ladies associated with the firm suddenly vanishing into thin air, but he hadn't, alas. He said he'd ask his son and report back although we're not to expect anything."

"Never mind," Alasdair said. "It would have been too much to hope that he'd have solved that part of our problem for us. Do carry on."

"This jigsaw piece that may only work when it's connected to another part of the puzzle. I don't promise it's related to your security threat but it could be." Morgan took a sustaining nibble. "Do you know whom I mean by Queen Salote?"

"I've heard of her," Jonny said. "Queen of one of the pacific islands, I think. Fiji? Samoa? My geography is hopeless, I'm afraid."

"Tonga." Alasdair and Toby spoke in concert.

"Toby, you elucidate while I fetch an atlas," Alasdair said, "because I'm not a hundred per cent certain where the island is, given how far the Pacific stretches."

104

"Thank the lord we only had to fly over the channel," Toby replied. "Anyway, Sir Ian—the head of Landseer—once had the privilege of meeting her. The conflab was something hush-hush concerning the war against Japan, and he told us all about it, although that 'all' was no doubt only what he was allowed to relate. Queen Salote is an impressive woman and not only in strength of character, being apparently even taller than Alasdair."

"Sir Ian took much delight in telling me that." Alasdair, holding the relevant page of the atlas so that everyone could see it, pointed to a spot on the map.

"Oh," Toby said. "Tonga's even more remote than I imagined."

"Half the world away." Alasdair passed the atlas to Jonny.

"Thanks." Jonny scrutinised the location before handing the atlas to Morgan. "If you held a grudge against this lady and wanted to act on it, better to wait for her to come here than for you to go there."

"A difficult journey indeed, although one can see the potential geographic importance of such a place in times of conflict." Morgan, as though this was a children's party and they were playing "pass the parcel", gave the map to Toby. "According to Dennis, they—being both Messrs Herbert and Chapman themselves—didn't like Queen Salote supporting the British and their allies."

Toby gave a derisive snort. "I dare say they also don't like the fact she *isn't* British. Or a chap. Or the same colour of skin as they are."

"Indeed, but it's apparently more than that. Dennis's son reckoned that pair would rather have had the island—Tonga—overrun by the Japanese. It apparently would have solved a few problems, although he never was privy to what his employers reckoned those problems were."

"How did Dennis's son hear this? Alasdair asked. "If it was by applying his ear to a door he shouldn't have been applying it to, don't be afraid to tell us: I suspect we'd have done the same had we been in that position."

Morgan grinned. "I believe it was a mixture of hearing the two principals speak quite openly—for example when they gave their opinion on Queen Salote—and subsequently being told of their pre-war affiliations by one of the secretaries who was a longstanding employee. I don't think the latter information was for general consumption but said employee was glad of a friendly ear to vent her frustrations into."

"Morgan, you're proving a treasure trove," Toby said. "Anything else?"

"Yes. On another occasion, Dennis's son heard one of the principles talking about how somebody needed to make a statement and show what they were made of. Given the context of the conversation, and the fact that he didn't at the time know about the Mosley stuff, he'd believed the man was talking about something relatively innocent like making a speech in parliament. When he mentioned it to the same secretary I referred to earlier, she gave him one of those 'you poor chap' smiles and told him he didn't know the half of it but not to worry his young head over such things. He said he couldn't not worry, which lead into her telling him that Chapman had a contact outside the firm who got used for unsavoury jobs, some of which ran pretty close to the wind. She had once returned to the office late to pick up something she'd left behind and blundered into a meeting between Chapman and this chap discussing what sounded horribly like an upcoming act of violence."

"What did she do?"

"Smiled sweetly, grabbed her stuff, left and never referred to it again, apparently. Unfortunately, she hasn't the

106

capacity Dennis's son had for finding a new position: a very well-paid job and an aged parent who relied on her entirely."

"She might be a useful contact within the firm should we need one," Toby said. "I'd be happy for her to vent into my ears, although God forbid that we should inadvertently be the cause of her losing her position. That's the most valid reason I've yet heard for keeping one's trap shut."

While Alasdair sympathised with the viewpoint, the mention of job loss puzzled him. "It doesn't sound as though she's been given the boot for what she heard, so why should she lose her job for talking to us if we employ our usual discretion?"

"It was less her being rumbled for snitching to us, than this business leading to the firm closing. I was having an overabundance of conscience." Toby ran his hand through his hair.

"Was it hearing about acts of violence that made Dennis's son leave?" Jonny asked. "By the way, does he have a name and I missed it due to the excellence of this port?"

Morgan inclined his head, probably in lieu of a shrug, which he'd no doubt have felt was beneath his dignity. "He must have a name but Dennis didn't use it and I didn't press him. He may have his reasons for not divulging it."

"Quite." Alasdair would have loved to know what they were.

"To answer the other part of the question," Morgan continued, "I believe all these things built up. The final straw was when he discovered what kind of clients they liked to defend. Apparently he was only privy to that when he'd been through a probationary period."

"We may need to speak to Dennis's son if all else fails on the missing person's front," Toby said. "The timings may work out that he and Alexandra overlapped."

"I'm sure Dennis would be pleased to facilitate that, sir. The same would no doubt apply if you or the police wished to discuss what the son heard. Dennis is a true patriot—in the best sense of the term—and would be horrified if he thought that any mischief was being intended for Her Majesty's great event."

"Excellent. It will be a treat reporting all of this to Firestone. Queen Salote will no doubt be attending the coronation, so this all fits together with a possible attempt at disrupting that event." Jonny raised his glass in Morgan's direction. "Thank you."

"Absolutely," Alasdair chimed in.

"My pleasure to help. An occasional treat and none the worse for that." Morgan quickly hid a delighted smirk. "Shall I leave you to your discussions, sir?"

"If you wish," Alasdair said. "I think we're winding up now."

Morgan rose, saying that he had things to attend to and wishing them every success in pursuing the business. Once he'd gone, Toby said, "Brilliant idea of yours to pick his brains, Alasdair. I wonder why Dennis wouldn't give his son's name, though? Unless he did and Morgan's been sworn to secrecy."

"Who knows." Alasdair shrugged. "Dennis didn't want to reveal it until he'd checked with the man himself? Feared that Mrs Dennis would scold him for embroiling their boy in our business?"

"Perhaps it's just an embarrassing name," Jonny suggested, "chosen in a mad moment of whimsy or patriotism. Gengulphus. Mafeking. Pointless speculating about it, I guess." He stifled a yawn. "Are we done or is there more to thrash out? I feel the need of my blameless bed."

Toby pursed his lips. "The last little bit to iron out—for the time being anyway—is how much we say to Mesdames Crouch and Richards when we go in search of Alexandra among their roll calls."

"We'll certainly need to be canny, as it were," Alasdair agreed. "Ignoring anything about the coronation—which I don't think we should touch on with them at present because that risks starting a panic—it'll look damned odd if we suddenly start asking after a particular woman."

"They'll think that one or both of you fancies her?" Jonny chuckled. "Although maybe that would help with the smokescreen you put up between you and your devotees."

Toby snorted a loud protest. "It won't help if she actually fancies one of us, rather than simply admiring our acting ability, because she'll then be heartbroken when she realises that wasn't our motive. Hell hath no fury and all that."

"While I agree, I can't help thinking that such a drastic strategy could flush her out," Alasdair said, then raised his hand. "I'm not suggesting we employ it unless all else fails."

"I think honesty's the best policy, if you'll excuse a cliché. Or as much honesty as we can muster in the circumstances," Toby added. "What if we simply say that one of Alexandra's friends has lost touch and is worried about her? That carries the air of authenticity and isn't threatening."

"Unless Alexandra is told that and assumes it's Lloyd," Alasdair pointed out. "If she's already got wind that you were invited to his Monday meeting, she might smell a rat."

"Then we say a female friend. We don't need to mention Moira by name. We could also say that if Alexandra doesn't want to be contacted, a reassurance to us of her being safe and well, via Miss Crouch or Mrs Richards would be enough. With the proviso that we can be certain said assurance wasn't issued under duress and came from Alexandra herself rather than someone else covering their tracks. Those two ladies are sensible enough to be told that Alexandra may not want to be found by her old pals, and we also know how much they trust us not to arse about with their precious time."

"I can imagine they have to be both sensible and strong of character to keep those clubs running without fights breaking out," Jonny said.

Alasdair produced a mock horrified look. "Fights? Are your crowd inclined to fisticuffs, then, Toby? Mine are far more refined."

Toby poked out his tongue. "So are mine, but Jonny's got a point. I've heard that petty jealousies can spark over who has accumulated the most time speaking to us or who is the most devoted fan. I've seen Miss Crouch nip them in the bud before they can fester—and that's with me present—so I dread to think what goes on behind my back."

"You're no doubt better off not knowing." Jonny rose. "And now, I really must go."

"Shall I ask Morgan to drive you home?" Alasdair said.

"Don't bother him. He's gone above and beyond already tonight and I can pick up a cab easily enough. I promise I'll report back anything that needs reporting." With that assurance, Jonny donned his coat and had reached the front doorstep when he said, "Carstone. His death must have been an accident, if he was a devout Catholic. Mortal sin and all that." He waved and headed off.

"He's not daft, that lad," Toby said, as they returned to their seats after waving their guest off. "Thinking of Carstone and Landseer, there's yet another job to add to the list. We'll need to get Sir Ian's permission to proceed with this, if it turns out there's any risk to our lives and limbs, which there might be if we're duelling with anarchists and acts of violence. I'll need to update him on Lloyd's group so we can morph one into the other although the permission part needs more urgency."

"Agreed. We should do it before we speak to Geraldine, as a matter of courtesy, although the fan club stuff can proceed, I'd say."

"Talking of fan clubs, I don't know if I've ever told you that I often wonder whether—given the membership of these groups seems entirely female—there's an equivalent group for the male of the species. They'd have to keep themselves undercover, perhaps, for obvious reasons, unless they meet openly with the pretence of worshipping the ground Fiona walks on. Although that would risk attracting members who really do pine for her."

"It wouldn't surprise me if there *was* such a clandestine group, perhaps to admire the whole range of attractive male actors rather than just us. If so, they'd no doubt be delighted to know that we have an eye for the same, although in our case a very limited selection. I don't want anyone but you." Alasdair left his chair, to sit on the arm of Toby's. "Filming starts tomorrow, alas and alack for our love life. A chaste kiss and then out the door you go, Mr Bowe."

"Alas and alack indeed. We can't have the king looking raddled tomorrow."

"I'm only the heir to the throne in the scenes we're filming, so I'm allowed to give off a hint of a young rake, although not too much of one. A night of abandon with you would exceed acceptable levels of debauchery." They shared a sufficiently passionate kiss to produce a warm glow, then Toby availed himself of Morgan's chauffeuring duties, leaving Alasdair to mull over all the strange developments of the evening.

What had started with trying to find an explanation for the unexplainable had become something prosaic but much more serious. Alasdair turned to the hall mirror and found himself addressing it as though he were giving a speech to camera. "We should hand this over to the police and then leave well alone, if we had any sense. While we're not unaccustomed to physical danger in the service of our country, tackling anarchists is different flying a spitfire. But we promised to find a missing woman and I'd hate to break a vow."

Was he trying to persuade himself or practicing his speech to Sir Ian? And if that danger included a threat to Toby, would Alasdair still be as enthusiastic for the chase?

Chapter Nine

The next morning, Toby had set the alarm earlier than he needed, in order to be ready for the Landseer car's arrival. He wanted to ring Miss Crouch and she'd made it plain to him that the best time for calling her was before she left for work. And if Miss Crouch made it plain, nobody was going to argue with her, not even her favourite actor.

"Mr Bowe," she said, on answering the telephone, sounding bright as a button. "You're up with the lark."

"I'm afraid so. I have filming today but before that, I'm on investigating business. We've been asked to find somebody who may or may not have gone missing. A young lady called Alexandra Cummings who apparently is a member of the excellent fan club you run, hence me ringing you at this unearthly hour. Her friend—a lady of my acquaintance—is worried about her." Why did "lady of my acquaintance" sound horribly like a euphemism for girlfriend?

"We have at least one Alexandra among the membership. Sorry to be wishy washy but I don't have all the details such as surnames at my fingertips."

"Now that surprises me, Miss Crouch. I thought you'd have everything stored in that remarkable brain of yours."

She snorted. "Save the flattery for one of your starlets. I have all the spare capacity of my memory strictly reserved for my patients. Ask me about one of them, and I could give you chapter and verse. That's why I make everyone at the club wear name badges when we convene."

"There's me thinking those badges are purely for my benefit when I visit." Toby chuckled.

"I no doubt said it was. Like I say at other meetings that it's to help any new or occasional members, so they can feel more at ease. You're the only one who knows it's for my benefit."

"I'll keep your secret."

"I believe you." Miss Crouch's chatty tone became professional again. "What's this young lady like?"

"According to her friends, fairly nondescript. Pretty, soft spoken, of average height. She has brown hair and brown eyes. Might have an unusual interest in the weather," Toby added, in case that rang a bell. "She might have a foot in two camps, as it were, being also a member of Alasdair's fan club."

"I see. I'm afraid I'm not aware of anyone who goes to both sets of meetings, but it's possible they would keep it quiet in case of a fight about which of you or Alasdair is best. Someone with a foot in both camps might be regarded as either a traitor or a spy."

"This conversation's turning into a bit of an eye opener. When I see Alasdair at the studio, I'll let him know about this internecine strife. He'll be as shocked as I am." Although would he, given that Mrs Richards could be telling him something similar?

"Some people are…let's say fixated. You have no idea how cutthroat it can get around who occupies the front row of chairs when you come to one of our meetings. However, I digress. Let me check my records for your Alexandra, although I'm afraid I won't be able to root through my files until this evening."

"Take as much time as you need." Although surely it would be a relatively easy job. There couldn't be that many women in the fan club, could there? "If you could please let me know what you discover either here if it's in the evening or via the Landseer office if you ring during the day. I'll tell them to expect a call. And you must expect a call from me

114

because this counts as duty above and beyond. I owe you a bottle of champagne."

"There's no need for that, although I'd be silly to refuse. Wish me luck."

"I wish you every scrap of luck in the world." Especially if it meant he got one over on Alasdair by finding the necessary address first.

Chapter Ten

At the studio, making the most of one of the few times that he was available, Alasdair put a call through to Mrs Richards, crossing his fingers that she'd also be free to speak to him. He used her home number, which she'd given him in case of emergencies—such as his falling ill and having to pull out of a commitment to address a meeting. Or announcing his engagement to some lucky lady and wanting to ensure that his devotees had prior warning and didn't faint with shock when they read the news. The latter had been Mrs Richards's suggestion and Alasdair had greeted it with what he hoped was the right mixture of alacrity and coyness.

"Oh, Mr Hamilton," she said on picking up the telephone and hearing his greeting. "You don't usually ring me—is everything all right?"

"All is well, Alice, and how many times must I remind you to call me Alasdair?"

"Old habits die hard, I'm afraid. How can I be of help?"

Alasdair smiled: there was no nonsense with Alice. "I'm trying to track down one of your members, for a friend of a friend. Bit of a complicated story but I felt sure you were the person to help her."

"Is this one of your cases?" She asked gleefully. "Happy to oblige if I can."

"Yes, it is. A young woman called Alexandra Cummings, who we think is a member of Toby's fan club, as well. It's a friend of *his* who got to know Alexandra via a totally different club—I told you it was complicated tale—but she's not attended recently and so folk are concerned that she might be ill."

"Well, off the top of my head, I believe we have two members called Alexandra, although I don't think either has the surname Cummings. One comes to every meeting—even breaking her leg six months back didn't stop her—and she was there when you visited us recently. The other stopped attending in January or February."

"That sounds like it might be her, although that non-attendance could be coincidence. Not having seen a picture of the missing lady, I wouldn't know if she was the broken leg one, whom I must have seen. Odd about the surname being different, though. Is there anyone else called Cummings, who perhaps uses her middle name when she deals with you?"

"I'm afraid not, although there may be a simple explanation for the surname not matching. If Alexandra is recently married, or recently divorced, she might still use her maiden name with us. I can even imagine someone employing different names if they attend both yours and Toby's clubs, so nobody can twig they're shouting for both sides." Alice chuckled. "You know how cagey people can be."

"I certainly do." Such behaviour would be in keeping with membership of the *Monday Evening Association*. "We have a description, although not a very specific one. She's of medium height, had—has—mousy hair and brown eyes, was said to be pretty and soft spoken. In her late twenties perhaps and always neatly turned out. And I apologise for the *had* and *has* part. We're hoping nothing's happened to her, obviously, but that uncertainty must have been playing on my mind."

"Her friend must be very concerned for it to have rubbed off on you. I'm afraid that description could apply to either of the Alexandras I have in my mind, if one stretched the late twenties to early thirties so it included the woman with the broken leg. That assumes Toby's pal is as bad at guessing ages as I am." She giggled again. "Some women never look their age, for better or worse, and if I didn't have my records I wouldn't have a clue."

That meant the one who was closer in age to Richard's guess had disappeared from the fan club. "The other Alexandra: do you know why she stopped coming to your meetings?"

"I'm afraid not. My predecessor as chairwoman used to ask people directly, after they left us, but on the last occasion it led to unpleasantness. The woman concerned had decided she'd gone off you—I know you're sensible enough for me not to have to gloss over the fact—and now preferred Stewart Granger. Unfortunately, news of that switching of allegiance got out and led to an almighty hoo-hah amongst our membership, including one or two unnecessary and unpleasant letters being sent to the woman who'd left. We put a stop to that, and I put a stop to asking folk directly once they'd made a decision. So, unless the departing person volunteers the information, I simply don't know why they've gone. We're all grown-ups with the right to make our own decisions, so the group needs to accept they've done so and move on."

"That sounds eminently sensible." Perhaps it would be for the best for Moira et al to do the same, were it not for the *Herbert and Chapman* business. "Now, you obviously keep member details. It would be wrong of me to ask you to give me these two women's addresses, if you have them, but might I impose on you to ask them to contact me via the office at Landseer. You can tell them what I said about Toby's friend being concerned for their welfare and wanting reassurance. They'll no doubt know which group is involved, so can guess at the friend's identity."

"Of course. I'll make sure she knows it's not Mr Bowe's appreciation society we're referring to. Actually, Mr Ham— Alasdair—if you don't mind, I'll ask the Alexandras to reassure *me* that they're well and I'll report their answers back. There may be a jolly good reason why the young lady concerned has disappeared and hasn't let her friends know where she's gone." Mrs Richards sighed. "Perhaps it might be best not to mention Toby's friend at all. I'll say it's us at the club who are worried."

"That sounds a splendid idea." Maybe he should suggest to Toby that he get Miss Crouch to do the same, unless he'd already been in touch with her. "A final question. Does one of these women show a particular interest in weather forecasting?"

"Not that I recall. Should she have done?"

"Toby's friend said she did, that was all. It's probably not relevant. And now, I've taken up quite enough of your time. Thank you for being so understanding and so helpful."

"It's a treat to be involved in one of your investigations. I hope I can give Toby's friend the reassurance he or she needs."

"She. Although not one of Toby's *lady* friends, if that makes sense." He should stop now before the pudding became too obviously overegged. Alasdair made his goodbyes, then sat for a moment to assimilate what he'd heard. Two possible candidates for the missing woman, although the broken leg surely ruled one of them out if it was coincident with the time Alexandra still attended the Monday meetings. The matter of the surname gnawed at him, though, especially when he took into account the level of pretence that abounded within Lloyd's little gang. Maybe Cummings *was* an alias, although Jeff having known Alexandra through work surely ruled that out. It struck him that a different and more vexatious lie could have been employed: perhaps she'd never been a member of Alasdair's fan club—or Toby's—and had put up the pretence for reasons of her own, as the others had done concerning their

119

powers. In which case, their trail was going to go cold almost before it had the chance to warm up.

***

The actors' plan had been to make an appointment with Sir Ian for the first available time that suited all parties, but as luck would have it, that Tuesday morning the great man himself made one of his regular yet spontaneous visits to the set. Sir Ian liked to keep an eye on all his productions, no matter how much he trusted the actors and vast array of other staff involved. He had a nose for spotting when something wasn't quite as it should be and the earlier he could ensure that a film would pass muster, by identifying an issue and dealing with it, the better.

On this occasion, all seemed to be well. He watched a couple of short scenes being filmed, nodding happily as they progressed, then when everyone broke for refreshments he joined them for a cup of tea and a chat.

"Excellent playing, as usual." Sir Ian said, beaming at his three stars, who had clustered around him. "I have every confidence this will be a winner."

Profuse thanks broke out all round: nobody liked to think they were saddled with a stinker and Sir Ian's judgment was to be trusted. Alasdair asked, "Has all the business with *Naughty Nelly* been settled or is it a sore topic?"

"The censor is satisfied at last. We took out what he regarded as the worst bits, which means we've got some others past him. The kind of lines which look fairly innocent on the page but are dynamite in the execution, especially with a knowing glance or a leer." Sir Ian grinned. "We've assured them that all the publicity will make it plain that the eponymous Nelly is the historical Miss Gwyn, which seemed to appease. Never have that issue with your films."

"Long may that continue." Toby—who'd manoeuvred himself to Sir Ian's side—said in a low voice, "Might we have a word, in a minute? We've an update regarding that *Monday Evening Association* meeting I got invited to, and it's turned out to have led us into a new case. A potentially serious one."

"Of course." Sir Ian glanced at his watch. "Now?"

"Perfect." Alasdair bowed elaborately to Fiona, in a style befitting his costume. "If you could excuse us a moment."

"Of course. I could do with seeing my dresser, because this thing—" she indicated a place on her bodice, just under her ribs, "—is like an instrument of torture. How and why women wore them I couldn't say." She sashayed away, while the three men headed for Alasdair's dressing room, where Toby wasted no time in giving a brief account of why they now had a logical explanation for the group members' so-called powers.

"Sounds like a plot from one of our comedies," Sir Ian observed, as the story concluded. "Misunderstandings and cover-ups all round, with a healthy thread of romance running through."

"We had a similar thought, because throughout our dealings with this group, various elements have felt somewhat unreal. The case we've been led into feels all too horribly real, though." Alasdair continued with a swift run through regarding Alexandra's disappearance and her having overheard an unsettling conversation at work.

"I've heard of *Herbert and Chapman*, when they helped defend an actor from a rival studio." Sir Ian's moue of disapproval spoke volumes. "Fingers in some unsavoury pies and possibly fascists to boot."

121

"Definitely fascists, according to a reliable source. That fact may be directly relevant to what she heard being discussed, which sounded like a threat to disrupt the coronation." Alasdair's insured eyebrow registered disgust.

"The coronation? The miserable sods." Sir Ian must have been deeply affected, because that was the strongest form of swearing he usually employed. "Any idea what this plot consists of? And before you answer that—stupid question no doubt—have you told the police?"

"Young Jonny Stewart is doing so today, possibly right now if not already," Toby reassured his boss. "If he warns us off because it's dangerous, we'll step back. Now, to answer the first part of your question, we're not certain what the threat is, but it may involve Queen Salote. We have evidence that they don't like her, or her wartime allegiances or something else about the great lady."

"The absolute bastards." Sir Ian excelled himself on the swear word front. "She's a magnificent woman, as beautiful and as brilliant as our own queen. They could run the world between them, if allowed to do so. Queen Salote will be here as befits her station and no doubt will be part of the procession, so it would be easy enough for a determined person to pick her out. Shades of Archduke Franz Ferdinand and look at the mess that helped stir up. If I could get my hands on these people beforehand, they'd regret they'd even considered such a thing."

"We'd join you." Alasdair jiggled his eyebrow in disapproval. "Although I've had to keep reminding myself that in British law, it's a case of innocent until proven guilty. Even if Messrs Herbert and Chapman were discussing such a thing, they may never have intended the plans to come to fruition. How many people say things like, 'I could kill you,' with never an intention of carrying out the threat? Idle words."

Sir Ian harrumphed. "Well, I hope the police take this seriously. If they don't, let me know and I'll pull some strings. I still have contacts."

"We'll do that," Toby said, "although Superintendent Firestone isn't the short of man to ignore such a lead if it comes onto his radar, especially from a reliable source and we'd count ourselves as that."

"Let's hope you're correct. Anything else?"

"Back to matters *Naughty Nelly* related," Alasdair said, "we've run across Charles Carstone's name on the fringes of this inquiry and he's become a bee in both our bonnets. We know that he was potentially going to be named in a couple of divorce cases, which makes it suspicious that he died under the wheels of a train before that happened. Yet he was a Catholic and wouldn't have risked his mortal soul."

Sir Ian, face grim, nodded slowly. "My thoughts exactly. I also feel some guilt about his death, because he came and confessed what was going on and how he'd taken up professional help as a precaution. I'm afraid I made the studio's position clear, so when I heard about his accident…well, I wish that his rescuer had been able to save him. It may have meant the end of his involvement in *Naughty Nelly* but I'd rather his life had been saved."

"Indeed. Sadly, he may have made the wrong choice in his professional help. *Herbert and Chapman.*"

Sir Ian shuddered. "Keep me informed on all fronts, then. I don't want either of you ending up under the wheels on the Central Line or indeed any other."

Once Sir Ian had left, Alasdair said, "Do you think that warning was specific or simply a good exit line?"

"The latter. If he knew of a particular threat, he'd have passed it on to us."

"Hmm." Alasdair frowned. "Where *has* the time gone this morning? I've been meaning to ask if you'd had any luck with Miss Crouch."

"Not yet. She's going to rummage through her rotary card index or wherever she keeps the members details and get back to me as soon as she can."

"She's happy to give you an address?"

"I assume so. I was going to suggest she did the contacting but the matter didn't arise." Toby had his hand halfway to ruffling his hair when he remembered he was wearing a wig and his dresser would slap said hand for disarranging it. "How about you?"

Alasdair exhaled in a frustrated manner. "Mrs Richards is going to contact her two Alexandras on our behalf although I'm not holding out much hope. One suffered a broken leg six months ago so she's probably not our woman and while the other candidate is promising—on the grounds that she's stopped attending the fan meetings—she doesn't have the right surname. Neither of them do. In fact, nobody at the club does."

"Lummy. I suppose Alexandra might be using a different name for a legitimate reason? Like some actors adopt an alias."

"Perhaps. Mrs Richards and I came up with several explanations for the discrepancy, but none of them sit well with me, given the context of the story."

"I don't blame you." Toby didn't like this at all. "More subterfuge, do you think, only this time from Alexandra? Either when she joined your fan club or when she joined Lloyd's mob? Although the latter seems less likely, given that Jeff knew her at work and would surely have spotted any mismatch in names."

"Who knows? At least I trust what our two ladies say, although whether I believe one hundred percent anyone else involved with this case—present company, Jonny and Morgan excepted—I increasingly doubt. It wouldn't surprise me if there are more layers to peel off this especially smelly onion."

"A very apt analogy." Toby edged towards the door. "The Landseer publicity office is bound to have cuttings related to Carstone's inquest. I'd be interested in the name of that aspiring good Samaritan. Might be interesting to get his or her view. Now, to end on a lighter note, Miss Crouch was saying she felt that devotees wouldn't necessarily admit to being members of both our clans, as 'twere. Not to their fellow members."

"Yes, I got that impression, too, from Mrs Richards. A great rivalry." Alasdair chuckled. "I now have visions of our most loyal devotees smiting each other with a glove and arranging for pistols at dawn to defend the honour of which of us is best." He dropped his voice. "Just as well we don't feel any need to have that fight. Equals always."

"Equals." Toby opened the door, shook Alasdair's hand—not the kiss he'd have liked to have shared but acceptable in the circumstances—then headed for the toilet. His cup of coffee had gone straight through him, as his mother would have put it, and a stroll to the facilities and back would allow his mind to get out of investigating mode and into acting again. Although given that in the next scene he merely had to hang around in the background looking decorative, it would be hard to keep his thoughts away from the apparent lack of an Alexandra Cummings on Alasdair's fans' roll call. And speculating whether there'd be one on *his*.

***

Tuesday night, Toby shut his own front door with a profound sense of relief. Much as he'd have loved to spend

125

an evening doing absolutely nothing other than smooching with Alasdair, they'd seen a lot of each other recently. Which meant they'd been seen together a lot and a short while spent apart, except for on the sound stage, wouldn't hurt in the preserving-their-reputation department. Anyway, they had tasks to execute.

As Jonny had left the previous evening, he'd offered to call with an update on any conversation he managed to have with Matthew Firestone. Toby had equally offered to ring Jonny, ostensibly on the premise that he wasn't sure what time he'd be home from the studio, but actually because he didn't want to be twiddling his thumbs waiting for the call. Better to take the initiative and to take it at the first opportunity.

Fortunately, Jonny was at home and able to talk at Toby's first attempt at telephoning. After receiving a brief update on the fan clubs side of things, Jonny said, "Plot thickening all round. You'll be delighted to know that I was able to speak to our esteemed constabulary pal this very morning and he's most grateful I did. If he had any prior knowledge of a plot against Queen Salote, he was keeping it to himself and the same goes for the disappearance of Alexandra. He says we can keep digging—on both counts—if we wish but to be extremely careful. He doesn't want to face the wrath of either your fans or the clan Stewart for having caused injury to their flowers of manhood."

"That serious? What does he know that he's keeping under his hat?"

"I asked him something similar and he said there was nothing specific, but any matter like this makes him fear the worst. Take that as you wish."

"I will." With perhaps a pinch of salt about the "nothing specific" part.

"Interestingly, the firm of *Herbert and Chapman* has come into his distant view previously, being on the fringes of objectionable stuff, although nothing that he or his colleagues could pin them down for. Matthew, fair man that he is, said that everyone has the right to be defended in court and, for example, sticking up for a child molester doesn't make you one yourself, but the alacrity with which Messrs H and C leap to defend said people gives one pause. He knew about their sympathies, as well, and you can imagine how those sit with him."

"I bet he's pleased to have a potential reason for bringing them to book. Anything else?"

Jonny sniffed. "Only that the upcoming events have apparently brought a few of the regulars out. You know, little old ladies who are sure they've witnessed a gang planning something awful but who in reality are either starting to lose their faculties or are possibly lonely and in need of a friendly conversation. Then apparently there's the chaps who want to confess to the worst kinds of crimes, either past or future. Every instance has to be taken seriously, but it's a drain on the police's time."

"Yes. Too easy to dismiss them all as time-wasters and then find some clever soul has hidden a real crime by confessing to it among a trail of false ones. Like a plot Mrs Christie might use." Toby stifled a yawn. "You've done well, young Jonny. Now, please excuse me if I have to depart, but it's been a long old day and I have more job to do before I can curl up with the Light Programme and a good book."

Only his intended reading matter was the press cuttings about Carstone and his accident.

"What a glamorous life you lead." With a chuckle, Jonny put down the telephone, leaving Toby to the tender ministrations of his man, North, who had a light supper ready to serve whenever it was needed. Now was the perfect moment, as Toby's rumbling stomach advised him: hopefully, he could get the whole repast consumed before Miss Crouch called.

He was just finishing the last soupcon of cheese, tucked up in his favourite chair for radio listening, when the telephone rang and North sprang into action to answer it.

"Miss Crouch?" North's deep, melodious voice sounded from the hallway. "Yes, Mr Bowe is expecting your call. Let me inform him."

Toby let himself be informed. North wouldn't have appreciated entering the sitting room as Toby was exiting it: a gentleman's gentleman had to discharge his job properly.

"Miss Crouch," Toby said, as he took up the receiver. "Thank you so much for calling."

"My pleasure. Now, we appear to have three Alexandras among our membership, although none of them have the surname Cummings. Did I note that part incorrectly?"

"You did not. After I spoke to you, I learned that she might go by more than one name and I'm hoping that's only the surname as opposed to the Christian name or else we've no chance of pinning her down. Can you eliminate any of your three?"

"The first one on my list is too old to match the description you gave me, so unless your informant is wrong, we can discard her. The next one I think came to the last meeting, the one you attended. It was her first and I particularly remembered her because of how tall she was. Too tall for the woman you seek."

"I feel like Goldilocks. This lady is too old, the other too tall."

Miss Crouch chuckled. "I'd pay good money to see you as Goldilocks. Perhaps you'd consider it for one of your charity pantomimes. So, we have the third Alexandra, a

Miss Munsey, about whom I have a note which helps me place her. She'd not long been coming to the meetings when she offered to help with any jobs that needed doing—there's a fair amount of admin at times—and one of the longer-standing, more mature, members took umbrage. She said that time in the ring should count in cases like that and that Alexandra should get in the queue. I felt sorry for the poor girl, because she was only trying to be helpful and I told her privately that I would certainly call on her if she was needed. In fact, I went out of my way to make sure I had a few small tasks to give her, which she did admirably. That's a long-winded way of telling you why she sticks in my mind."

"Be as long-winded as you like, as long as we get to identifying her correctly." Toby recalled the remark Alasdair had made at *The Swan with Two Necks*, about Alexandra Cummings might have been using an alias. If that was a bow drawn at a venture, it had hit the spot. "Was Miss Munsey at the recent meeting?"

"No. In fact, I doubt she's been there since January or February. Sorry to be vague, but I don't keep a record of who comes when. The aforementioned older lady and her pals seem to do that unofficially for themselves."

Yet another group Alexandra had left. "Has she let you know why she no longer comes along? You can be honest and say that she's gone off me and wants to throw her cap at some other actor."

Miss Crouch gave a derisive snort. "As if anyone would do that. Mr Bowe, I know that you're used to exercising discretion, with your work alongside the police and all that, so I can air a suspicion."

"Air away. You have my promise of secrecy. Unless, of course, this is a matter the police have to be informed about." Toby tried to ignore the unpleasant thought that

129

employing discretion might concern Miss Crouch having discovered something that he and Alasdair wouldn't want discovered, namely their relationship. There'd be no blabbing to the police in that instance.

"I wondered if she was expecting a baby."

"Oh." That was a possibility they'd not considered. Hadn't Richard said something about Alexandra glowing at the last meeting she'd attended? What if that had been due to her condition rather than her upcoming change of employment? "What made you think that?"

"Her face. I saw a possible mask of pregnancy there, if a confirmed bachelor would know what that is."

"I don't, but I'll look it up forthwith."

"It's a darkening of the skin. That's all I have to base my theory on, because she stopped attending before her waistline had a chance to become too noticeable. Assuming it was expanding, of course. I could be wrong."

A practiced eye such as this hospital matron possessed would have been less at risk of error than a laywoman—or layman—though. If this was *the* Alexandra, then either his promise of confidentiality or his duty to Moira was going to have to go by the board and the latter looked the likelier. He and Alasdair would have to tell her that they knew why Alexandra had gone off and that was all they were prepared to say. "Would you know if she's either married or recently widowed? That could explain why we have two names for her. Although I don't suppose she'd hide herself away in shame in that instance."

"I wouldn't know about her marital status. She's listed as Miss Munsey, that's all."

"I see. Well, that leaves me with the challenge of finding a way to tell my mutual friend what's happened to Alexandra without actually telling said friend what's happened. Assuming what we think has happened *has* happened." Toby chuckled. "If that makes any sense. I've been working hard at the studio and I'm losing coherence."

"It makes entire sense. I'm sure you'll find a way to reassure them, especially if we can pin down what's going on and it's nothing sinister. Would you like her address or would you prefer I made contact?"

"In any other circumstance, I'd suggest I send you a note that you could forward to Alexandra, asking her to get in contact with her old pal. However, time is of the essence, so if you feel you could trust me with Miss Munsey's address, I'd be very grateful. I can tell you, in strictest confidence, that this business might be more serious than a missing person's case."

"Ah." The nod Miss Couch was no doubt giving was almost audible. "I won't ask you to expand on that, because I know you paddle in some murky waters, investigation wise. Pencil at the ready?"

"Poised over the paper as we speak." Toby jotted down the address—a road in Finsbury Park—thanked Miss Crouch for being a marvel, reminded her that a bottle of champagne would be coming in her direction and then ended the call so he could contact Alasdair with the news. Frustratingly, when he put a call through to his lover, the line was busy, Alasdair probably engaged in his own detection tasks. No doubt any discussion could wait until morning, unless Alasdair uncovered a bombshell, in which case he'd surely be sharing that later. Toby could use the time to plan the next step: would he be writing to Alexandra via the Finsbury Park address or visiting himself?

Or was this a job better suited to Jonny, who had the benefit of a face that didn't look out from dozens of film posters all over London?

And who, Toby reminded himself with a frustrated sigh, could go out and about any time he wanted with his chap

Roger, frequenting establishments that Toby and Alasdair could never be seen entering. Sometimes fame and fortune proved a tough account to pay.

He settled down again, picked up the file of press cuttings and worked through them, ready to make notes as he went along, although his page became only sparsely occupied apart from obvious things like the date of February the fifth. The reports gave no hint of what had troubled Carstone, nor any mention of Messrs Herbert or Chapman, although there were conflicting accounts of whether he'd been talking to a woman while he waited for his train. Inevitably, the array of witnesses couldn't quite agree on what had happened prior to the tragedy, except that the actor had edged his way towards the platform edge, as though keen to be first on the train. Among the most convincing witnesses was the man who'd attempted to save Carstone—James Salt—and the person who'd saved Salt's life, one Robert Archer. There were fuzzy pictures of them with some of the newspaper reports, probably syndicated given their similarity and the type of photographs that could have been of anyone.

Why did something about the names ring a bell, though? *Mr J Salt.* Surely that was one of the names he saw at Herbert & Chapman's office, one of those he was going to ask his nephew about and which had subsequently gone out of his head. That lapse didn't matter now. The surname wasn't common so gave a potential link between the firm and the moment Carstone had died. He quickly scanned back through the other reports, which said that Salt and Archer didn't know each other and were simply there to travel home at the end of the working day.

What that coincidence of name signified, Toby couldn't tell, but he was going to have to discuss it with Alasdair that evening, or he'd burst.

Chapter Eleven

Alasdair headed straight for the bathroom when he arrived home. The first few days of filming a new project always seemed to leave him sweating and in a state he'd describe as frankly disgusting. Before he could face putting a call through to Geraldine, he'd need a shower. Not that she'd be able to see—or smell—the condition he was in, but a man had his standards to maintain and to be clean in this context was like wearing the correct undergarments for an historical film. No-one in the audience would be able to spot if you had 1950's underpants on, but the actor would know and—according to the costume department—the way one moved oneself would be different. He thought of poor Fiona and her discomfort with her bodice and was grateful he didn't have to endure such an instrument of torture.

He'd just come down the stairs, clean and refreshed, when the telephone rang.

"Mr Hamilton? Mrs Richards here."

"Lovely to hear from you. And it's Alasdair, please."

She chuckled. "Old habits die hard. I have a surname for the Alexandra who no longer attends our meetings. Munsey. I don't have a note if she's a Miss or a Mrs, although I don't think she wore a wedding ring so go with Miss. I wrote to her—and to the other Alexandra, who's called Chilcott, just in case—as soon as I put the phone down from speaking to you, so we'll await a response."

"Many thanks." Alasdair started to make notes. "Now, I may be reading too much into your tone of voice, but it sounds as though you might have more to tell me?"

"I do indeed. I confess I didn't leave matters there, because that struck me as being most remiss. You're a busy man and anything I can do to help chivvy this up—without sticking my oar in too far—seems only right. So, rather than put the letters in the post, I decided to take them round myself this afternoon, to the two places I'd addressed them to. On the off chance I might see one of the women concerned. I hope you don't mind?"

"Of course I don't. I admire your taking the initiative." Especially if it had paid dividends.

"That's a relief. Anyway, don't get too excited, because I didn't manage to see either lady, although I did make some progress. Alexandra Chilcott's mother was weeding their front garden when I called, so I gave a precis of our conversation, which ended with her saying she'd pass the letter on but as far as she knew, her daughter hadn't cut off ties with anyone. Mothers don't know everything, of course."

"Quite so." Apart from Alasdair's mother, who had known about his romantic preferences possibly before he did. "Did you happen as well to meet Miss Munsey's mother? And that's not easy to say: I'm so pleased I don't have it in my current script."

Mrs Richards giggled. "Quite a tongue twister. No, when I went to her digs in Finsbury Park I didn't come across her mother, but did turn up something more intriguing. I can quite see how you and Mr Bowe find investigation so enthralling. I felt like Miss Climpson and, like her, being a lady of more mature years than your good self, I can get away with asking questions that a younger man couldn't."

"I bet you were just as efficient as Miss Climpson." Dorothy L Sayers had got it spot on in her depiction of the underrated usefulness of older women. "What did you discover?"

"Initially that the landlady made a lovely cup of tea, had a light touch with a rock cake and was probably lonely and therefore appreciative of someone to chat to. That's relevant, because I think it made it easier for her to be frank with me." Mrs Richards took a deep breath. "Alexandra gave notice and moved out weeks ago. She left no forwarding address other than a place where she could pick up her mail. By the time that emerged, Mrs Carson—the landlady—had my letter in her hand and promised she'd forward it. I couldn't exactly snatch it back and say I'd go there myself in order to have a nose about."

"A wise decision. Especially as we have a young chap helping us on the case and that's exactly the kind of thing he would be very good at busying himself with." Assuming they had all the necessary the details. "You didn't by some wonderful chance get hold of this forwarding address?"

"I'm proud to say that I did. I'd already told Mrs Carson how I was connected to Alexandra through your fan club, which also helped establish a rapport between us, as she loves your films and often chatted to her ex-tenant about them. I mentioned the times I'd sent a letter on club business and said I'd have more to send so if I could have Alexandra's address, that would save the landlady work. She looked at the envelope I'd given and said she recalled my handwriting, describing it as elegant, so knew I was telling the truth therefore was happy to oblige. The forwarding address appears to belong to a shop in Stoke Newington. Ives and Co in Church Street. Mrs Carson thought they may be a tobacconist."

"Thank you. This is certainly becoming reminiscent of a pre-war crime novel. If we send our colleague along, will he run into Lord Peter Wimsey?"

"Or your pals Coppersmith and Stewart? It *is* intriguing. There's more, though and it's a touch delicate. Mrs Carson harboured a suspicion that Alexandra might be pregnant."

"Aha." That might well explain why she'd been hiding herself away from her friends, rather like—who was it?

135

Sarah or Elizabeth? —in the bible. "What evidence did she have for this suspicion?"

"Alexandra putting on weight around the waistline, although that's hardly definitive. She had apparently been sick a couple of times in the morning, which sounds more like it. Also, when she moved out she had a large, heavy trunk and was about to bring it downstairs. Mrs Carson, not wishing to risk harm to any baby, but not wanting to air her belief, forbade her simply on the grounds of weight. Alexandra didn't kick up a fuss, despite being a modern young woman, most independent, which makes it sounds as though she too was being extra careful. And then—I quote—a nice young man in overalls came to the door with a van parked outside. He was clearly helping her move so he hauled the thing down the stairs. All of it circumstantial evidence, I suppose, but suggestive."

Suggestive indeed. Although Alexandra might have developed had a dodgy back, or something equally unconnected to being with child. It would however explain her making herself scarce, if she wanted, say, to start a new life, with a husband, a wedding ring and an upcoming first anniversary, the last of which would be fake as could the first two. Nobody would know any different in a strange area. "Your Mrs Carson sounds a mine of information."

"She was, although she reiterated that the pregnancy part wasn't proven. I said that if it *was* true, it raised the question of whether Alexandra could already have gone into a nursing home, but Mrs Carson didn't think a baby could be due quite yet. Although she could be in for observation, of course. My sister got hauled in six weeks before her due date because her blood pressure was sky-high. Sorry, I'm digressing."

"No need to apologise. We bachelors don't necessarily know this kind of detail, so we'd be at risk of jumping to the wrong conclusion. Thank you for reporting everything back so promptly."

"Not a problem. If you need anything else, let me know."

"I will certainly do so." After Alasdair ended the call with the usual pleasantries, Morgan appeared in the hallway, asking if he was ready for his omelette. "Give me ten minutes, if you could. I've just finished with one formidable lady and have another to tackle. Once that's done, I'll be needing refreshment."

"I wish you the best of British luck, sir." With the nearest he'd likely get to a sly grin, Morgan retreated to his pantry.

Alasdair went through another set of pleasantries after getting through to Geraldine, although she was quick to cut them short with a, "Are you calling to discuss those peculiar people you and Toby told us about?"

"Only at one remove. You'll be delighted to know that their claims were made up, for a mixture of reasons including wanting to impress each other and, we suspect, needing to feel of use. Their real intent was for us to locate a missing friend, and they think we'll be able to because she was a member of our appreciation societies." For some reason, it didn't feel right to use the term "fan clubs" with Geraldine. "To cut a long story short, we subsequently ended up with a link to a possible planned disruption of the coronation. We've reported it to the police, but I seem to recall you mentioning your cousin was involved in the planning for the event."

"And you wondered if he should know about it as well? Probably very wise. I'm not entirely sure what he does—except go on about a lot of rather tedious detail about the nuts and bolts of things—but he could always pass the

137

information on to the right person. Would you like to meet him?"

"Please. If he wouldn't think it odd for two actors to be buttonholing him with what's, frankly, not a lot of concrete information."

"I think he'd rather you *did* if there's any chance of disruption, as you so tactfully put it. Forewarned is forearmed and while I have every admiration for our police, they can't have eyes and ears everywhere. And we're running short of time to forestall any unwanted actions."

"Exactly. Would you like to know more before you speak to him?"

"Not now. After the event…literally…then you and Bruce—that's his name—can regale me with the story. Let me put a call through to him now, if you'll be so kind as to give me your number. Will you be at home for the rest of the evening?"

"I will. Although could you please ask him to give me half an hour to get myself fed or I'll be incapable of rational thought."

"I will do. You need to stoke the brain up to deal with such matters. Oh, and before you go, let me thank you for contacting me once more regarding one of your cases. It's so nice to feel useful."

"My pleasure."

Once settled with his omelette, which was a triumph of the egg cooking art, Alasdair planned what he'd tell Bruce. It wouldn't be like addressing Matthew Firestone, whom he knew well and who'd automatically have a sympathetic ear, although surely one could assume that Geraldine would give some background to her cousin, outlining why the two actors had glowing credentials in the amateur detection field. Perhaps Bruce would already know of his cousin's involvement in their most recent case and be prepared to trust what he was told.

Which would be what, exactly?

Maybe it would be wise to avoid all mention of the *Monday Evening Association*, apart from in the vaguest way where it touched on how he and Toby had become involved in this business in the first place. Best, perhaps, also to avoid mentioning anything suspicious about Alexandra's disappearance, given that they now had a possible, entirely prosaic explanation for it. He'd concentrate merely on the *Herbert and Chapman* stuff.

You, sir, are an absolute dolt, missing the obvious.

It wasn't unusual for Alasdair or Toby to have a sudden clarity of thought during an investigation: an idea that was so blindingly apparent that it seemed ridiculous they'd not considered it before. This time, it was the question of what Lloyd's role in the business. Lloyd, whom Toby—always a good judge of character—had disliked, who was cousin to Chapman and who was allowed free use of the firm's premises for his club. Was he a sympathiser to their beliefs? Did he know about the plans regarding disrupting such a notable occasion, whatever those plans might be? Most importantly, should his name be mentioned to the authorities, given that Alasdair's suspicion was based on nothing more than a family connection?

The omelette was a mere memory on the lips and Alasdair was well settled in his chair with *Smallbone Deceased*, in an effort to clear his head by concentrating on the delightful Henry Bohun, when the telephone rang. With a call down the hallway of, "I can answer it, Morgan!" Alasdair picked up the instrument, to be greeted by a deep, pleasing voice, much as he imagined Bohun might speak.

"Mr Hamilton? Bruce Martin here. Geraldine's cousin."

"Call me Alasdair, please, and many thanks for ringing me. Did your cousin explain what this is about?"

"Only in as much as it touches on your amateur sleuthing. I hope the word amateur isn't an insult—Geraldine is most impressed with your abilities, and those of Mr Bowe. She says that what you have to tell me is important."

"We believe it is, although I'm afraid it's going to sound awfully thin. Let me start with something concrete, which is that we've already reported what we know to our contact within the police force."

"Glad to hear it. What did he say?"

"I don't know." Alasdair felt even more of a dolt. "We've some else working with us and he was discharging that duty today. I've not heard his report yet."

"I see." What Bruce saw wasn't clear and his tones had become less encouraging. Working as a team meant the workload was shared but it did have its disadvantages in terms of not being abreast of everything, and Alasdair felt that now. "I believe my cousin has helped you in a previous case. She says you're both much more intelligent than you come across on screen. Which I also hope you don't find an insult," Bruce added, in what sounded like a hurried afterthought.

"I'll take it in spirit intended." And with a carefully adopted air of generosity. "To cut to the important bits. In the last fortnight we've been approached by a group of friends who are ostensibly worried about a missing acquaintance and wanted to see if we could help locate her, because she's a fan of ours. That's how it started, anyway. As we peeled back the layers of the story, a coronation connection came up. Part of a conversation this missing woman overheard at work about people planning some kind of disruption to the event."

140

"Do you think that these two elements are linked?" Bruce sounded more serious. "That she's been taken off and dealt with in some way for hearing what she shouldn't? Or gone into hiding?"

"Possibly, although we've made a lot of progress on her side of the story and have an unrelated, highly plausible explanation for why she may have hidden herself. That could be a cover, of course. As you know, where people are concerned, motivation can be complex."

"Quite. How did she overhear this planning happening?"

"As a result of a picking up a telephone at her then employers, a firm of solicitors come investigators, name of *Herbert and Chapman*."

"That bunch?" Bruce's tone of voice suggested a raised eyebrow. "They have their fingers in some unsavoury pies. The defendants they represent are not ones my cousin Geraldine would choose were she in their shoes and neither would I."

"If that was all they got up to, it wouldn't be so worrying. We know, from another reliable source, that the two principals were involved with the British Union of Fascists and still bear the same sympathies."

"Ah. I knew Chapman had knocked about with Mosley pre-war and sometimes acted as one of the Blackshirts but I didn't know it about the other one. It doesn't surprise me that they still believe in their cause. Those unpleasant leopards rarely change their spots."

"We've heard from this other source that they've also been sounding off about Queen Salote and their dislike of her and that another employee accidentally came across Chapman and person unknown discussing an upcoming act of violence. Whether the two are linked and whether they hate Queen Salote because of the colour of her skin or some other reason, we don't know. We felt that all these elements potentially meld together to make something nasty. Admittedly, they may have no connection and the statements overheard were nothing more than hot air or related to something else. I said this stuff was awfully thin."

"Less thin than you believe to be the case, Alasdair. The identity of the firm alone adds considerable girth to it." Bruce sniffed. "Who's your police contact? I feel the need of liaison."

"Matthew Firestone. He's a superintendent at Scotland Yard. Although whether he'll deal with the matter himself or pass it on to some other agency, I wouldn't know."

"Leave that with me. I simply want to make sure we're working together and not tripping over each other's feet. Anything else for me to get my teeth into?"

Time to draw a bow at a venture. "I have some other names of people who are vaguely connected to this business, in that they are members of a fortnightly club that meets at the *Herbert and Chapman* offices. I was going to list them in case their names ring any bells."

"What sort of club is this?" Bruce suddenly sounded on the alert.

"A cross between a support group for misfits and one for lonely hearts, or that's the impression we get." That seemed a bit harsh, but avoided a long explanation. "Run by a cousin of Billy Chapman, name of Lloyd Conway."

"Oh yes? Small chap, a bit full of himself?"

"I've never met him, although Toby Bowe has and I think the description would fit. Toby didn't like him."

"If it's the chap I'm thinking of, I'm not surprised. I can rely on your discretion?"

"Absolutely. Although I can't promise I won't be sharing what I hear from you with our police contact, nor with Toby. Or indeed with Jonny Stewart, who's part of the missing person investigation."

"Did I mishear that, Alasdair? Jonny rather than Jonty?"

"Yes. The great-nephew of the great man. He's taking the role of police liaison this time, hence my vagueness earlier as he's not yet told me what transpired."

"You're forgiven. I had the pleasure of working with Messrs Coppersmith and Stewart during the last unpleasantness and the latter mentioned he had family members following in his footsteps including the nephew who's a judge. We digress, though." Bruce didn't sound bothered at the digression. "Lloyd Conway got himself into trouble during the war by making outrageous claims about what he—and other people—could do. Bizarre powers."

So, this behaviour was nothing new? "That fits in with this club he runs. Supposed to be, on the surface anyway, a group of people with odd abilities, although we've discovered that three of the members are merely pretending, for reasons of their own."

"None of this surprises me. When Conway first appeared on the radar, he was thought to be either eccentric or mentally unwell but he was holding down a perfectly good, perfectly effective role contributing to the war effort, so the powers that be decided he was probably harmless. He'd been trapped in a bombed building, early in the Blitz, so it was thought he had a touch of shell shock."

"That would explain a lot."

"Yes. I thought the same. I never met him at the time, but when I was told about the case it stuck in my mind because there are Conways in our family, although no relation to this chap. After the war, I happened to meet him and he tried to persuade me that *I* had some extraordinary ability that I could put to use for the greater good. I don't, apart from a useful brain and the knack of analysing things and making connections and I'd hardly call that extraordinary."

"Lloyd did the same thing to Toby, who had a similar answer for him, only *his* real skills were to do with flying." Alasdair, feeling his eyebrow begin to rise, forestalled it. No point in overusing one of his greatest assets with nobody to see it. "Lloyd seemed convinced he was right."

"Perhaps he's been saying that to his cousin, Chapman. Maybe the latter believes he truly possesses some unique ability and it feeds his visions of grandeur."

Visions of grandeur. Hadn't the same expression been used about Lloyd?

"Perhaps Toby could butter up this chap Lloyd," Bruce continued, "to see if he knows anything about what his cousin's up to."

"That's a good idea. I'm sure he could summon up the courage." Alasdair chuckled. "Let me pass those other names I have in front of you, given how successful we've been so far. Group members Moira Matthews, then two chaps called Richard and Jeff, for whom I have no surnames."

"They don't ring a bell, but I'll jot them all down even if they appear to signify nothing at present. One can never be sure as to what will be meaningful in the long run."

Whatever Bruce's role in the event preparations, he appeared to be more than simply a logistics man. No surprise, if he'd been working Jonty and Orlando during the war doing something that probably required a lot of brain. Had they inadvertently found—or, to be accurate, had Geraldine steered them towards—the very person they needed on the inside?

"Excellent. Add to your list Alexandra Cummings, who may go by the name Munsey. Or vice versa. The aforementioned woman who did the overhearing when she worked at *Herbert and Chapman*."

"Added. Anyone else?"

Alasdair was about to say there wasn't, when a name popped into his head. "Charles Carstone, the late actor. Believed to be one of *Herbert and Chapman's* clients at the time of his death."

"Ah. He was making a film with Landseer, I believe, when he fell under a tube train? I saw the story in the paper." The light way in which Bruce spoke implied he knew a lot more than he was willing to divulge at present.

"Yes. Strictly in confidence, he may have been dreading an upcoming pair of divorce cases in which he was threatened with being named as co-respondent. Carstone is—Carstone was—a devout catholic, believe it or not, as was his wife, so he went to get advice in case the balloon went up."

"He went to the right place for avoiding scandal. Old hands at that game. Quite likely old pals of his, too."

"Really?" That would explain a lot.

"In so much as Carstone was well in with Mosley pre-war, so it's entirely possible he ran into one or both of that pair. This was before he was on his way to becoming a successful actor, at which point he dropped all such associations like a hot potato. None of this is common knowledge."

"No." It had even escaped the notice of Dennis's son and therefore Morgan. Interesting that it had also evaded the beady eye of Sir Ian, who'd have dropped *Carstone* like a hot potato had he known. Not views of which Sir Ian approved, although if Carstone had gone to him to plead the error of his ways, stating how his previous beliefs had been stupid and how he'd soon learned enough to cast them off, the head of Landseer might well have forgiven him. Such a change of heart could have been manipulated by the publicity department into a story of redemption. "Carstone must have been desperate to risk re-opening the relationship with *Herbert and Chapman* if word could get back to the studio that they were fascists."

"I heard he was in deep despair. The biggest chance of his career and the likelihood it would all fizzle out with the divorces business." How did Bruce know these things? Time to probe him.

"Where does all this information come from? Sorry to have to ask, but we've learned not to take anything on face value, even if the source comes with a sound recommendation."

"Such as Geraldine's?" Bruce chuckled. "You're quite right to question my credentials. I can't give you any details, for reasons which will become obvious to a bright chap like you, but during the war, one of the jobs I had involved keeping an eye on British fascists and I've had to do some since. Is that enough to persuade you?"

"It'll have to be," Alasdair said with good grace. "Now, is there anything else we can do to help with this possible threat of sabotage? I know we're only actors but it's surprising how often that seems to help. Either because folk are so familiar with us they address us almost as friends, or because we come across as a pair of silly asses whom it can't possibly hurt to gossip with."

"I've no doubt about *your* credentials and that any silly ass persona is all a clever act. But—and I'm sure your police contact will say the same to Jonny—please don't press this any further. We'll do what needs to be done."

How vexatious. "I understand. We'll still have to press on with the issue of the missing woman until we're sure we have the correct explanation, but we'll be concentrating on following the address trail and trying our best not to stick our noses in where we shouldn't." Alasdair made the promise through gritted teeth and with his metaphorical fingers crossed. If, for example, Alexandra volunteered

146

some information about her ex-employers, the conversation couldn't simply be shut down.

"That would be appreciated."

"Hold on a minute. Earlier in this conversation, you suggested that Toby talk to Lloyd about his cousin. Does that still apply?"

"Ah." Bruce sighed. "On calm consideration, perhaps not. I don't want to have to face the wrath of your fans—not least my cousin—should anything happen to you." With which he made his goodbyes, leaving Alasdair to wonder exactly why this business was expected to be so dangerous.

And why Bruce had changed his mind about probing Lloyd.

Chapter Twelve

As Toby had anticipated, the telephone rang once more that Tuesday evening and it was no surprise to hear Alasdair at the other end of the line.

"Sorry it's late, oh heart of my heart, but there's news to share," he said, in a voice redolent of weariness tempered by excitement.

"I have news to impart, as well, and it's never too late in the evening to compare notes. Anyway, there might not be a chance tomorrow morning, given the way the schedule works." Toby and Alasdair were shooting separate scenes and having to cram costume fittings in between, because some newly written outdoor scenes demanded different clobber. Opportunity for sleuthing would be scarce. "There'll be the journey to Cambridge in the afternoon for the local premiere, but that feels too long to wait."

"Quite. And I believe our car is also collecting Alexander Rattigan, so we won't be able to speak with the same freedom. He's a good egg, but we don't want to risk him repeating what we say and causing a general panic."

"Do you want to toss a coin for who goes first with their news, then? I'll I trust you to flip it and not cheat."

Alasdair snorted. "It's certainly too late for that nonsense. You go first."

"Jonny's spoken to Matthew, who is vaguely aware of our nasty pals and will be putting the investigational wheels in motion concerning what they're up to. Interestingly, the police aren't short of people saying they've run across a conspiracy being planned which then turns out to be eyewash. I do feel sorry for them. Anyhow, there's no prohibition on us regarding further poking about. On which subject, the admirable Miss Crouch tells me that the likeliest candidate for our Alexandra is called Miss Munsey and lives in Finsbury Park. I have her address."

"The surname part isn't news and I'm afraid she doesn't live there any longer." Alasdair sounded horribly smug. Just as well he wasn't in the same room or he'd be getting a punch. "Said Miss Munsey has moved out to parts unknown and left a forwarding address for her post. A tobacconist's shop in Stoke Newington."

Toby whistled. "Well, that's a turn-up. A wicket for the Hamilton team all right. Do you know why she upped sticks, though?"

"I think I do but I'll pretend I don't, as I don't want to be on a hat trick ball."

"Most gentlemanly. Miss Munsey was quite possibly up the duff, although I was given no proof of that by Miss Crouch. It was merely based on her not inconsiderable medical opinion."

"An opinion apparently seconded by Miss Munsey's erstwhile landlady, centred on a couple of episodes of morning sickness. You know, it's a shame we haven't got Miss Crouch and Mrs Richards working on the *Herbert and Chapman* angle. With those two, Bessy and Geraldine pursuing the case, Matthew Firestone would have all the information he needed within the hour." Alasdair chuckled. "Difficult for us chaps to compete."

"Unfair competitive advantage." Toby chuckled. "In re Alexandra, I can't help feeling slightly cheated, should it turn out that she's simply hiding what people in the past might have called her disgrace."

"Because that's too prosaic an explanation? I've had the same thought and castigated myself for it. Better that reason than her being done away with because of what she overheard. Which may still apply, we should remember. No grabbing at the first piece of proper evidence, if that's what it is."

Toby nodded. "If this *does* apply, though, it takes two to make a baby, or so I was taught many moons ago. No practical experience of my own."

"It does. Your point being…"

"Who's the papa? Dennis's son? The chap she was arguing with? Please God it's not Lloyd."

"Hold on. I've got some notes here." A rustling noise. "Mrs Richards spoke to Mrs Carson, the aforementioned landlady. *She* reckoned that when her tenant moved out, a young chap in overalls came to help her. Of course, he might also be Dennis's son and—or—the man she had the row with. If we could find him, we might find her, although there's not a lot to go on, in either case."

"True. I was simply being ultra suspicious and wondering if it could have been one of Chapman, Herbert or even Salt, although that's based on nothing other than the dislike I've built up for them, despite never having met them."

"It's not an unreasonable idea. Boss gets employee with child and either finds a reason to dismiss her so his indiscretion doesn't follow him into the office every day. Or he slips her a douceur in order to go off, have the child and perhaps get it adopted. Or dispose of it completely with a nurse in some back street who offers such a service."

"All of which says we should follow up on your tobacconist—who may have some light to shed on things, please God—and I propose we get Jonny to tackle that angle. He's not possessed of a well-known face, for one thing, and if the person doing duty behind the counter is female, he can exercise that undoubted charm of his on them. Spreads the workload, too and we don't want to freeze him out when he's already proved his worth."

"Agreed on every count. What excuse could we suggest he has for being on Alexandra's trail that wouldn't risk him being slung out on his ear? He can't say he's an old flame, because surely the tobacconist would wonder if Alexandra was using a poste restante address to ensure he didn't know where she was." Alasdair gave what sounded like a stifled yawn. "And unless whoever gives her the letters is blind, innocent or obtuse, they must know that the woman who collects the post is expecting, unless the baby has already arrived."

"Hm." Toby should have anticipated this added complication. "What if Jonny says he didn't realise Alexandra was expecting and is desperate to see her and ask for her hand?"

"Same applies. If he suggests he's the baby's father, it begs the question of why Alexandra should run away and favour disgrace over shaming him into marrying her. Too suspicious all round."

"The whole business begs the question of why she hasn't married the papa, irrespective of who he is. Unless she has, of course, and needed to keep it a secret from her— or his—family because they don't approve. Or," Toby added, suddenly recalling the book he'd read recently and had now loaned to Alasdair, "it's like in *Smallbone Deceased* and she won't marry as a matter of principle."

"Oh, yes. I've just reached that bit. Life imitates art?" Alasdair took a deep breath. "Then what about Jonny playing the 'noble sacrifice' part? The type you excel in. He could say that he knows Alexandra's expecting a baby and while it can't be his, the father is a swine who's left her to face the consequences of their joint action—don't snigger— alone and that he wants to offer his hand and so preserve her honour."

151

"Will he be prepared to say all that? I mean, given the notable family he comes from, doesn't he risk his reputation, if both the shop assistant and Alexandra believe him and he's sued for breach of promise? We could accidentally have hit too close to home if she's desperate to get a ring on her hand."

"I'm sure Jonny isn't going to be bothered by that and the Stewarts strike me as the kind of family who'd be able to overcome any difficulty should it occur. Anyway, all Jonny has to say is that he was putting on an act as part of an investigation and he'd have us—and Matthew, no doubt—to back him up."

Toby snorted. "And what if Alexandra has a most dedicated young man who hears of this slander and gives Jonny a punch up the bracket? Maybe we should leave it to Jonny to come up with a plan, because he's not short of brains. He can always consult Messrs Stewart and Coppersmith regarding a strategy."

"We'll be seeing them tomorrow in Cambridge, *n'est pas*? We should tell them how valuable Jonny's proving. Anyway, we're digressing, I'm tired and there's more to impart. I spoke to Geraldine, as a result of which her cousin, Bruce, rang me." Alasdair gave a summary of what he'd learned, including Carstone's pre-war political sympathies and Lloyd's making a nuisance of himself by insisting he knew about people's powers, ending with, "And that peculiar behaviour was possibly a result of having been bombed during the Blitz."

"A touch of shell shock? That puts a different complexion on things." It wouldn't make Toby like the man but he could sympathise. "That could have changed his perception of reality. I'm sure science has only scraped the surface of how the brain works and the effects of it going wrong. Maybe Lloyd has met people who've suffered a similarly traumatic experience and they truly believed they could do such strange things, which bolstered his beliefs. Maybe Alexandra was one. Now, talking of Carstone, I've been working through the file of cuttings the publicity department lent me. And guess what?"

"The hour's too late for 'guess what', hooligan. Tell Uncle Alasdair what you found."

"The chap who tried to save him at Chancery Lane was called James Salt. J Salt was one of the employee names I noticed in the *Herbert and Chapman* offices. It may be a mere coincidence, but it's an unusual name and given the way neither of us can shake Carstone from our minds, perhaps it means something."

"That could explain why Carstone's been bothering you: your subconscious remembering the name from newspaper reports on the inquest and linking it to the one you saw in the office, all without your realising that you were being nudged into connecting the two." Alasdair sounded distinctly perkier at hearing this titbit. "Would it be possible to fake pushing someone while looking like rescuing them?"

"Why not? Magicians practice that kind of misdirection all the time. We do, too, as actors. Were you never taught how to fake a strangling scene? If you were clever enough in the execution and afterwards produced just the right amount of wailing and hand wringing, you'd be convincing."

"Hmm." Alasdair considered the notion. "It would help if you had a collaborator, perhaps in the form of the person who apparently saved *your* life. As a plan it's audacious but possible, and haven't we been told that *Herbert and Chapman* were rather good at manufacturing a plausible scenario when defending one of their unsavoury clients?"

"Very true. That other chap was called Robert Archer, by the way, and he could also be one of H and C's merry men, for all we know. Should we ask Dennis's son or beard the lions in their den ourselves?"

"Doing any bearding could be tricky. What I hadn't got round to reporting back, because we got distracted by Lloyd's history, was that Bruce doesn't want us poking in our noses with them. He stated plainly that he didn't want to face the wrath of our fans if anything untoward happened and I don't think that was just a joke."

Toby whistled. "Very different to Matthew Firestone's viewpoint, but perhaps he's more aware of our track record and our ability to handle ourselves in a tricky situation."

"It was all rather odd, actually," Alasdair said, "because earlier in the conversation he'd suggested that you might pick Lloyd's brains about what his cousin was up to. Bruce said he'd changed his mind after further reflection, although I wasn't convinced it was merely that."

"Any inkling of what caused the about face?"

"Funnily enough, it was after we discussed Carstone. Might be a coincidence, but…"

Toby could imagine the eloquent shrug accompanying that statement. "What does this Bruce chap do, by the way? I'd assumed he was an equerry or civil servant but I no doubt assumed wrongly."

"He didn't say and I suspect pressing him wouldn't have got an answer. I guess it's something on the security side, because he'd been involved with keeping an eye on Fascists during the war, and he'd also worked alongside Messrs Coppersmith and Stewart with whatever they were doing. Add on to that the authoritative air he possessed and what Geraldine said about him. He tells her plenty about his job but it's all mundane details."

"I see. Like folk in war who were involved with something secret which they couldn't talk about, so told friends they were simply involved in a clerking role and would they like to hear all about it?" Toby's second cousin had done the same, pretending she was a mere clerk, when he knew all along that she had far too much in the way of brains to be confined to such a mundane role.

"Exactly the idea I had. Anyway, I told Bruce we had a missing woman to find and we'd be continuing in that particular quest. He didn't issue a ban on that." Alasdair yawned. "Sorry. I need my bed."

"You get away to it. Give me that Stoke Newington address and I'll call Jonny to get him on the trail. We'll have to explain how things may have turned on their heads in more ways than one, so I'll brief him on the Bruce stuff as well as Mrs Richards's Miss Marpling. As for us, what next?"

"Despite what Bruce said after his change of mind, I'd like to follow the Lloyd angle. See if he's more deeply involved in this mess, if we can do it without touching on *Herbert and Chapman*."

"You *must* be tired. Fat chance of that given his relation to Billy Chapman."

"You don't fancy going back to the meeting next Monday? Ostensibly to give everyone an update on Alexandra, but really to probe Lloyd? You don't need me to tell you what to do."

"Ask him out for a drink, ostensibly—as you put it—to make amends for not having the power he was sure I had?" Toby chuckled. "I'd have to work myself up to that. I'd happily go and see the doorman, though. Not any time on a Monday, to avoid the risk of seeing the rest of the gang. I could pick his brains on all counts, including the matter of Lloyd—whom he clearly doesn't like so might be willing to dish any dirt on. Then I'll turn the conversation to Carstone. What were *you* thinking of doing that won't incur Bruce's wrath?"

155

"Assuming I don't wake in the morning with a better idea, and assuming you wouldn't mind me slightly treading on your toes, I'd like to talk to one or more of Moira and the lads. On the same subjects as you're going to tackle the porter about." Alasdair yawned again. "Goodnight sweetheart. I'll be no use in the morning if I don't get my shut eye."

"Then you go off, sweet prince. I'll be doing the same once I've tried to catch young Jonny."

Luckily, Jonny had not yet taken himself—with or without Roger—off to bed when Toby rang. "Sorry to call so late, but there have been developments."

"They must be important. Tell all."

Toby outlined the news about Alexandra Munsey, the information from Bruce, leaving for the moment the things he'd gleaned himself from the inquest reporting. "Which all means that, although it may be too soon to say for definite, our case of the missing lady may have turned out to be a bit of a red herring, while the threat of disruption to the coronation seems to have become something that only the proper authorities can handle. Bruce doesn't want us getting involved."

"What a spoilsport. Didn't you and Alasdair happily risk your lives every time you scrambled?"

"We did, but he clearly doesn't want us to continue indulging that daredevil attitude into peacetime. Anyway, there doesn't seem to be a moratorium on locating Alexandra, so we'll press on with that and if anything coronation wise turns up while we do so, we report it to Matthew, not Bruce." Toby harrumphed. "Although we may have something meatier to dig our teeth into, which we're not banned from probing."

"That sounds more like it."

"Yes, I thought you'd appreciate this. I've spent my evening going through everything Landseer could provide me regarding Charles Carstone, late actor of this parish. He who went under the wheels of a train in what might have been a cleverly masked suicide."

"The suicide theory that I reckon is a no go because of his Catholicism?"

"The very one. This death might just turn out to be murder, unless Alasdair and I are so obsessed with finding violent crime lurking everywhere that we've misread the slender clues."

Jonny whistled. "Well, that's a turn up. I never thought of wondering if you could make a murder look like an accident. What's brought you to that conclusion, apart from a naturally suspicious nature salted by relevant experience?"

"A name. And one that's rather coincident to what you just said. James Salt. Does that ring a bell?"

"Let me think. Was that one of the names on the desks at the *Herbert and Chapman* offices?"

"Correct. J Salt, anyway. James Salt was the person on the platform with Carstone who tried to save him and who was himself saved by a chap called Robert Archer who was, according to all the reports, standing next to him when this happened. If we could somehow prove they knew each other, which wasn't admitted in court, it could be an indication of dodgy business afoot."

"Hm. Playing devil's advocate, Salt might have had genuine reason to know Carstone through his being a client of the firm. Chancery Lane isn't that far a walk from Clarence House, so they might have innocently gone there together at knocking off time, in order to journey home. Salt might even have been asked to keep a watch on Carstone, if somebody at the solicitors was concerned that he was in such a state that he might harm himself."

157

"All good points, but that client connection isn't mentioned in any of the reports. They state that neither man knew Carstone, so either it isn't our J Salt or they've deliberately kept things quiet."

"As they keep their location quiet. This Bruce chap hasn't banned looking into Carstone's death, has he?"

"No. Although remember that he told Alasdair that Carstone was another Mosley-ite, until his career started to take off and he wisely eschewed those connections. Alasdair also got the feeling that the mention of Carstone might have prompted the warnings about poking our noses in, although that might be him reading too much into things. It becomes habitual when you play Holmes and Watson too much."

"I expect it does. Right, give me that address where Alexandra has her post sent and I'll try to drop in there tomorrow. If I take an extended lunch hour, I can make up the time later. I'll report back tomorrow evening."

"Alas, you won't find us here then. We're off to see your aged relative for the East Anglian debut of the film in which I portray him. They're entertaining us at St Bride's."

Jonny chuckled. "Watch out for the claret, then. It can be powerful stuff and we wouldn't want your adoring fans to see you pie-eyed. I'll call on Thursday, if that works."

"Excellent. I hope that we'll have things to report to you, too. We've that day off from being actors, so we'll turn detectives, instead."

Although what Alasdair was going to contribute was a moot point. The vague idea he'd spoken about, talking to Moira again, felt increasingly like a smokescreen. What idea was buzzing around that beautiful head of his and how would it be in line with the promise to Bruce that they'd not be sniffing around the firm of *Herbert and Chapman*? Or had Toby fallen into the trap of reading too much into everything?

Chapter Thirteen

Wednesday had proved an excellent day, one which Toby had enjoyed every moment of. All Landseer studio business had gone well, the drive to Cambridge turned out to be smooth and untroubled, and the meal at St Bride's—claret and all—had turned out to be both delicious and entertaining. The premiere itself was a huge success, with Jonty Stewart charming all and sundry, especially Fiona who managed to much of the evening on his arm. Stewart and Coppersmith had also proved a hit with the gentlemen and ladies of the press, their picture being splashed over both the arts and society pages of the classier newspapers. Toby hoped that he and Alasdair would be as handsome and charismatic if they reached their age.

Now it was Thursday and the three principals had a fallow day, with any filming on the new production being confined to background shots, which would be awash with extras, and those scenes involving minor characters. While Fiona was probably going to spend her time seeing her handsome nobleman—who'd hopefully be amused at the way his uncle had monopolised her in Cambridge—Toby and Alasdair would be putting on their metaphorical deerstalkers. They'd be having a debriefing on the case that evening, probably followed by a hurried de-briefing of another sort, before they headed to their respective beds.

After a lie-in and a glorious breakfast, Toby dropped into his tailors to pick up a new set of pyjamas, then made his way to Eagle Street, hoping that Clarence House wouldn't be under observation by Bruce's boys, which would risk earning himself a black mark. His conscience was fairly clear, because he wouldn't be going anywhere near the third floor nor would he be asking the porter about Messrs Herbert or Chapman. Not directly, anyway.

By the time he'd got his new pyjamas wrapped and tucked under his arm, Toby had also got the approach he'd take with the doorman—whose name he'd remembered as Fred—firmly wrapped up, as well. He made his way along Eagle Street with a spring in his step, raising his hat to several ladies and one striking looking chap who shouted greetings along the lines of, "Hello, Dr Watson."

"Back again?" the doorman said, as soon as Toby entered the lobby. "I thought, from the way you left his nibs's meeting that evening that you and your pal had shaken the dust of this place off your feet good and proper."

"I meant to, Fred. That was what his nibs called you, wasn't it?" Toby waited for the confirmatory nod before continuing. "The trouble is, I needed to come back to get some information: the things one has to do in the name of amateur detection. It's a damn sight easier playing Holmes and Watson onscreen than off."

Fred rolled his eyes. "Don't come over all Gloria Swanson. That's as bad as *him*."

"Him? Do you mean Lloyd Conway?"

"That's the one. They're all a right shower, him and his pals on the third floor. It's lucky that they're the exception, because if all the tenants were like them, I'd be out of here." Fred drew himself up in his chair. "But there's two DFC's and the son of a VC among the other occupants and better people you couldn't wish to meet."

Toby, momentarily wishing he'd had the foresight to be wearing his medals, pressed on. "Fred, you sound just the person to give me the information I need, in strictest confidence, naturally. We need to keep an eye and ear in case his nibs, as you so splendidly referred to him, or any of his acquaintances turn up."

Fred jerked his thumb towards a door behind him. "We can talk in my cubby hole. I can keep an eye on the door and an ear on the telephone from there."

"Much appreciated." When they'd entered the inner sanctum—which was well provided with a window looking into the lobby and a mirror to cover a potential blind spot by the main entrance—Toby lowered his voice. "*Herbert and Chapman*. I had no idea, when I came here that Monday, exactly what the firm was like. I've since discovered their business reputation and that nobody has a good word for them. I can understand why."

"Their clientele must have a good word for the firm, but some of those are hardly an advert for decency or good judgement." Now Fred dropped his voice. "I'm not going to mention some of the people I see going up there. I know that's where they're headed, because even if they hadn't had to sign in, they look shifty."

"I don't remember signing in," Toby said.

"You don't need to, either side of official opening times."

That was interesting: might *Herbert and Chapman* entertain some of their clients—or co-conspirators—out of hours?

"Still," Fred continued, "in or out of hours, people have to ask where the blessed place is, like you did. Daft, not having a proper nameplate outside or a notice in here."

"Clearly feeling they have something to hide."

"Not just the business they conduct, I'd say. Who they'd vote for, if they got the chance." Fred snorted contemptuously. "I don't suppose it'll come as a shock if I said that there's a chap works for them who…well, guv'nor, his politics are the kind that decent people like us took to the skies or seas to fight against."

Toby tried to look surprised. "Nazis? Fascists?"

161

Fred nodded. "Home grown ones. If you run across a bloke called James Salt, go in the other direction. Mr Bowe, I remember when the Blackshirts marched through the East End—or tried their damnedest to. Salt was marching with them. He must have been barely old enough to shave but I remember him."

"You must have an extraordinary memory, then." Or Salt had a striking appearance. Toby would have to look back through inquest related articles because he was sure they held a picture of the two supposed heroes, although so blurred that it could have depicted anyone. The pair were hiding their lights under bushels, one of the reports had said, true heroes who didn't seek the glare of publicity. No wonder they'd been so reticent, if they were in shady business up to their necks.

"I've always had a knack for recalling faces, even if only seen the once, and Salt's got a distinctive kink to his conk which you couldn't miss, although I had another reason for remembering him. Would you forget if you saw a young squirt of a thing, fists ready for action, squaring up to a woman old enough to be his granny, and just because she'd tipped a bucket of water on him? It was only because our side stood for common decency that he got away without having his hide tanned."

Toby whistled "It must have been awkward when you first saw him here."

"Not for him it wasn't, because he didn't recognise me. I don't suppose he really saw any of us that night. We were just a group of people he'd never met but decided he didn't like. I'm not Jewish, and that's just stating a fact, but I was standing shoulder to shoulder with my friends. I guess to Mr Salt and the rest of them we were just a mass of vermin." The story was related with a surprising lack of rancour, a simple account of what had happened. "It wasn't awkward for me, either, because I know what he is and I'm keeping a watch on him. I daresay they're all cut from the same cloth up there on the third floor."

"I daresay you're correct. Do they ever have visitors out of hours or hold other meetings in their offices? Lloyd's little group of followers excepted, because they seemed a pretty decent lot to me, if a bit odd."

"They do hold meetings in the evenings and the odd weekend afternoon, Mr Bowe. Seeing clients, they tell me, if it's one of my shifts, so I can make sure the visitors get up there all right. Not sure what happens if it's one of my colleague Ted's shifts. We Cox and Box in here, which suits us fine, both being widowers. We *Fred and Ted* you could say."

Toby chuckled, pleased both that he'd come on the right day and that he'd been right about out of hours business. "What happens when one of you is on holiday? Do they find a chap called Ned or Red to fill in?"

"They use an agency. I like your idea though. Maybe I should tell them to make sure the names of the blokes they use rhyme with ours."

"Do you think these folk visiting out of hours really are clients?" Toby asked, feeling he was making progress.

"Some may be, because they must have some who don't want to be seen sneaking in here." Fred tapped the desk. "One of your lot was here. Charles Carberry. No. Carstairs. Something like that. I'm better with faces than names. I did see him on the stage, in *The Merry Wives of Windsor* and he was very good."

Toby hid his surprise at the choice of play. Why shouldn't Fred enjoy a bit of the bard? "Was it Charles Carstone?"

"That's the fella. He was here a good few months back, a couple of times, including a Monday evening when

Conway's lot weren't in. He had to ask where to go, like you did, so he mustn't have been here before. Carstone gave me the impression he was trying to pretend he was still Falstaff, but underneath that jolly exterior he seemed like a worried man. Scared, if that's not going too far." Fred paused, scratching his head.

"Scared?" Toby could understand anxiety, if there was the risk of these divorce cases blowing up in the press, but would that go as far as fear? Yet Fred didn't seem like the sort of bloke who'd exaggerate.

"I could have been wrong, but that's what I thought at the time. Maybe that should be no surprise, because it wasn't just Billy Chapman in there with him. Salt as well. Perhaps he had as little time for Mosley's mob as I did."

Toby didn't share what he'd been told about Carstone's former political leanings. "I'm glad I've never had the pleasure of meeting either of those gentlemen. Is there a chap called Archer who also works for *Herbert and Chapman*, would you know?"

"There isn't, as far as I know. There's a Mr J Archer who's in the theatrical agent's office, because I see post for him when it's my shift and I'm on sorting duty. One of the agents in training, if they have those things."

"I believe they might." That was annoying, although this Archer could know Salt through working in the same building. Unless the newspapers—by their own error or by someone else's manipulation—had stated his initial wrongly, or he even used his middle name in everyday conversation and signed in with his other initial. Was that clutching at investigational straws? Best to press on. "Changing tack, does Lloyd Conway ever come here apart from his Monday meetings? Or do any of the others from that little gang," Toby added, for the sake of completeness: no point in being blinkered.

"Conway does sometimes, of an evening. I don't know what he does up there: it's been when the partners have both been working late and that's all I can say. The others I've not seen, although they might have dropped in here when Ted's working. Anyone else I can help you with?"

"A young woman called Alexandra Munsey. Or possibly Cummings. She seems to go by two surnames and we don't know if one is her maiden name and one her married, for example. She used to come to Conway's meetings—she worked for *Herbert and Chapman*, too," Toby raised his eyebrow in a manner that would have done Alasdair proud, "but she left."

"I remember her. Cummings. Not married, because there was no ring, and not the sort you would forget in a hurry. The kind of girl you might call ordinary until she smiled then you realised how just pretty she was. Nice with it, always finding the opportunity to pass the time of day with me. I thought she'd seen the light, got fed up with them and found a better placement. She said as much when she left although I don't know where she's working now."

"When did she leave here?" This case was perilously short on actual dates, as opposed to vague mentions of "a couple of months ago" or similar.

"February. I know because it was around my birthday." Fred left his seat, then flicked back through the brightly coloured calendar that hung on the wall. "Friday the twentieth and my birthday was the nineteenth. I made a joke about it not being the present I'd have chosen, one of my favourite customers going. She said she might be back with a better present but she hasn't produced one yet."

"She still might." Did that imply she'd return with a ring on her finger and a baby in her arms, for him to coo over? Toby jotted down the date: solid confirmation that any plot being hatched in this building must have been gestating a while. Interesting also to compare that with their other definite date, the fifth of February, when Carstone had gone under the train. Were the two events linked or merely coincident? "That February was an awful time for us at Landseer. Not one I'd want to repeat. Did you read in the newspaper about Carstone's accident?"

"He fell under a train?" Fred had raised his eyebrow on the word "fell". "I did. Not speaking ill of the dead, but just being honest, I assumed he'd jumped. Because of whatever he was having to consult Billy Chapman about."

"Not an unreasonable assumption. I wonder—" Toby paused. A visitor had arrived and Fred needed to deal with him. Once the man had signed in and begun to climb the stairs, Toby emerged from the inner sanctum. "I've been keeping you from your duty. I'll resume my rightful place the other side of the desk."

"You sounded like you were about to ask me something when we got interrupted."

"I was leading up to doing so, yes. I was wondering how many folk have formed a similar opinion on Carstone's death. I know I used to think the same, but I've revised my opinion." Toby leaned forward. "How far can I trust you, Fred? We're entering murky waters and while you seem a decent bloke but the war taught us that didn't necessarily mean a jot."

The doorman drew himself up in his chair, his back ramrod straight. "I hope I know when to keep my mouth shut and my ears open, sir."

"Good man." Toby dropped his voice once more. "I've been re-reading the reports on Carstone's inquest. One man tried to save him, and then another chap had to save the would-be rescuer. They were called James Salt and Robert Archer."

Fred frowned. "Now I see why you asked about them. That's either a big coincidence with the name Salt or it's our pal upstairs. Not the chap from the agents, though, unless the newspaper got the name wrong."

"You're right." Toby sighed. "May I have a look through the visitors' book? I promise that you can rely on my discretion if I see any names that I recognise. I'll forget them immediately unless they're relevant to our investigation."

"I shouldn't really, but if you take it through the back into my cubby hole, where you'll be out of sight, I'll sit here and act like nothing's going on. I can come and get the book if I need it."

"You're a Christian, sir. Much obliged." Toby turned to the start of the book, to find the entries beginning at the start of March. That was after the relevant date, but in the interests of doing a complete job, he decided to scan it, although that proved unsuccessful, with not a single name of interest turning up. He stuck his head round the door, then handed Fred the current signing-in book. "Sorry to be a pain, but I think I really need to see the previous volume, if you have it?"

"It's on the shelf, in date order and labelled, Mr Bowe. Help yourself to whichever you need."

"Much obliged, once more." Due to Fred and Ted's efficient system, Toby soon found the relevant volume, and a quick scan of the first and last entries showed it would likely cover the period he needed. He worked through the pages speedily but efficiently, once again scanning every entry—particularly the visitors to *Herbert and Chapman*—looking out for any names of significance.

There was no mention of Carstone, so he must have attended out of hours or met them off site.

Toby was delighted to find an entry on January the twenty second that read, *Name: Mr R Archer. To see: Herbert and Chapman*. It might still be merely coincidental, but he couldn't help a sense of excitement mounting at having potentially fended off the death blow to his idea. The secretary who had blundered into a discussion about an upcoming violent act: what if that had been a murder rather than a terrorist attack?

Toby resisted going straight to the date Carstone was killed, leaving the potentially best bit to last. So, keeping that page unread, he ploughed his way to the end but nothing else sprang out at him, apart from the lack of further visits from Archer. Now it was time to open the special page and see if his theory could be revived.

"Fred!" Toby leaped off his seat and into the lobby. "Look at this and say my eyes aren't deceiving me."

"If you're reading the name R Archer, who's come to see them upstairs at three in the afternoon of February the fifth this year, then you're not mistaken."

"Thank you." It was only one of the names he'd been hoping to see, though. "I was half expecting to read that Carstone was also here on February the fifth, which would fit in with him being at Chancery Lane tube station on the way home when he was killed. Alas, he isn't listed there."

"What time would that have been?" Fred asked.

"He was killed around six o'clock in the afternoon."

"Ah. If he'd been here first his name should be in the visitors' book, as long as he didn't find a way to sneak in without me or Ted knowing. To give him time to walk there, he'd have still been within business hours." He checked the page again. "That would have been Ted on duty then, because he's signed the bottom of the page as being a true record. He's sharp as a tack, so if Carstone was here on that day, he'd surely be in the book."

"It's rather rude of me to ask, but what happens if you or Ted have to answer a call of nature? Could anyone sneak in then? I'm just covering all angles."

"Quite rightly, but we've also covered all angles. There's an arrangement with Brown and Bassett, who have offices on this floor. We ring over to them and young Billy, the office boy, or one of the others comes across and covers for me if I have to nip off. Otherwise, I have my lunch or a cuppa in my cubbyhole and keep an eye out. Same applies with Ted."

That was that, then. Unless Carstone had done something like clamber up the fire escape—if there was one—but that seemed unlikely.

"Then we must conclude that Carstone couldn't have been going home from here with Salt and Archer for company. I'd got it into my head that they were maybe deputed to keep an eye on him in case of him doing something silly."

It seemed like his lovely theory about Salt and Archer being involved in Carstone's death had been prematurely resuscitated, even if Toby could equate the Archer in the book with the Archer at Chancery Lane. Because if the murder was set up in advance, rather than being opportunistic, how could they have known that the victim would be at that station at that time? Still, he wasn't going to give it up just yet. What if the end of official office hours was five o'clock, thus giving ample time for Carstone to have been briefly here before he was killed?

"What time do you shut your signing-in book for the evening?" Toby asked.

"Six o'clock on the dot Monday to Friday, one o'clock on Saturdays."

Damn.

"It looks like I gave you an answer you didn't want to hear, Mr Bowe."

"You did, Fred, but if it's the truth I have to accept. I'd made the mistake of putting together a theoretical sequence of events without much in the way of evidence and the time the book shuts was vital." Toby sighed, deciding it the only hope was to take a different tack and that hope looked slim, as well. If only he could find, instead, a convincing reason why Archer and Salt could be sure their intended victim would be on that platform when they wanted him to be. "How can you arrange for a man to be in a certain place at a certain time? It's not like putting an advert in the paper to notify Joe Bloggs that if writes in he'll hear something to his advantage."

"I'd fix him up a date with Fiona Marsden," Fred stated, without hesitation. "Make it plausible that she'll be waiting for him at such a place at whenever o'clock and most men would grab the chance of being there. Even if it's only to have a look at her close up and see if she's as lovely in real life."

"She's a total peach, Fred: Alasdair's a lucky boy when he's filming with her." Toby paused: weren't there reports that Carstone had been talking to a woman on the platform shortly before his accident? "I like your idea though, so I'll expand on it. Why would you arrange to meet Fiona on a crowded platform rather than in some intimate little restaurant?"

"Because it possibly looks more innocent, for one thing. If you had a table for two at you swanky café, with the whole candles and violins nonsense, everyone would know you were up to hanky-panky." Fred grinned. "I knew a bloke who used to meet his fancy piece where it was crowded but not on home turf. Told me it was in case he was ever spotted, so he could say it was total coincidence that he and the bird were both there, and then he planned to follow that up by asking whether it wouldn't have been more sensible to choose somewhere quiet if he was playing about? Easier to brazen it out in those circumstances."

That idea could be feasible. Especially if the person concerned was already in disgrace with his wife and needed his excuses ready. Although who could have played the "Fiona" role in Carstone's case? Toby eyed the visitors' book again. "You've no record of employees coming in and out?"

"I'm afraid not. Their firms might have. Why? Are you still thinking about Mr James Salt?" Fred's hint of insult flavouring the title "mister" would have done credit to the best low comedian at Landseer.

"No. I was wondering if Alexandra Munsey, sorry, Alexandra Cummings, is somehow tied up in this. Given how her leaving the firm was hard on the heels of Carstone's death. Would she be the kind of girl who'd let herself be used as bait if her employers—or her colleague—asked her to? I don't mean bait to entrap some chap into, if you'll excuse the crudity, dropping his pants when he shouldn't. Simply to get him to the right spot at the right time."

Fred ran his fingers through what was left of his hair. "If you'd have asked me that before today I'd have said you were barking up the wrong tree. She was too nice. But while you were working through the visitors' books, I've been having a think. I still think Alexandra wouldn't do something like that of her own accord but she might have been persuaded. Before she left, she seemed out of sorts so I asked her if she was all right. She said she didn't know if she was or not. She'd been asked by her boss to do something that she thought was above board and had ended up involved in matters she wouldn't have touched with a barge pole if she'd known beforehand. At the time I thought it was to do with one of their clientele because I know that *Herbert and Chapman* sail pretty close to the wind when they're defending someone. The nastier the case, the closer they sail. Maybe it wasn't that."

"I fear you might be right. No proof of it, though, until and unless we can get her to tell us." Seemingly evidence that she felt betrayed by her boss, however. "One final question and it may seem bizarre. This time when Alexandra was upset, did she make any reference to the upcoming coronation? Or, indeed, did she say anything peculiar about it at any other time?"

"I don't think so, Mr Bowe, but it's funny you should say that, because another thing came to my mind when I was having a think. Not the coronation, but the month of June. The day Alexandra left, when she came to say goodbye to me, remember I told you she said something along the lines of having made the wrong choice in coming to work here?"

"Yes."

"Well, there was more. One of those throwaway lines like you have in your Sherlock Holmes films that turns out to be a big clue to what was going on. I always think I've scored a hit if I spot one."

Toby nodded. "Landseer has some clever script writers. And you've picked up one of those clues in real life?"

"I'm not promising I have, because I can't see how it could apply to Charles Carstone or the coronation but I'll tell you anyway. 'I don't want to be in those offices come June,' she said. Meaning her former employers."

"Interesting. Perhaps she planned, once she was well clear of this place, to tell the police something she knew about Carstone's death." Toby didn't believe that to be the case, but he'd realised he was at risk of spreading rumours if he kept plugging the coronation issue. If the public needed informing of a potential threat, that was up to Matthew, Bruce and the like.

"Ah, it's easy to tell you've got practice at this, because you could be right about her reporting something, sir. See, she also made a remark about how if the whole thing blew up in their faces it would serve them right, and she'd be laughing. I assumed she was talking about one of their unpleasant cases coming to court, but now I see it could be to do with that actor's so-called accident."

"It could. Only let's keep mum on that for the moment, shall we? In fact, I'd rather you didn't say anything to anyone about what we've discussed. Except the police, of course, if they come calling. We don't want to flush out the game before we have the guns lined up." Toby grinned, pleased at the analogy, even though he wasn't a hunting or shooting man himself.

"You have my word on that. And you can be certain I'll make a statement or stand in court and swear to everything I've told you so far. Every word's been true."

"Thank you for the reassurance, Fred, although on first impressions I'd expect nothing less." More than satisfied with what he'd learned, Toby fished a pound note out of his pocket. "Please don't be offended at being offered this. Treat your mates to a pint and think of both justice and Britannia. You might have acted in their interests today."

Chapter Fourteen

Alasdair, much to his frustration, hadn't woken on Thursday with any brighter idea than the one he'd told Toby about talking to Moira again. All the things he'd have liked to do—such as going to the Clarence House offices and inveigling himself with one of the members of Billy Chapman's staff—had been embargoed and he'd had to settle for what seemed like second best. If nothing else, he now knew what Toby's characters always felt like in the Landseer films. As for the interview with Moira, Alasdair wasn't even sure what the point of it would be, apart from giving her news about Alexandra and then introducing the subject of Carstone, Salt and Archer, but he had to be doing something. Even more frustrating was the feeling he'd had since speaking to Toby that there was a throwaway comment he should be following up but the wretched thing wouldn't spring to mind.

As soon as it was decent, he rang through to the number Moira had given Toby and was pleased to discover that she would be free to meet him for lunch. He made it clear it was to discuss the case, which was probably unnecessary although bitter experience had shown that women—of any age—did sometimes get the wrong end of the stick and believe his intentions were romantic. She suggested they meet in an understated but pleasant restaurant not far from Trafalgar Square, where she was known and therefore could be sure of being found a table somewhere, no matter how busy the place happened to be.

When Alasdair arrived there, a minute before the appointed time, Moira was already waiting at a table and if the owner was surprised at finding a film star frequenting his premises, he was too well trained to show it. Perhaps she'd forewarned him of whom her guest was. She and

Alasdair shook hands in a business-like manner, ordered their food and got down to business.

"Let me update you on what little we've discovered so far about Alexandra," Alasdair said. He didn't mention the possible pregnancy as he wanted to be sure that actually was the case—and that Alexandra would want the news shared—but emphasised that they were sure the lady concerned had moved. "We've got Jonny on that part of the trail, possibly as we speak. We can reassure you all that, unless her landlady was lying, Alexandra was fine when she left Finsbury Park and she had a nice young man helping her with her luggage."

"Oh, that *is* a blessed relief." Moira, smiling, studied him for a moment. "I'm sure there's more you could tell me, but I won't probe you on it because you clearly won't tell me All I'd ask is that you'd please let me know more when and if you can."

"I can promise you that. Now, there are some further things you can help us with. We're fairly sure the Alexandra we've located is the right one, because of the fan club membership, although she's called Munsey. Or that's the name she goes by at both those clubs, which don't have anyone at all called Cummings as a member. You wouldn't have an explanation for that?"

"No." Moira frowned. "How odd. We've always known her as Cummings—I suppose Jeff could have been aware if she used a different name at his work but if they barely knew each other from there she might have known she could use a false surname with us. I'm sure Jeff would have told me if he knew different."

Would he, however, if he fancied Alexandra and wanted to keep what he knew hidden to protect her? "She never dropped any hints about being married and now divorced, for example?"

"Not that I remember. Hold on." Moira picked up her handbag and opened it. "The restaurant has a telephone and I'm sure Guiseppe will let me use it. I have Jeff's number and can try to catch him at work."

"Please do."

Alasdair waited patiently, aware that he was attracting the odd glance from people at other tables and smiling at them in a friendly way if they caught his eye. One always had to remember who ultimately paid for him to indulge his investigational whims although he was relieved to see Moira returning, especially as she appeared to have news to share and she had a waiter not far behind bearing their meals.

Once they were settled again, with the wonderful aroma of pasta and sauce wafting up at them, Moira said. "I have a sort of solution for the name dilemma."

"Excellent. You can tell me once we've done a bit of justice to this." Alasdair feared that the incipient rumblings from his stomach would become so loud that the other patrons would hear them and his image suffer.

They ate for a while in silence until a natural break arose, as Moira took a drink of water. "So, Jeff. In one of those bits of serendipity that life seems to like throwing at us, he was chatting with one of his colleagues only yesterday and Alexandra got mentioned. I suspect Jeff himself made sure she did, because he's always been overfond of her." A hint of bitterness at that fact couldn't be hidden. "Said colleague, whom Jeff reckons didn't like the girl which may or may not make her a reliable source of information, told him that Alexandra was a bit of an inverted snob. The surname she was born with was Munsey-Cummings but she only uses half of it, the half depending on the circumstance. Therefore, she's both Miss Munsey and Miss Cummings."

"Oh." Another anti-climax in the Alexandra department.

Alasdair's reaction must have been obvious, because Moira said, "I know. Rather frustrating to find a mystery bears such a simple solution and I'm afraid there's more to come which doesn't help. This woman said Alexandra had told her she had an old flame she was trying to make a clean break from. And now I feel awful because that's exactly what one of you suggested when we met at *The Swan with Two Necks*. It feels like we've sent you on a wild goose chase."

"Don't feel bad about it at all. I'm not convinced we've got to the bottom of why she went off." Alasdair knew he was saying that as much to persuade himself as Moira. "Anyway, in the process you've opened up other things to look into. Regarding which, again, I can't give too much detail at present."

"Spoilsport."

They returned to the important matter of clearing their plates, after which Alasdair said, "What I can tell you is that we've notified the authorities about the coronation stuff you told us about, and they're taking it seriously, which wouldn't have happened if you hadn't called us in." Especially as Moira et al seemed so cowardly about notifying the police themselves. Maybe Alasdair now had an explanation for that reticence, though. "Actually, did Lloyd ever mention that he'd made a bit of a nuisance of himself during the war, telling said authorities that he could detect other people's special powers?"

"He did. Or at least he had a good moan about it, going on about how nobody had taken him seriously and what was the use of telling the powers that be anything important when they just laughed at you. I think that's one of the reasons we three were so reluctant to go to the police ourselves. What if they could connect us up to him and thought we were just time wasting like he'd been?" Moira pushed her plate away, then clasped her hands together on the table, clearly distressed. "I'm sure it seems silly to you, Alasdair, but Jeff in particular feels any blow to his self-esteem very deeply. His wife left him during the war, because they couldn't have children and she reckoned it was all Jeff's fault. She gave him a terrible tongue lashing before she went, one that he still thinks about. It doesn't help that he could never talk about some aspects of his war work. Nobody knows what a hero he really was."

"I understand." As would Geraldine and Bessy, who had mooted such an idea.

"Thank you. Then he developed this stupid crush—quite hopeless, in my opinion—on Alexandra, which led him into making up that story about what he could do. He wanted to impress her."

"And did that in turn lead to you and your small change, so you could join the club he was in? You like him, don't you?"

"I think he's wonderful. I just wish he'd stop moping about the women who've ditched him and realise there's one here who wouldn't." She hurriedly fished a handkerchief out of her cardigan pocket and blew her nose. "I'm so sorry. I hate being soppy but the unfairness of it all does get to me. Anyway, when Alexandra left, it was like another blow to him. If the police had laughed him to scorn about the overheard conversation, he'd go into a slough of despond."

Alasdair had at last realised that being laughed at, albeit in a polite way, was a real possibility, given what Matthew Firestone had told Jonny about people making groundless reports.

He should get matters away from romance and onto Lloyd again. Alasdair may have been good at comforting an emotional Fiona onscreen but here he felt out of his depths. "I should get Toby to give Jeff a jolly good talking to.

Getting back to Lloyd, did he ever mention that he thought his cousin Billy Chapman had special powers?"

"He did." Moira visibly brightened as the subject moved away from Jeff. "Apparently Chapman was delighted that somebody else had realised the capabilities he possessed. Lloyd told us about it when he discussed his own being snubbed for what he had to offer. How his cousin's powers hadn't been appreciated by the powers that be and how that was an opportunity missed as they could have been used to great effect in the war."

"For which side, though? Us or them?"

"Ah, there's the rub, Alasdair. Whatever else Lloyd is, he's a true-blue patriot, but I'm not sure I could say the same about Billy Chapman. Part of Lloyd's threnody on his being disregarded was that if powers aren't used for good they could end up being used for evil. He didn't specifically say so but I thought he was referring to his cousin. But I suppose he hasn't used them to the country's disadvantage or Lloyd wouldn't still be friendly with him." Moira paused as the waiter came to take their plates, then said, "I'm getting myself in quite a muddle. Chapman can't have powers, any more than we do. It's that business about Jeff playing on my mind. Pull yourself together, Moira."

The arrival of the manager—who seemed to be called Luigi—to take their dessert order allowed Moira to compose herself before Alasdair reopened the discussion. "You're not that muddled, because Chapman may not think they're bogus. He might be as self-delusional as Lloyd is."

"It wouldn't surprise me, from the little I know."

"Did Lloyd ever mention what his cousin's powers were alleged to be?"

Moira rolled her eyebrows. "Influencing the weather, which is oddly close to what Alexandra was supposed to do. Even more potentially useful, in a time of war, which is why

179

Lloyd was so agitated about not being taken seriously. But it's all stuff and nonsense, isn't it? Unless Chapman went to the other side and was trying to ensure that D-day couldn't happen by making the early June weather so lousy. That was a joke, by the way. I don't believe anyone could bring in a rain front, either with science or by willpower."

"I knew you were being frivolous. Sometimes it's the only way to counter such nonsense." Still, such a coincidence of weather events could have persuaded Chapman he was having an effect: who knew what self-deceptions a delusional man was prepared to swallow. "Perhaps he thinks he can call down a disastrous lightning strike on Westminster Abbey during the coronation, setting the place and all its occupants ablaze. He'd surely think that the police couldn't foil that, short of executing him, because if it's all to do with his mental influence, he could do it—sorry, he would *believe* he could do it—from a prison cell. And if we're in that territory it won't give the authorities much to get their teeth into in terms of arresting him."

Moira blenched. "Wouldn't it be awful if he's the one person Lloyd has lit upon who actually does possess a supernatural power and we just think it's nonsense."

"Agreed." Perhaps Matthew Firestone should be forewarned. Not that Alasdair actually believed in Moira's hypothesis, but maybe self-belief could perhaps be as dangerous as actual ability.

As they awaited the apple pies and coffees they'd ordered, the chat turned to such bland topics as the man in Moira's office who was obsessed with their Holmes and Watson offerings and his speculation about whether their next film would see them returning to Conan Doyle. This welcome conversation allowed Alasdair the opportunity of naturally introducing the matter of Charles Carstone. "I do feel rather guilty when I think of him, because his tragic death was the reason we were able to get the Cambridge film out so promptly and therefore crack on with the new offering. Capacity in the tightly run Landseer production system."

"How interesting. I'd never real thought about how much work of different sorts must go into making a movie. No wonder the list of those involved is so long."

"That's just the tip of the iceberg. If they named everyone, not only all the extras but those who work behind the scenes, the list would feel interminable." Alasdair sighed. "It's a funny old business where we've ended up benefitting from Carstone's death, but I dare say if he'd been in the same position he'd have said that one simply cracks on, like we did in the war. Was Alexandra a fan of his, as she is of us?"

The arrival of the apple pies, awash with cream, gave Moira the opportunity of considering the question. "I don't remember her mentioning him, although she was rather a starstruck type and she spread her watching favours far and wide. Don't take this amiss, but the time she mentioned being in your fan clubs she also went all swoony over Leslie Howard and Dick Powell. Others, too, whose names I don't recall, although I'm sure Carstone wasn't one."

"Toby will be mortified to discover she's been spreading her affections so widely," Alasdair said, gleefully. "Although it'll be a relief to him that Carstone wasn't one, as he wasn't quite in the Leslie Howard mould."

"I'd agree with that." Moira took a spoonful of pie. "I really don't know how they get their pastry so light."

"It's an art beyond me, although my manservant Morgan produces something almost as good. He won't reveal his secrets, though, apart from saying cold hands are key."

"Cold hands, warm heart, my mother used to say." Moira paused, spoon half lifted. "Wasn't that one of Carstone's films? Set in a POW camp?"

"*Cold Hands, Warm Heart*, yes. I rather enjoyed that. Wasn't Carstone the chap who kept everyone's spirits up and at the end we discovered that his wife had left him just before he was captured?"

"Yes. He took the part beautifully." She took a mouthful of pie and then frowned. "Do you know, Alexandra *did* mention him to me. I'd quite forgotten. At the end of the last meeting she attended, we walked to the underground together because it was raining and I'd come out without a brolly. She had hers so you can imagine Lloyd swanking about how that proved she knew what the weather would be so had come prepared. Alexandra was as unimpressed as I was, so we left him to his gloating."

"If I may interrupt, was it Chancery Lane station you went to?"

"No, it was Holborn. The distance from Clanfield House is much the same. On the way, the rain eased, so we paused to put the umbrella down, right by a poster for an upcoming film. Funny how you can forget something for ages and when you recall it again, it's as clear as day."

"The mind's a rum kind of beast. Please continue."

"Well we looked at this poster, which was quite hideous, so not one of yours, and Alexandra made an offhand remark about having had her fill of movie stars. How she'd once met one at the Eagle Street offices and he'd been a bit of a letch. I'm sure she said it was Charles Carstone. If it wasn't, I apologise to his ghost and it was someone similar."

Alasdair nodded. Another little piece of the jigsaw helping to create the overall picture. "Talking of those offices, she didn't happen to mention working there with either a James Salt or a Robert Archer?"

182

"Mr J Salt, yes. I don't know if he's James. His desk is in the main office foyer where we meet on Monday evenings and Alexandra pointed it out, saying he was one of the folk *Herbert and Chapman* got to do their dirty work. Given what you told us about their clientele and the cases they handle, I'm now guessing that she meant Salt was mixed up in that kind of sordid stuff."

"That seems most likely." Or in even dirtier work.

A waiter appeared with their coffees, which nudged them into finishing of their apple pies.

After Moira had consumed the last scoop, she said, "I should finish the story about that night at Holborn station. When we got down to platform level, Alexandra had a bit of a funny turn. I wanted to take her back up, because it can get a bit claustrophobic down there and a few minutes fresh air are just the job, but she laughed it off. Said that if she went up she might never have the guts to come down again, which seemed odd. She insisted we go on and, while she was a bit unsteady on her feet, she got onto the platform, we caught the northbound tube and then she seemed much happier. She alighted at Finsbury Park, all smiles and waves. That was the last time I saw her."

Was that "funny turn" another confirmation of Alexandra's medical condition? The waiter returned to clear their plates, with Luigi the manager in tow to ask if they had enjoyed their meal. Moira launched into fulsome—and genuine-sounding—praise of the pie pastry, while Alasdair truthfully said that the coffee was as good as any the capital had to offer.

With a delighted smile and elaborate bow, Luigi asked Moira if she'd like to join a small party he was hosting on June the second as he could promise a wonderful view of the coronation procession from the apartment just upstairs from the restaurant.

"Would you care to join us, Mr Hamilton?," he added. "There's plenty of room and my lady guests will be eternally grateful to me for inviting you."

Alasdair inclined his head as nobly as he'd be doing in the new film. "I truly appreciate the very kind offer but I already have something similar lined up with a very old friend and she'd not only be mortified if I stood her up, she'd quite possibly slap my legs." That was not a million miles from the truth, because Toby's mother had arranged a prime viewing spot for them from the moment the coronation date was announced and while she might not resort to physical violence, he'd never hear the end of it if he changed his arrangements. He took the very welcome cue, though. "I'm particularly looking forward to seeing Queen Salote. Sir Ian, the head of Landseer, met her during the war and can't praise her highly enough."

Luigi nodded. "If her photographs do her justice, she's a stunning woman. I—" Alas, whatever he was about to add was forestalled by the arrival of a waiter with a query.

"I'm pleased Luigi was interrupted," Moira said, when he'd hastened away, "because your mention of Queen Salote brought to mind something I saw in the *Herbert and Chapman* offices a couple of meetings ago. I was emptying some tea leaves into the kitchen dustbin when I saw a photograph crumpled up in there."

Alasdair forced himself not to slap the table and break out into a smug grin. That was it, the thing he'd wanted to follow up that had been stuck at the back of his memory: Moira making reference to things she'd seen in the dustbins at Clanfield House. "Was that what you meant at *The Swan with Two Necks* when we were discussing their unsavoury clientele?"

"Yes. You do have a good memory, don't you?"

"Not as good as I'd like it to be." As the bin business had proven. "Please go on."

"Well, being a nosy baggage, when I saw this discarded photo I picked it out and uncrumpled it. It was a photo of a regal personage I couldn't put a name to for reasons which will become apparent, but it could well have been Queen Salote or a similar monarch from a commonwealth nation. The nasty thing was that the photograph looked as though it had been used as a target for someone throwing darts, which is what made the face so hard to recognise."

"How horrible."

"Quite. I'd found similar things before that had clearly been used for darts practice and then discarded, but never a photograph of a person." Moira shivered, and then drained her cup, perhaps finding the excellent coffee a comfort. "When I was still looking at it, feeling rather stunned, Lloyd came in and I showed it to him. He seemed equally shocked, especially as he thought his cousin might have been responsible. Apparently Billy Chapman had always been a dab hand at darts."

Dab hand? A flurry of thoughts came into Alasdair's mind, beginning with whether you could put poison on an ordinary dart and then throw it with enough accuracy to hit a specific person riding in a procession. Not necessarily from amongst the crowds lining the streets but from the kind of elevated vantage point Moira would herself be occupying. If a dart wasn't viable, could that accuracy of aim allow you to lob an incendiary device or grenade into a carriage?

Matthew Firestone needed to know about this genuine skill that Chapman possessed, and he needed to be told as soon as possible.

Chapter Fifteen

Thursday evening, as Alasdair awaited the arrival of his light of love, he basked in the wonderful aromas wafting from the kitchen, where Morgan was producing something miraculous involving the slow cooking of an obscure cut of beef. Once Morgan was sure it could be left, *he'd* be leaving for his club and Alasdair, Toby and their fellow investigator could serve themselves at leisure while they discussed their news.

Morgan had not been gone more than five minutes when Toby knocked at the front door and he and Alasdair hadn't been more than two minutes in a clinch when the knocker sounded again.

"I bet that's Jonny," Toby said, swiftly straightening his hair.

"Then his timing is to be deplored." Alasdair grinned, as he went to open the door. "Jonny. How goes it?"

"Very well, up to a point." Jonny's nostrils quivered. "That smells glorious. Whatever it is, I need its reviving powers."

"That bad? Let's get you a small glass of something and you can tell all." Alasdair closed the door and ushered them into the living room, where a decanter of sherry awaited.

"Thank you," Jonny said, as he accepted a glass, "and thank you for inviting me here, rather than doing this over the telephone. Roger is working all hours God sends at present, and I'm feeling at a bit of a loose end. It's frustrating, as well, to sit on one's hands when I want to get out and properly question people about things. The denizens of *Herbert and Chapman*, for a start."

"Is that why you need reviving?" Toby asked. "A case of investigator's irritation?"

"More a case of policeman's tongue-lashing. Matthew wasn't best pleased when I rang him earlier," Jonny said, settling himself in his chair. "I had no idea you'd both called him before I did, so I got through to a rather grumpy individual. He says we should co-ordinate in future and only bring one set of news."

"Sorry about that." Alasdair made his best apologetic gesture before taking his seat. "He was fine with me, but he's probably got a point."

"I wondered why he sounded a tad exasperated when I called him," Toby said. "I thought it was pressure of work. You must have caught him first, Alasdair, if he was all sweetness and light with you."

Alasdair grimaced. "*Mea culpa.* In the circumstances, we should let Jonny go first with his briefing, on the understanding that we'll neither of us be grumpy with him, but eternally grateful for his help."

"Much obliged." Jonny grinned, raised his glass, took a sip and continued. "Earlier today, I discharged my duty regarding the Stoke Newington tobacconist, so you have the story hot off the press. I'm lucky to have an employer who admires Lord Peter Wimsey—as well as admiring the aged great uncle—meaning he wasn't averse to allowing me an hour or so for amateur 'teccing, especially after I explained I was working alongside the men who helped pin down the *Grey Assassin*. I also dropped a hint that the commission involved acting in the national interest and promised I'd tell him all about it when in a position to do so. I hope that was all right?"

"If it means he might give you more time off if necessary, then it's more than all right," Toby said. "The 'when in a position to do so' can be extended for a jolly long time if need be, especially if friend Bruce puts a moratorium on all news even after the event."

"Yes, spoilsport that he is. I'd thought if those circumstances prevailed I might simply say we'd kept the queen safe and leave it at that. Anyhow, as we'd speculated, it *was* a female shop assistant and so I piled on all the charm I could manage. I didn't need to use any of the ploys we'd mulled over, because once I gave the name Stewart, Enid—said lady—asked if I was related to Jonty. She'd apparently seen your film last night and knew it was based on real people. She'd seen an item in a screen magazine regarding your latest venture, which featured a photograph of the aged relative in his younger days and she thought I bore a resemblance to him."

"That's handy. Straight into her good books, I hope," Alasdair said.

"Indeed. I assured her I was indeed related to himself and gave her some background on both the aged relative and the pair of you. That worked like a charm, although I did have a dodgy moment when she told me she believed that every word of your film was based on true events." Jonny rolled his eyes, in a manner reminiscent not of Jonty Stewart but of the latter's partner, Orlando Coppersmith. "Especially when she asked if Dr Coppersmith had gone on to marry the character that Fiona plays."

"Ouch." Toby winced. "What did you tell her?"

"I decided to put on a deadly serious face and tell Enid—in strictest confidence, because it was a heartbreaking story that Coppersmith didn't want spread—that the lady concerned, for whom the false name Margaret had been used in the film, died tragically young of tuberculosis. Dr C, distraught, had vowed never to take another sweetheart." Jonny placed his hand on his breast. "Gentlemen, I not only brought Enid to tears, I earned myself a cup of tea and a slice of excellent fruit cake. Over which she asked if I was on a case, like you and Toby often are. I assured her I was, one that involved locating Alexandra, at which the floodgates of information opened. It turns out that she never picks up her own post, not after for the first time. Ever since it's been done by a chap, who—the first time he arrived—came with a letter of authority written in Miss Munsey's fair hand."

"Isn't your friend Enid suspicious?" Toby asked. "How does she know that letter wasn't forged?"

"Because Alexandra had forewarned her that her brother would be coming in future. My lovely purveyor of tea, cake and gossip said that this chap came with quite a sob story. His sister Alexandra was with child, which is why she didn't want to carry on getting her mail in person. All her family had disowned her—except him—and she dared not show her face in the family home, and so on and so forth. Enid says Alexandra was very pleasant the one time she spoke to her and hadn't seemed ashamed of her condition, but the young woman was wearing a large, floaty type of cloak so could have been hiding a considerable bump. Enid put that all more delicately than I have, of course."

"Hang on," Alasdair said. "Something about this doesn't add up. Why do I think Alexandra's an only child?"

"Because Jeff told us that," Toby replied. "He said something like it being the reason why she'd found the Monday evening group such a help."

Jonny nodded. "Exactly what I thought. Not that I told Enid I knew that. I simply asked her for a description of said chap, which she was happy to provide and which means the letter collector isn't Lloyd, unless he's managed to cover up that large hairy mole on his cheek and lost a dozen years. The supposed brother is my age, although taller, darker and possessed of no distinguishing features. So that rules out Jeff and Richard, too, except if Enid is short sighted or useless at guessing ages and I don't believe she's either."

189

"You honestly thought it might be one of that pair?" Toby asked.

"Given what we've heard these last few weeks, nothing would surprise me. If, say, Richard had inveigled himself with Alexandra, would he let Jeff know? And the fact that Enid said this chap is called Nicholas means nothing. If he's a false brother he could be using a false name."

"You could be right about the name irrespective of him being too old for Richard or Jeff. I also reckon you're spot on about Richard not telling Jeff in the event that he and Alexandra were involved with each other, because Moira says he carries an unextinguished torch for her. Much to Moira's annoyance. As complicated a situation as one of our plots." Alasdair sniffed. "if this Nicholas is younger, who could he be? We seem to be the only younger men associated with this case."

"Apart from the chap Alexandra was seen arguing with," Toby reminded him. "I suppose she might be living with her bloke out of wedlock and telling all the world he's her brother, for appearances' sake. Oh, and what about the young man who came to get her trunk when she moved from Finsbury Park? He's a second, unless he's the aforementioned arguer."

"There's a third," Jonny said, with a hint of triumph. "Somebody we've had information from, albeit at third hand. Dennis's son."

"Of course," Alasdair said, a touch grudgingly, annoyed at not having remembered him. Any evidence that this chap is...no, I'm being silly. There must be, given your smug expression, Jonny."

"My pal Enid was telling me all about him. She seems to like chatting to her favoured customers, among whom I now include myself. I bought some of her most expensive cigars for my father before leaving."

Alasdair grinned. Handsome young men both, no doubt—Jonny and Nicholas—although he wouldn't judge Enid for that. Why not enjoy that aspect of her work?

Jonny pressed on. "She was saying that you couldn't judge people by appearances, because she'd never have guessed that Nicolas's father would have been in the business of keeping a public house. It may be coincidence, but there again…"

"How vexatious that Morgan's not here," Toby said. "If he's anything like North, he wouldn't want to be contacted at his club or wherever he's enjoying his evening off."

"Quite," Alasdair replied. "It'll have to wait for his return, because he works damn hard and his free time is sacrosanct as far as I'm concerned. I'm more than happy to leave a note for him, however. I can appraise him of the developments, partly so that he doesn't put his foot in it with Dennis, but also in case he can see a way to wheedle a name out of his old pal. Jonny, does Nicolas come to the tobacconist at a regular time or day to collect the post?"

"Great minds think alike, Alasdair, because that's what I asked Enid. Yes, he's apparently regular as clockwork twice a week. Half past twelve on a Wednesday and roughly a quarter past five in the afternoon on Saturdays. I wondered if the former coincided with his work lunch hour and the latter was on his way home from seeing the Arsenal."

"Oh yes, we're back in Highbury territory, aren't we? I wonder if anyone else finds the coincidence of the *Herbert and Chapman* name ironic."

"Anyone with an ounce of sense would, Toby," Alasdair said. "Although the Gunners can't be at home every Saturday so Nicholas can't always be on the way home post-match."

"No, but he might be waiting to listen to the football scores on *Sports Report* before he heads out, and that would mean he lives locally."

"In which case, Nicholas might support Sheffield United or any other team. You're getting carried away with yourself, young Toby and diving down alleyways." Alasdair slapped his thighs then rose. "And we should be getting ourselves some dinner, to power up the old brain cells."

The next few minutes were spent serving up the casserole and accompaniments, then taking them through to the dining room where a bottle of a decent red wine had been coming up to a nice temperature for drinking.

Once they'd started to do some justice to a meal that deserved proper attention, Toby said, "You rebuked me for going off on a tangent of deductions, but all three of us are getting slack. Nicholas *could* be Alexandra's brother, you know and the pub stuff is either the truth—we don't know that her parents don't keep a hostelry—or it's a coincidence, or another cock and bull tale."

"What about her telling the others she was an only child?" Jonny asked.

"Another lie, told to gain sympathy. 'Oh, I've been so lonely all my life, and you're all such a help.'" Toby uttered the last part in an unconvincing falsetto. "There are so many tall stories woven into this case that I'm finding it hard to believe anything at first sight. And, irrespective of what the lovely Enid said—do send us an invitation to the wedding, by the way and we'll make sure we console Roger—Alexandra could be being kept against her will."

Jonny nodded slowly. "I did like Enid—she's married, by the way, so I can't plight my troth with her—but I think it possible for her to be taken in by the lies of a charming young man. If that had happened, it would mean the collection of Alexandra's mail, and presumably the filtering of same, is part of the method by which she's being kept under control."

Alasdair looked up sharply from where he'd been loading his fork. "Do you really believe she is?"

Jonny shrugged. "I don't think so, but it's proper diligence to consider all possibilities. I'm sure there's also an element, it pains me to confess, of wanting a more satisfying—for us—solution to this mystery than 'girl gets in the family way and has to hide her interesting condition'."

"I might have a more satisfying solution," Toby said. "Or at least another reason for Alexandra wanting to move away from her old digs, which her previous employers would have had on record. It's all from my visit earlier today to see Fred. He was the rather sardonic keeper of the door at Clanfield House, if you recall, Jonny."

"I remember him well. How did you manage to get on his good side?"

"Simply by employing honesty, a touch of flattery and an appeal to his better nature. We're now as pally as you and Enid, although we're not having the banns read. Hold on, let me finish this." He cleared his plate, pushed it away and then launched into an account of what he'd discovered.

Alasdair listened, increasingly impressed, at the information produced. The fact of a chap called James Salt working at *Herbert and Chapman* and his connection to the Blackshirts was no great surprise, although evidence of an R Archer being at the company's offices on the day that Carstone died was very welcome. "Why does Lloyd visit of an evening?" he asked, when Toby reached that part of his account.

"No idea, and neither does Fred. Buff up his cousin's ego—and his own at the same time—with this powers nonsense?" Toby shrugged. "There's more on Alexandra, though. She told Fred, before she left, that she wouldn't have wanted to be with her soon-to-be-no-longer employers come June, which may be a coronation reference. Especially as she made a remark about things blowing up in their faces, which might be a veiled reference to an explosive device. She also said that she'd been asked by her boss to do something that she thought was above board and had ended up involved in matters she wouldn't have touched with a barge pole if she'd known beforehand. My theory is that she was used to lure Carstone to Chancery Lane station platform. The woman that some witnesses say he was talking to on the platform. Which is one of the reasons, maybe the primary reason, why she left the firm."

"That all calls for port and cheese." Alasdair went to fetch the items concerned while the other two insisted on clearing the table and doing the washing up.

Once they were all back at the table, Jonny resumed the discussion with, "Why hasn't Alexandra told the police about either the overheard plot or the actor's dubious accident? Is she as feckless as Jeff and the rest of them appear to be?"

"I can add to that. Over lunch today, Moira gave me a fuller explanation of why they sat on their hands," Alasdair said, with a twitch of his eyebrow he hoped would suggest he wasn't entirely convinced they'd picked all the layers off that particular onion. "All tied up with their individual self-esteem and the fact that Lloyd had been laughed at by the authorities during the war. They didn't want to be in the same boat, especially Jeff, who had a rough time of it with his ex-wife belittling him. If Alexandra felt the same and was worried that the police would find out about the *Monday Evening Association* with its peculiar claims and dubious leader and laugh her to scorn."

"There may be an element of that," Toby said, "but I've another suggestion. What if she was blackmailed, in effect.

194

Perhaps after Carstone's death she got a warning from Salt or Chapman along the lines of, 'Don't come forward for the inquest. In fact, keep shtum, because if you say what you saw at the station, we'll not only deny it, we'll tell the police how you were involved in Carstone's death. You lured him to the station on the promise of an assignation—we can prove that you're obsessed with film stars because of these fan clubs you've joined—and then when you'd got him nice and close to the edge of the platform, you tripped him up and over the edge. When we couldn't save him, we covered for you.' How about that?"

"They could have brought in her membership of Lloyd's club, too, as an example of her liking for flights of fancy," Alasdair pointed out.

"I'm not disagreeing," Jonny said, in tones which indicated he was about to do just that, "but how could they hope to make that a viable threat? What motive could they pretend that Alexandra had for killing Carstone when, as you say, she was devoted to film stars?"

Alasdair had been mulling over the theory, increasingly persuaded by it. "What you referred to as her interesting condition. They say, 'We'll tell the police that it was Carstone who got you up the duff and then refused to do the honourable thing because he didn't want to rock his own marital boat. That's why you've gone into hiding.' And so forth. That might have been enough to have scared her into silence and to have made her leave the firm."

"Good thinking, Alasdair. I'd like to develop the idea further," Toby said. "Which came first, Carstone's accident or Alexandra overhearing the phone call about the coronation? If it was the latter, could they have deliberately got her entwined in the Carstone case so they could hold that over her? Safer than bumping her off or making threats, perhaps."

"I feel the need of a written timeline, clarifying what Alexandra stopped doing and when, related to other things." Jonny chuckled. "The sort of thing Orlando might like, with dates on one axis, events on the other and seven or eight different coloured pencils to differentiate between the strands."

"You and Roger can produce one yourselves," Alasdair said, with a snort. "Don't forget that one thing happening after another doesn't imply cause and effect between them."

"No," Toby said, "but it could eliminate the reverse. For example, if I steal Alasdair's biscuit after he hits me, the assault can't have been occasioned by the robbery."

"The robbery could have been in revenge for the slap, though," Jonny pointed out. "Same sequence of events, different cause and effect."

"Which could also apply to what happened to Carstone. He falls under the train but it's due to Salt's actions, rather than his slipping causing Salt to attempt a rescue. After which, Alexandra's conscience causes her to quit her post." Toby drew a notebook from his pocket. "I spent a bit of time just before I came here going back through the reports of the inquest. Nothing—apart from Salt and Archer's testimony— would definitely preclude this new scenario being true. Even Carstone deliberately moving too close to the platform edge for comfort, which had been interpreted as his being in a hurry to get aboard, might have been him trying to get away from those two."

"Why should they want Carstone dead, though?" Alasdair asked.

"Maybe he seduced the wrong woman," Jonny suggested. "Chapman's wife or daughter or sister or cousin. Carstone didn't recognise the connection and the name only emerged when he was briefing them on his situation."

"That's possible," Toby said. "Alternatively, perhaps he arrived early for one of the out-of-hours sessions and overheard something through the door. Something incriminating about whatever Chapman and his pals are planning to do. They didn't trust Carstone to keep his trap shut or perhaps he even threatened to go to the police about what he'd heard unless Chapman did the decent thing and went to them and confessed all first."

Alasdair nodded. "The latter sounds more likely. Although they may have turned the tables on him as we're speculating they did with Alexandra. 'Tell the police and we'll say you're involved and how will that look in the publicity for *Naughty Nelly*?'"

"Do you know," Jonny said, "that also gives another motive for Carstone to take his own life. Yes, I know I argued against his suicide, but it may have been the last straw."

Toby rapped the table. "We need to turn some of this speculation into fact, which means talking to Alexandra. A note via the lovely Enid, perhaps?"

Jonny grinned. "Already done. Although as this conversation has gone on, I'm less and less sure of getting a response."

"We'll catch her somehow." Alasdair wasn't sure he felt as confident as he tried to sound. "Did you tell this to Matthew, Toby?"

"Yes. After I'd mentioned the vague 'Wouldn't like to be them come June, when it blows up' thing."

"What was his response?" Alasdair asked.

Toby frowned. "He made some joke about maybe *it* was going to be a bomb attached to a dart, which made no sense."

"It will in a moment," Alasdair promised. "What about the Carstone business?"

"Well, put it like this. When I told him we have a murder for him to look into once he had five minutes, he replied that he would be happy to oblige and that 1956 looked pretty clear in his diary. He's clearly worn to a frazzle with other priorities, poor lamb."

"Perhaps we can give him a nice case, neatly tied up with plenty of decent evidence, as a nice present for when he's successfully kept Her Majesty and all her guests safe." Alasdair passed the cheese board round again. "Anyone for coffee?"

Jonny shook his head, while Toby said, "No thank you. What I want is to make sense of the dart quip. Clearly you told Matthew something about it."

"I did. Along with the fact that Billy Chapman believes that he possesses the power to influence the weather—I suspect Lloyd gees him up on that one—and his proven talent with darts. Someone in the *Herbert and Chapman* office had possibly been using a picture of Queen Salote for target practice and the money is on Billy Chapman himself."

Toby raised his hand. "Hold your horses, young man. Where did you get this weather and darts stuff from?"

"From my over-lunch conversation with Moira, who's been nosing about in wastebins. It was quite an illuminating discussion, one way or another. I'll flesh out the tale." Alasdair gave his guests a summary of what Moira had said to him over their meal, from the double-barrelled Munsey-Cummings surname to Chapman's claim regarding the weather. "Remember how the heavens opened beforehand? I've heard we were damn close to deferring the whole operation. If Chapman was trying to muck the weather up then—or on other occasions—he could well have thought he'd influenced things when it was mere coincidence."

"Do you think he'll be dancing naked around Avebury ring, every night between now and June, waving his hands

198

and trying to summon lightning to strike Westminster Abbey and set it ablaze on the big day?" Toby gestured expansively, as though conducting the clouds like an orchestra.

"Possibly he might be doing that as a sideshow, but I had his ability with darts more in mind, which I was about to expand on but couldn't, owing to your theatrical interruption." Alasdair snorted, then recounted the tale of Moira and her poking about in the contents of the kitchenette bin. "If Chapman's got such an accurate arm, it raises the possibility of him standing on a balcony somewhere lobbing things into the parade with deadly precision. And if you think that's a flight of fancy, I wasn't the only one to have that idea. Matthew suggested something similar when I told him about it. However, chucking darts at a picture of Queen Salote isn't enough to arrest Chapman on, nor is anything else we have at present, unfortunately."

"Can't they pick him up forty eight hours before the event on some trumped up charge?" Suggested Jonny. "Then let simply him go—sorry guv, a witness misidentified you—when it's safe to do so because all the ceremony is over and done with."

"I suppose they could," Toby said, "but if it was a last minute arrest you wouldn't have time to try to interrogate him, or whatever Matthew does to get at the truth. In which case, you couldn't be certain Chapman didn't have a substitute lined up to do the deed in case of anything going awry."

"You're thinking that he might expect to be arrested?" Jonny asked.

"Not necessarily." Toby shrugged. "It's simply that if I was serious about causing a disruption, I'd have a back-up plan in place in case of, say, having a car accident in the run up. I know there's value in acting alone, because the more folk involved the more chance of someone blabbing, but it has its own risks."

"He's clearly not working entirely alone, if he had that conversation Alexandra overheard," Alasdair pointed out. "While we're discussing Matthew, I didn't mention to him anything on the Carstone business, given that he has bigger and more urgent fish to fry, but Moira did have some stuff to say that backs up what you were suggesting earlier, Toby. Alexandra told her she'd had enough of film stars and that she didn't like Carstone because she'd met him and thought him a letch. She also had a funny turn when she and Moira were heading down onto the platform at Holborn one day. I wondered if that was more evidence of Alexandra being in the family way, but it may have been memories resurfacing of being used to lure Carstone to his death. Various strands are starting to weave together."

Jonny stuck out his lower lip. "If I can't have a diagram of when and what, can I at least have an assessment of where we are because I still feel a touch befuddled. You're much more experienced in this sort of stuff than I am. Do you often find that for every loose end you appear to tie up another couple work themselves loose?"

"Frequently," Alasdair assured him. "It's sometimes the small threads that prove most annoying because you can't always weave them into the whole and you feel guilty about wasting time on them."

"I think it's high time we took stock." Toby rose from the table. "Let's clear up *these* bits and pieces—meaning the plates and glasses—before we try to clear up any mysteries."

Once the domestic duties had been discharged and they were all comfy in Alasdair's sitting room once more, Jonny said, "To me, we have a hotchpotch of knowns, unknowns and partially knowns and some of the things we think we're sure about are still a touch dodgy. For example, and starting with one of Alasdair's small threads, the Munsey-Cummings name now seems a blindingly obvious explanation for what had seemed a mystery. I've discussed the two names thing with Roger. I hope it's acceptable to chat things over with him, because he won't go blabbing and he's got a useful brain that squirrels away useful bits of information he's overheard or picked up."

"Men like us are used to employing discretion, so if you trust him then we will too," Alasdair said.

"Thank you. Anyway, we came up with every answer under the sun apart for the Munsey versus Cummings business, from that one. Although I confess I'm still not entirely satisfied it's the truth."

Toby nodded. "You have my sympathy. I've become horribly cynical about anything that members of Lloyd's club tell us, Moira not excepted. Still, we can only work with what we have."

"As I see it," Alasdair said, "assuming Alexandra is indeed pregnant, that part of the story is almost a red herring. A convenient if unusual excuse for cutting off ties, that she could use if challenged, rather than admit she no longer attends our fan clubs because she's had enough of film stars after her encounters with Carstone. Or have to confess that she doesn't go to Lloyd's meetings anymore because she doesn't want to be in the *Herbert and Chapman* offices or is sick of Jeff mooning over her."

"She could have stopped attending because of that funny turn she had in front of Moira, which she doesn't want gone into too deeply," Toby suggested. "Irrespective of what her motivation was for upping sticks, we're getting closer to signing off on our original commission, which was purely to locate Alexandra and confirm that she's safe. We're not

201

obliged to tell Moira and company why she's done a flit, even if we knew that for a fact."

"Agreed," Alasdair said. "The motivation only becomes relevant for us in relation to either Carstone's death or whatever Chapman's up to. So, starting with the former. Apart from what was reported at the inquest, which is also to be taken with a pinch of Salt—excuse pun—if the evidence comes from the two would-be rescuers, everything else related to what happened to him at Chancery Lane is circumstantial."

"And our only hope of making it more solid is to get a statement from the girl herself." Jonny shrugged. "Circumstantial or not, it's all adding up to something damn suspicious."

"Which could also apply to the second part, the coronation threat. Again, what we have is hearsay and indirect evidence but as you so eloquently put it, Jonny, it also amounts to something damn suspicious, albeit not a thing we're supposed to be poking our noses into." Alasdair steepled his fingers to his chin. "Which brings me to one of the other ends that still need tying up. Why did Bruce change his mind midway through our conversation about whether we should pursue the Chapman angle? I can only think that's tied up with Carstone, because the volte face appeared to happen after I mentioned him."

"The name might have jogged his memory," Jonny said. "If Bruce also suspects the actor was killed, he needed to warn us against getting too close and perhaps ending up being disposed of. If we're talking loose ends, *I* want to know who Alexandra was arguing with in the street and whether that was, for example, James Salt who was trying to get her to do something. Which could suggest that the argument was related to the Chancery Lane lure scheme."

"I hadn't thought of that possibility." Toby nodded in clear approval of such an excellent idea. "*I'd* like to know how much Lloyd is involved in all this, given that Fred told me he visits the Clanfield House offices out of hours and not just on meeting nights. Maybe the mention of him—and recollection of his wartime eccentricities—put Bruce on guard."

"Quite possibly," Alasdair said. "We've mooted going to interview him, but I'm increasingly reluctant to do so, as more of the story emerges. Quite possibly he'd report back to Chapman and any gains we make would be offset. I wonder if his extra-curricular visits could be anything to do with Chapman's power-over-the-weather nonsense? Which is strangely close to Alexandra's alleged weather-related gifts, of course."

"Although his claims of what he can do are unlikely to be a bit of bravado on Chapman's part, as distinct from why the others say they can do what they can't. What a tangled web." Toby sighed, then blew out his cheeks. "One other thing I'd like to know, among many, and it's something I should get a definite answer for, is what you reported to Matthew Firestone, young Jonny. It couldn't have simply been Enid's stuff about a supposed brother, although if it was, no wonder you got sent away with a flea in your ear."

"I'm not that daft. I should have told you earlier, but we kept going off on tangents and it's nothing definite, which is why Firestone was a touch lukewarm about it, so don't get over-excited. Nothing to do with my pal Enid, either, because this time my informant is the person with whom I'd really love to have my banns read, but alas never will." Jonny smiled ruefully. "Roger has an old pal from schooldays called Neil, who lives outside of Manchester, so when he's down here on business they tend to meet for a drink, a meal and a catch up. He rang yesterday evening to say he's about to spend some time in London and to arrange their chinwag, which is likely to be either tomorrow or Saturday."

Alasdair couldn't help mentally consulting his diary, because despite Jonny's warning about not getting excited, his thumbs were pricking.

Jonny continued. "Neil works in the armament business. Newly manufactured and ex-services surplus. He's part of his company's high level sales team, so gets to deal with foreign governments and representatives of the same, which is a job that requires a lot of discretion and a huge dollop of common sense. The ability to smell a rat, as well, because not every potential sales contract apparently leads back to someone you'd like getting their paws on your weaponry."

"I can imagine," Toby said. "What's the 'nothing definite' regarding which we have to restrain our enthusiasm?"

"It involves one of Neil's clients. Roger says his friend is mainly coming to London for a meeting at one of the embassies—we're not allowed to know which—but there's also a more informal chat planned either for tomorrow or Saturday with a private individual. This chap says he's working for an important party in an unnamed yet friendly minor nation who's interested in smaller and less expensive weaponry. Perhaps items that have already seen service and are no longer needed in a time of peace."

Alasdair sniffed. "That private individual sounds rather dodgy to me."

"To Neil, as well. It's not unknown for his company to be approached in this way, for good or ill, which is why *he's* been sent to scope out this prospective customer while he's in London on more important business. If he isn't convinced by the individual in question, then all deals will be off and maybe a word dropped in the appropriate authorities' shell-like." Jonny grinned. "This is where Roger thinks we come into it."

"Doing the scoping?" Toby asked, markedly puzzled at why they should be asked.

"Not exactly. You see, while Neil didn't mention this possible client's name—that being unprofessional, even when chatting to an old pal—there were some things he said which made Roger's ears prick. Meeting person unnamed at a place on Chancery Lane, because that's near his office. Said person wanting the order filled by the end of May, as his original supplier has let him down and if the goods can't be delivered by then, he's not interested. Suggestive of our man Chapman, eh?"

"It certainly is," Alasdair said, "although let's temper our enthusiasm with remembering that it *is* only suggestive. Unless you've something else to add, Jonny, knowing your capacity for keeping the best for last."

"Guilty as charged. This mysterious customer apparently offered as character reference a couple of the great and good, including a peer of the realm. While no names were mentioned, Neil told Roger that he'd heard what the son of said peer got up to with minors and that rather tarnished the gilt on any reference. Does that remind you of anything?"

"What Morgan told me about *Herbert and Chapman's* clients." Alasdair nodded slowly. Three links could still be coincidental, but the potential connection was becoming stronger.

"So, Jonny continued, what this all adds up to is whether you're free on Friday evening or sometime on Saturday to talk to Neil, assuming Roger can get such a meeting set up?"

"My diary's as clear as a nun's," Alasdair said. "What about you, Toby?"

"I'm free tomorrow but booked on Saturday afternoon." Now frustration had replaced puzzlement on Toby's handsome face. "Although as soon as I get the chance tomorrow, I will try to unbook myself, because I wouldn't miss this for worlds. Do we need to involve Matthew or the dreaded Bruce in such a meeting?"

Alasdair pursed his lips. "I'd say not, at present. We know that the former is run off his feet and I'm sure that applies to the latter, as well. As Jonny says, the details are suggestive of Chapman, but it could be a damp squib and our reputation with the authorities could go plummeting if we distract them with nonsense at a time they don't need distracting."

Jonny's eyes were twinkling, in evident delight at restricting involvement to themselves. "I agree. We can always ring them if matters take an unexpectedly dangerous turn."

"Exactly. Well done Jonny, and well done your Roger. I think there's nothing we can do or say to trump that, this evening." Toby yawned and stretched all four limbs, like a large cat. "It's hard work, this detecting lark."

"It's also getting late and while I've a cold bed awaiting me until Roger returns, you two no doubt will have one to be warmed up in the best way possible." Jonny eased himself out of his chair. "I'll keep you appraised of any communication from Alexandra."

As they reached the hall, with a leave-taking set of handshakes and shoulder pats all round, the sound of a key in the lock heralded the front door bursting open and the entrance of Morgan. He appeared uncharacteristically red about the cheeks, a colour that didn't seem entirely to be due to the temperature of the outside air.

"Excuse me, sir," he said sheepishly, "I fear I have been led slightly astray."

"You're allowed to be sometimes." Alasdair replied, slapping Morgan's shoulder. "Been celebrating something?"

"Some excellent news for my friend Dennis. He's going to be a grandfather." Morgan beamed, watery eyed. "And if it's a boy they'll name it after Dennis's father, Nicholas, which was my father's name, so it's rather taken me aback."

Alasdair affectionately cuffed his manservant's shoulder, feeling a touch of Lord Peter Wimsey's surprise at hearing that Bunter was possessed of a parent. "You had every reason to celebrate, then. And you can't imagine how pleased we are to hear about the name."

It might all be a huge coincidence, of events and family names, but it could equally be one of the nice juicy facts their investigation so badly needed.

Chapter Sixteen

The romantic part of Toby's night with Alasdair turned out to be significantly delayed—as did Jonny's departure from the house—given that they needed to digest the news they'd got second hand from Dennis and then measure it alongside the information they had to impart to Morgan.

The manservant could still give them no indication of Dennis's son's name, nor that of his girlfriend, but the other details they had about the upcoming birth matched with what Jonny had discovered from Enid. Including the fact that the grandchild would be born hard on the heels of a hastily arranged marriage, which was due for the week after the coronation. Morgan promised he'd try his level best to elucidate a name for either or both parties, because he could now play the card detailing how this might relate to an investigation bearing on national security which would appeal to the man's patriotic streak. He'd emphasise that Alasdair was part of a group trying to eliminate red herrings, and reassure Dennis that they were keen for his prospective daughter in law to be eliminated from any connection to the miscreants.

"I won't mention Carstone," he'd said, "because that might scupper any chance of candour from Dennis. I wonder if that's why there's been this coyness about names, rather than a baby who'll be born just in wedlock."

"It could well be," Toby had replied, "if he's been so candid during the celebrations."

"That might have been the beer loosening his tongue," Morgan had admitted. "I hope it's had a longer lasting effect. I'll endeavour to provide an answer by the end of tomorrow, at least in terms of the son's name, but maybe on other fronts. Perhaps I can try persuading Dennis to broker a meeting with Alexandra."

"An excellent idea." Alasdair had expressed their thanks, told Morgan to leave a message at the studio as soon as he had anything to report and then had brought the evening to its close.

The next morning, both men travelled separately to the studio so they'd arrive at a sensible time interval apart, and not have to face questions about why they'd been together at such an early hour. It wasn't unknown for Landseer to arrange a sympathetic chauffeur who'd turn a blind eye to picking both actors up from the same place at an early hour but that degree of licence was also on hold for the moment.

During the journey, Toby mulled over whether they'd made a breakthrough on both cases or had simply landed on two sets of coincidences. If this was a book—or possibly one of Landseer's more intricate plots—then either or both apparent correlations would turn out to be accidents of chance, whereas there'd be an actual solution that would neatly tie up and interlink both mysteries. A solution that Alasdair might work out onscreen when playing Sherlock Holmes, his logic based on a chance remark or two which had occurred in the first reel.

Had they missed such a connection here, a piece of information that they hadn't slotted into its correct place? What had Jonny said about links? *Different cause and effect, same sequence of events*. Maybe *he* and Roger would already be putting together their colour coded chart, working things out in a scientific manner and finding that piece of wisdom applied here. If they concluded—and could prove—something outrageous like Alexandra having killed Carstone, Salt having genuinely tried to save him and Messrs Herbert and Chapman encouraging the woman to go into hiding to protect her, Toby would eat his hat. In the meantime, he would rely on his sub-conscious brain mulling things over and hope that if a revelation came, it wouldn't come in the middle of a scene he was filming and risk ruining the take. He had his reputation as a supreme professional to maintain.

He worked hard at keeping up that professionalism all day, trying not to think about the imminent arrival of a message to himself or Alasdair from either Jonny or Morgan. It was entirely possible that on the one hand Dennis wouldn't play ball—or was too hungover to talk to Morgan—and on the other that Roger had subsequently discovered Neil's prospective client had no connection whatever to *Herbert and Chapman*. Either that or Neil had refused to be interviewed by them. Still, Toby covered all his options by seeing Sir Ian as soon as he could, an interview which included sounding the studio head about an idea which came into Toby's head as they spoke and which he'd share with the others as and when the need arose.

When the anticipated communication did arrive, in the form of a note asking one of the two actors to telephone Jonny Stewart as soon as it was convenient, Toby took advantage of having half an hour free to make the call. He left a message to that effect for Alasdair, who was in the middle of filming a scene with Fiona. The great Mr Hamilton, darling of the upper circle, would have to accept that disadvantage of being the leading man, a role he played on the screen if not in their completely equal personal partnership.

"Jonny, returning your call," Toby said, once the telephone call was connected. "How goes it?"

"Very well." Jonny certainly sounded chipper. "It looks like we might be on tomorrow, around twelve noon. Did you manage to get yourself free?"

"I did. I was down to attend a relatively minor studio engagement, but as soon as I explained to Sir Ian what was potentially on the agenda, I found my diary suddenly being cleared for Saturday and permission to leave whenever I want to tonight, should that be required. One's patriotic duty trumps even one's Landseer obligations, although he'll be pleased to know I won't be tinkering with his filming schedule."

Chances were, if fulfilling that patriotic duty meant a dastardly plot being avoided and that story eventually came to public light, Sir Ian would be dropping subtle hints about his stars' involvement in it. He could imagine the statement now. *Landseer, quite rightly, can neither confirm or deny whether Mr Bowe or Mr Hamilton were involved in foiling this dastardly plot. However, given both men's outstanding war record and sense of loyalty to the crown, it would be no surprise that they would readily perform their duty should it be required of them.*

"Are you still there?" Jonny asked.

"Yes, sorry. Going off on a flight of fancy. You have my entire attention now."

"I was asking whether Alasdair's been roped in instead of you."

"No. Sir Ian guessed we'd want to work in tandem so he'll make sure nobody tries to pull him in as a last minute substitute. We have some up and coming young actors who'd no doubt welcome the chance of scrubbing up and putting on a show. Is the game definitely afoot?"

"It is. Roger spoke to Neil—very circumspectly, of course, because while he trusts this chap implicitly, he didn't want to risk starting a rumour and a panic. Wise old bird, Roger."

Obviously the love of Jonny's life, as well, given the adoring way his name was always spoken.

"As a result, Neil would like to have a council of war before he meets his client. Forewarned is forearmed and all that. Roger hasn't detailed exactly why you have such an interest in the chap but he's confident you can be candid with Neil face to face."

"Has Roger obtained a name for Neil's potential customer? Not that the latter would be eliminated if he called himself John Smith, because he might employ an alias."

"In order, no and I agree. Any name discussion is being saved for when we meet in person, too. Roger gets the impression Neil wants to have all the evidence lined up before committing himself to divulging any details. He's apparently apologised in advance if he ends up wasting your time."

"It'll be no waste at all. Red herrings to eliminate and all that." And the added bonus of one of the less enticing Landseer functions to be avoided. "Does Neil know that his buyer might well be a fascist?"

"He does now, by which I mean after Roger had a little word. That's why he wants to chat to us before he goes to dinner with said buyer tomorrow, because he won't be selling a balloon on a stick to any of Mosley's mob, past or present. Anyhow, be at *St Bride's Tavern* near Blackfriars— I thought you'd appreciate the name—at twelve noon tomorrow. Roger has some connection there and they'll organise a back room where nobody can disturb us. It's fine if you arrive before official opening time because we count as a guests of the landlord." Jonny snorted.

"I'm already looking forward to it. See you then." Toby put down the receiver and went to find Alasdair.

The actor wasn't to be found on the studio floor nor in his dressing room. Toby nabbed the continuity girl, Priscilla, who reckoned he'd nipped off to make telephone call to his valet who'd left him a message earlier.

"He seemed dead keen on replying as soon as he could, Mr Bowe," she said with a giggle. "I bet he's arranging a date tonight."

"You could be right. He's a one, our Mr Hamilton." Toby joined in the laughter, which was brought to an abrupt end by a stern voice sounding behind them.

"Who's a one? Whoever it is, you two are having too much fun."

Toby swung round to find the possessor of the voice was Alasdair, grinning broadly and clearly in a good mood.

"Why shouldn't we? And you're the aforementioned one, sneaking off to make mysterious phone calls that leave Priscilla here on tenterhooks. We reckon you were arranging a secret assignation."

"Priscilla!" Another voice, genuinely stern this time, sounded across the studio floor.

"Sorry, must dash." The continuity girl scurried away, unable to hide her reluctance to do so. The date story would no doubt be all round the production team by the end of the day, which was an added bonus for maintaining the two actors' continued charade.

"Cilla's a nice girl, but I'm glad she's gone. I have news to impart," Toby said.

"So have I. Morgan's worked the oracle. Dennis was keeping quiet about the young couple's names because of the potential shame and disgrace of their predicament, apparently. However, the mention of our patriotic involvement in a matter of vital national importance has proved, as Morgan predicted, the key to unlocking the informational door. They are indeed called Nicholas and Alexandra."

"Very regal, if unfortunate, given what happened to their Russian namesakes." Toby shuddered, thinking of what had

213

happened to the Russian royal family and the upcoming ceremonies for their blood relative.

"I hadn't thought of that." Alasdair's uninsured eyebrow signalled a sudden, similar disquiet. "Anyway, Morgan says he's promised Dennis a pint or two of beer in return for his candour and also asked him to arrange a meeting with Alex, whom Dennis knows goes all swoony over the pair of us, which is more evidence that it's the right woman. Apparently, she's always wanted to meet either thee or me."

"If she'd carried on attending our fan club meetings she'd have managed that without any ado." Still, Toby wasn't going to balk at using the fact to their advantage. "My news is from Jonny. Roger's orchestrated a get together with Neil, twelve noon sharp tomorrow at *St Bride's Tavern*, which is not a hostelry I know but is probably in the vicinity of Blackfriars bridge. He's also arranged a private room for us to meet in, so that we can talk candidly and Neil can make sure he's not potentially selling arms to some nasty piece of work."

"Whereas *we* want to make sure that he is? I'd also love to know precisely what this customer wants to buy. Some lobbable grenades, perhaps, or a professional version of a Molotov Cocktail." Alasdair lowered his voice. "I have to tell you I was struck by an attack of scruples earlier and decided to try to contact Bruce about this new development. Luckily for us, there was nobody to answer the call."

Toby grinned. "You didn't deliberately use the wrong number to facilitate that outcome?"

"Of course not." Alasdair appeared horrified at the very suggestion. "My conscience is clear on all counts. Including the fact that we didn't go looking for this interview with Neil. It merely dropped in our laps."

"What would you have done if Bruce had answered your call?"

"Told him about said drop and laps and then invited him along to any meeting that we booked with Neil, details to be provided once they were in place. I don't feel the need to contact him again now that I have those details. What if he's out at a meeting and I waste my entire day trying to get through?"

Toby appreciated the logic of that piece of thinking. "My decks are clear for tomorrow, thanks to Sir Ian, with whom I had another productive conversation. I can't say anymore at present, because I'm waiting for confirmation from him, so don't press me on it yet. Let's say it's a bit of belt and braces for an idea I've had."

"Hmm." Alasdair eyed him for a moment. "I suppose I'll have to hold myself in readiness for the great revelation."

"You will indeed. Console yourself with thoughts of everyone looking at you sidelong and wondering about this secret date of yours. Cilla's bound to spread the word." With which Toby performed an elaborate bow, suitable to both their characters in the upcoming film, and headed off to prepare for his next take.

Chapter Seventeen

Late morning on Saturday, Toby arrived early for their appointment at *St Bride's Tavern*, which proved to be a nice little pub with a comfortable, well-lit back room and none of the affectation of *The Swan With Two Necks*. This was the genuine article.

Alasdair arrived hard on his heels.

"You look a touch flustered. What's up?"

"A mare's nest, I hope." Alasdair shrugged off his coat and settled himself. "I thought I was being followed. I came on the tube and another chap got into the same carriage. I didn't think anything of it until he got out at Chancery Lane with me. Then he seemed to take the same route, keeping behind me, but he went off towards Ludgate Hill while I swung round here."

"We'll keep an eye out for him when we leave. Maybe there'll be a taxi chase."

The door opened again and Jonny entered, accompanied by a handsome man around their age whom Toby assumed was Neil, until Jonny introduced him as Roger. Toby had got it into his head—from the way that Jonny spoke about him—that Roger was significantly older than his partner, but if he was a year or so the elder that was all. He did, however, have an air of maturity about him that contrasted with the youthful exuberance of Jonny, which was perhaps why the latter referred to him as 'old Roger' although that could be an affectation. Roger was a stunner, though and there could be no surprise about Jonny having fallen for him.

"Pleased to meet you," Roger said, sticking out his hand. "Sorry if this turns out to be a mare's nest."

Toby shook hands enthusiastically. "I promise you, it'll be worth it whatever happens. This conflab has saved me from a studio function that would have seen me surrounded by starlets and while some men might think that a dream come true, it fills me with anxiety."

"I think we can all sympathise with that," Alasdair said. "It's fine playing a part for the screen but when that has to continue all the time, it's wearing. Artificiality in every word and deed."

Jonny tapped the table. "That reminds me of the pub we met Moira in. The one that reminded us of a film set. I might be able to help clear that up. Or rather, Roger can."

"Don't get excited, because I'm not handing you a vital clue or anything so grand, I just wanted to confirm your ideas about *The Swan with Two Necks*. I hadn't realised that was where you and Jonny had gone to meet your mysterious pals until I'd got a couple of glasses of red wine into him and the whole tale came out."

"Half a bottle of red ensures candour?" Toby sniggered. "We'll make a note of that and tell his aged relative. Jonty or someone else in his family might have cause to employ it."

"Steady on there!" Jonny exclaimed. "Play fair. Go on with your story, Roger and no more snitching out of school."

"Sorry." Roger's grin clearly showed he was anything but. "You thought the place felt synthetic, somehow? Well, to an extent it is. I know someone who goes there a lot and the place is deliberately decked out to remind demobbed folk of the messes they were used to during the war, in an effort to recreate the sense of camaraderie people felt then. It's supposed to be popular with ex-servicemen and women, even though it's years since VE and VJ days. Finding something they've lost in peace time."

"No wonder our three lost souls feel at home there," Toby said. "There were plenty of people who found it hard to adjust after the Great War and it's the same now. You know, I keep thinking about Bessy and Geraldine, who were our escorts for the recent film premiere, Roger. A pair of ladies, more on the mature side than our usual dates, whom we came across during our last case. The degree to which they must understand people is astonishing because the ideas they batted about have come to fruition again and again in relation to Moira's crew."

"Indeed," Alasdair replied. He appeared to be on the verge of waxing lyrical on the topic but was interrupted when the door opened and a tall, thin chap entered the room. This had to be Neil, from the greeting Roger gave him prior to performing the usual introductions. Despite having the sort of build that suggested a stiff gust of wind might blow him over, Neil had an air that made it clear that he was a man who would stand no nonsense. He also exuded an air of bonhomie perhaps suited to a career which must combine salesmanship with diplomacy and the ability to say "Sorry, no.".

"Thanks for agreeing to see us," Toby said, as they shook hands.

"I was about to thank you all for making time to see me. Thanks for this, too." Neil took his seat and then grasped the half pint of beer which Roger had ready on the table for him. "I hate going into any meeting half cock and that seems particularly important this time, given that Roger here seems to think there might be something dodgy about my prospective customer. I understand this might link to a case you're investigating?"

"Yes," Alasdair said, "We have two cases at present that are twining themselves around each other. Your prospective client—if he is who we think he is—could be involved in both. To clarify, we're looking to solve a past crime and also prevent a future one, the latter being the more urgent. All of which comes with the caveat that a man is innocent until proven guilty because much of the evidence we have for who's involved in both cases is circumstantial. Forgive us if we don't explain all until we can link your man to ours."

Toby made a mental note that when Alasdair was too long in the tooth to play the love interest, he'd be perfect as a judge in a courtroom drama.

"I appreciate your discretion." Neil took another swig of beer. "You'd do well in my line of work, so if you ever tire of acting, let me know. Give me a name for this chap, and I'll say nay or yea."

Alasdair, evidently delighted with the complimenting of his discretion, said, "Billy Chapman."

Noticeable relief swept across Neil's face. "I'm afraid— for you, not for me—that's a nay. Not a name I recognise."

"Oh." Jonny's expression resembled that of a child on Christmas morning who's opened his present to find a lump of coal, not the toy drum he wanted. "Then it looks like all the clues we've had are red herrings."

"I think we need to apologise for wasting everyone's time," Roger said.

Toby raised a hand. "Belay that. Those clues could also point to other people. Here's some more names for you, Neil. We'll start with a Mr Herbert, Christian name unknown. James Salt. Robert Archer."

"Robert Archer?" Neil hastily laid his glass down. "Your nay has become a yea. I think you'd better tell me what you know about him."

"Alas, very little," Toby said, not bothering to hide his grin of satisfaction. "We can start with the death of an actor, though, and a mention of Archer at the inquest."

He gave a summary of what they knew about Carstone's death, then what they'd surmised—and why— leaving out only Alexandra's name. "Therefore, our conclusion at present is that this tragic death was a murder made out to look like an accident and Archer is involved. That's not primarily why we're here, though. Alasdair, do you want to pick up the urgent part of the case?"

"I will. It starts with an overheard conversation about a threat of disruption to the coronation, between Billy Chapman and person unknown."

Jonny raised his hand. "Hold on. *Two* overheard conversations. We keep forgetting the one the secretary blundered in on, which talked about an act of violence. Either or both of those discussions could have featured Archer as the second party."

Alasdair nodded. "You're quite right. Because we weren't allowed to follow up on her, I'd put the secretary out of mind." Alasdair detailed what the two women had heard, matching this with what those present had discovered about the characters of Messrs Herbert and Chapman, including the strange contents of the bin and how this all related to what Dennis's son had reported. He concluded with, "We've already informed both the police and a friend of a friend who is involved with coronation planning. The latter was the one who insisted we didn't get too close to the firm. Back off or act at your peril—you know the sort of thing."

Neil raised an eyebrow. "This sounds like something out of a thriller." He didn't appear perturbed, though, so perhaps his experience with selling arms had taken him onto similar territory.

"What kind of arms is Archer looking to buy?" Toby asked.

"Small materiel, in a relatively small quantity. He says it's on behalf of a foreign potentate, to equip his personal bodyguard, so Archer wants predominantly firearms, plus a range of items such as grenades, body armour and the like. Does that sound like what your man might want?"

Toby stuck out his bottom lip. "Grenades fit in with the practicing darts bit, although I'm not sure about the rest."

"If it is *our* Archer," Alasdair said, clearly beginning to worry that they'd gone down the wrong track, "then the scale of what he wants is concerning. We were thinking it would only be a few grenades to lob into a parade. Although if he simply wanted those why not ask around his dubious pals, because plenty of such things came home as souvenirs during the war, as did small arms or kukris and the like."

"Maybe they're only there to reinforce the bodyguard story," Jonny suggested. "It might look odd only wanting a handful of small explosives."

Neil nodded. "Yes, that could be so. As for accessing those items which servicemen sneaked home, Archer did tell us his original supplier—which he didn't name—had let him down, so he needed things urgently Apparently this no doubt non-existent potentate had an important visit abroad coming up. Having said that, if he's involved in a terrorist plot, then it's a surprise he should be going down a legitimate channel by contacting us, unless he had no other option and he knew we could supply him at short notice. It's not long until the coronation, so it may be Hobson's choice."

"What about the trail back to you afterwards?" Alasdair asked. "Granting that if nobody could prove a connection between the man who buys the goods and the man intending to do the deed, Chapman, they might think themselves safe."

"His name appears in Fred's signing in book," Toby pointed out, "although they could plead he was simply a client and how did they know what he was up to? We should still consider that, if he wants all that stuff, this thing could be larger than one man lobbing Molotov cocktails at one carriage in a parade."

"All guns blazing—literally?" Jonn's eyes widened. "Wouldn't they be taking a hell of a chance, to get away with all the crowds there'll be? Many of whom saw active service not that long ago and who won't be averse to getting stuck in."

"Perhaps Chapman and co aren't bothered. They might want to be martyrs for their cause." Toby shrugged. "I could never fathom the minds of people like that."

Neil rapped the table. "So, gents, what action do we need to take? I'm not bound by the order to back off, but I am bound by my duty as a citizen. Could I ask for the name of your police contact and where's best to reach him on a Saturday? I've a feeling he's going to be interested in a report of my upcoming conversation."

"Matthew Firestone and via Scotland Yard," Jonny said. "If he's not there they'll contact him for you. He's my godfather so mention of this conversation and those involved won't come as any surprise."

"What about Archer?" Alasdair asked. "How will you leave things with him to ensure he doesn't realise he's been rumbled?"

"I have my ways. It's not the first time I've had to do something like this and I'm sure it won't be the last." Neil gave a rueful smile, one that also made it clear he wouldn't be elaborating.

"Then we'll leave things to the professional in his field, Roger said. "I suppose we'll now gracefully bow out of today's action and await developments."

"Not so fast, said Toby, who'd been incubating an idea since the previous morning and felt that now was the time for it to hatch. "There's a connection with *Herbert and Chapman* that we haven't pursued, and we can go in initially on the Carstone side of things. It's someone we should have spoken to before but Bruce's embargo prevented us, as did our consciences. A lady whose job we didn't want to put at risk, given her personal circumstances, but I think I now have a solution for that problem."

"The game's afoot on her now, is it?" Alasdair asked, obviously having realised whom Toby meant and as keen as any greyhound in the slips to get cracking on a new lead.

"I think so. This morning, I had the confirmation I needed for us to proceed, and we're ideally placed geographically to get on with things. It's not far to Eagle Street and we'll just have to hope it's a Fred day, not a Ted day." Toby scanned the company, delighted to Roger and Neil's bewildered faces. "After that, we could be heading anywhere, so we'd better grab a quick bite to eat first."

***

On leaving the tavern, having had a round of excellent sandwiches at *St Bride's Tavern* to keep them going, Toby suggested Alasdair and Jonny went first while the rest kept an eye for suspicious characters, but if anybody was hanging around to spy on them, he or she was doing their job extremely well. They decided to walk to Eagle Street, because that would give them time to bring Roger up to date. The bloke wouldn't have as much information as they did—albeit that not amounting to much—concerning the secretary who'd blundered into a discussion she shouldn't have heard. Toby rectified the situation with help from the others, so by the time they'd almost reached their destination, Roger was as fully prepared as the time allowed.

"I understand why you wouldn't want to make life any harder for this woman," Roger said the briefing ended. "Are you going to enlighten us regarding your solution to that problem or will you continue to play your cards close on that?"

"The latter, I think, at least for the moment. It's not sheer cussedness, honest, so much as not wanting to jinx matters until we have her name, address and an assurance that she's willing to talk to us. Several things will need to line up for all that to be achieved." Toby gestured airily. "I also don't want prematurely to dangle so bright a lure that we're given misinformation simply so that the fish can grab for it."

"Nicely put," Alasdair said. "It's hard enough to tell from fact from fiction in this case. Who's that waving, by the way?"

"Where?" Toby glanced around him, then returned the wave. "Chap I saw last time I was here, who asked if the game was afoot. One of our aficionados, I guess, although not in Miss Crouch's gang, more's the pity."

"He is rather fetching," Roger said. "Shame he's heading in the other direction."

"Should we be worried about him popping up twice?" Alasdair asked. "He couldn't be James Salt, keeping an eye on us?"

"Not him. I've seen his and Archer's pictures in the newspapers and that chap's far too sylph-like to be either of them. Anyway, wouldn't any observer be unwise, drawing attention to himself twice running?"

With which they arrived at the door of Clanfield House, where Jonny pointed out the vexatious lack of a nameplate. "See? Trouble all round, that bunch."

On entering the building, the first thing that needed to line up clicked into place, because not only was Fred the man on duty, he seemed delighted to see Toby again.

"Mr Bowe!" he exclaimed, as the four men came towards his desk. "You're quite mob handed today. Have you come to start a card school?"

"Perhaps another time, as long as you promise not to fleece us of our hard-earned cash. Let me make the introductions. You probably recognise Alasdair and these other two reprobates are Jonny and Roger, our associates in detection for our present case." Toby glanced over his shoulder, checking that nobody else was in the offing. "We're working on that investigation this afternoon, Fred, and we need the help of a man who knows."

Fred, sitting up straighter in his chair, tidied away his newspaper. "I'll try my best, Mr Bowe."

"We'd like to speak to a lady who, for her sins, works for *Herbert and Chapman*. All we know about her is that she's a loyal and pleasant sort, with a parent who's unwell and who relies on her totally. Any help you could give us about finding said lady would be gratefully received."

"It would also possibly help to prevent somebody evading proper justice," Alasdair added.

"I think I can tell you what you need, but I have to admit I'm reluctant to divulge it, Mr Bowe and Mr Hamilton. The lady in question is not in a position to risk losing her job." Fred studied his hands.

"We know that," Toby said in his most sympathetic tones, "which is why I didn't ask about her the last time I was here. The situation's different now and I can promise you that she won't end up the worse off for agreeing to see us, because there's an elegant potential solution if the problem arises. Trust me, Fred." Trust Sir Ian, as well, who was—thank the lord—a man of his word and who also had a secretary who was never short of a bright idea.

The doorman considered for a moment, then nodded. "I'll tell you, but you can trust *me* never to forgive you if this goes pear shaped."

"Absolutely fair." Toby bowed. "I wouldn't blame you at all."

"Right, well I think the woman you want is Vera Brook. She and her mother live in a bungalow at Theydon Bois although I can't remember the exact address. I went there just before Christmas for a do Vera had to celebrate her mother's birthday but I'd need to go home to get the road and number because it's not stored here." Fred tapped his head then his desk. "The place is not far from the tube station, although that's no help."

"Is Miss Brook on the telephone?" Alasdair asked. "I've assumed she's a Miss, so sorry if that's wrong."

"She *is* a Miss and an independent one. I can help with her telephone number, though. Hold on." Fred—who'd looked a touch rueful at the word *independent*—scuttled into his little office, returning with a small book. "I keep odds and ends jotted down here of the off chance I'll need them. I've got Vera's number in case I ever had to ring home for her. Easier for me to say she's working late and not to worry rather than her getting delayed further making the call."

Patently obvious that Fred was happy to help Miss Brook and probably hoped to get another invitation to the house in Theydon Bois. "Can we make a note of that, please? If we can ring her now and nip over there as soon as possible, it would be very helpful."

"Feel free, Mr Bowe."

While Toby wrote the number down, Jonny said, "How ill is Miss Brook's mother? It might be useful to know so that we don't go blundering in with our size tens and saying what we shouldn't."

"She's not breathing her last, if that's what you're worried about." Fred, smiling, shook his head. "She's not gone senile, either. Mind as sharp as a pin and always cheerful, despite the pain and not being able to move as she'd like. The problem is she's badly crippled with arthritis and so can't fend for herself for more than a few hours. A neighbour goes in during the day to make sure she's doing okay when Vera's here but it's a burden on her, even if *she* doesn't complain, either."

"You've put our minds at rest," Toby said. And had there been more than a hint in Fred's reply that he was distinctly taken with both women?

Roger tentatively raised his hand. "Actually, I appreciate I'm the most recent call up to the detection squad, but might I make a suggestion? Rather than one of us ringing Miss Brook out of the blue, could Fred here do it and then introduce both us and our purpose? Surely that would increase our chances of winning her over?"

Fred thought for a moment and then gave a nod. "I think the best plan would be to have Vera talk to Mr Hamilton here, because that'll send your chances soaring. You're an actor she has a lot of time for, Mr Hamilton, whereas her mother has a soft spot for you, Mr Bowe. The old woman loves reading her film magazines."

Alasdair jiggled his eyebrow appropriately. "Does she indeed? We must ensure we make a good impression, then."

"Yes, don't let either lady down. Mrs Brook only gets out every couple of months because it's such a palaver to get her and any transport organised and then the effort takes so much out of the pair of them. Her favourite outing's being taken to the pictures, so you can imagine how much work that involves. She's a brave soul, though, and so is her daughter." Fred, evidently moved, fished out a handkerchief to blow his nose.

Was there an incipient romance going on, perhaps only foiled by Miss Brook's duty towards her mother, or was Toby reading too much into things? "We'll have to hope that when you ring they're not off at a matinee this afternoon."

"It'd be a rum go if they were out watching your latest, wouldn't it? When they could have had the real thing on their doorstep, eyebrow and all. Is it really insured or is that just magazine gossip?"

"Absolutely, Fred. If I lost this in an accident, my career would be over."

Fred, grinning, picked up the telephone receiver and had the call put through.

Toby and the others then had to suffer the inevitable frustration that went with only hearing half of a call, having to guess the other end of the conversation from Fred's responses and his facial expressions. Initial pleasantries were evidently followed up with a question about why he was calling and his reply—that he had Alasdair Hamilton in his lobby and that the actor was playing at Sherlock Holmes off-screen—was clearly met with disbelief.

"God's honest truth, Vera. You know from the newspapers how him and Toby Bowe like to do their amateur sleuthing. Well, he's on a case and needs to speak to you about it." Fred hastily handed the telephone to Alasdair.

"Miss Brook? Yes, it is me and not one of Fred's jokes. Oh, does he? Not this time, though. Quite." Alasdair perched his backside on the desk. "I'm calling to ask if there's any chance of seeing you today. We have some important questions to ask you regarding an actor who used to work for Landseer."

Toby resisted mouthing, "She can't see your eyebrow, no matter how well its's trying to convey both sincerity and concern, so don't bother."

Alasdair continued, oblivious. "No, not that one. You're right to say he blotted his copybook and yes, he's long gone form the studio, so he's of no concern anymore."

Roger, Jonny and Fred shared puzzled looks. Toby could have guessed who was being referred to but would keep shtum: if they didn't know already, then best not to enlighten them.

"Indeed, a *great* relief. This concerns another actor and I—we'd—rather discuss it in private. Yes, that's Mr Bowe and myself. We can promise you our utmost discretion and that nobody at Herbert and Chapman will come to know about it from us. Fred here isn't going to blab, either." There followed a prolonged pause from Alasdair's side of things, only punctuated with a series of "Hmphms" and nods. "I understand exactly how tricky things are. Nicholas, who used to work with you, mentioned it. We promise we'll make sure you're no worse off, should the very worst come to pass. I have Toby's assurance on that and he's always reliable. Yes, indeed. Dependable and constant offscreen as well as on. Oh, *is* he? He'll be pleased to know that. Yes, I'm sure he'd be delighted to oblige. Quite. Now, will this afternoon work?" Another frustrating pause until Alasdair said, "Excellent. We'll be there as soon as we can, if you could give me the address. Fred, helpful as he is, couldn't run to that. Yes, I'll tell him he has a memory like a sieve."

As soon as the address had been noted and the call ended, Toby leapt in. "It sounds like we were successful, but what was all that about people being delighted to do something?"

"I promised that when we visit this afternoon, you'll be thrilled to go and chat to old Mrs Brook, while I speak to the daughter, because apparently you're the old lady's absolute favourite. She'd be mortified not to have the chance of entertaining you."

"Does that mean I miss out on Miss Brook's interview? It hardly seems fair, given that it was my idea all along and I've done all the groundwork in order to make it possible." Toby knew he sounded like a petulant child, but he'd facilitated the brilliant way of ensuring that Vera wasn't left worse off. "I'm jolly well minded not to tell you the key part of the plan. I'll whisper it in Vera's mother's shell-like, she can reassure her daughter and you can all be left in the dark."

"Temper, temper. This isn't the spirit that got you through every time Jerry came over and you had to scramble," Roger pointed out, with such a huge grin that Toby couldn't help smiling, too. He was quite right, of course.

"I suppose I can sacrifice my desires in a greater cause but I will insist that someone comes along with me. Jonny, what say you regale the old lady with tales of the aged relative? If she's a film fan she'd love that. Might be her generation, too."

"I'll accept the sacrifice, as well. Although I insist that Alasdair gives us a full briefing afterwards." Jonny eyed his partner sidelong. "Can Roger go along with him to take note, whether mental or actual? Two sets of eyes and ears are always less likely to miss something."

"That sounds a splendid idea," Alasdair said. He turned to Fred. "Miss Brook says I have to upbraid you for not remembering her address. She also still has some reservations about this interview but seems to have been mulling things over these last few weeks. She said she's had a small crisis of conscience and will welcome getting some things off her chest."

Fred made a sweeping gesture. "You have my blessing then, gentlemen. Only if you upset her or it ends up that she finds herself out of a job, don't you dare come back here. I won't be answerable for my words then and the air will turn seven shades of blue."

"Message received loud and clear, Fred." Toby pitied anybody who found themselves on the wrong end of such a tirade. "We'll treat Miss Brook like the queen herself."

And hope that she shared the latter's sense of duty to a higher cause.

Chapter Eighteen

They took a cab out to Theydon Bois, despite the fact that the underground might have proved quicker. The risk was too great en route of Alasdair or Toby being recognised, cornered and—as had happened on one occasion in the past—pursued by adoring fans hell-bent on securing anything from an autograph to an item of clothing. There was a task to fulfil and nothing, even their paying public, much as they were to be cherished, could get in the way.

As the journey progressed from the city out to the leafy northern suburbs, Alasdair explained why he hadn't mentioned to Vera Brook that there'd be four people tipped out of the cab onto her doorstep. "I felt it was a delicate balancing act and that the sheer weight of our numbers could tip the scales the wrong way. Once we arrive there she surely can't give us our marching orders."

"What if she does, though," Toby said. "Jonny's flashing smile having failed to charm her and only thee and me being allowed to cross the threshold?"

"Then we'll give him and Roger a couple of quid and they can entertain themselves in the pub while we enter the lionesses' den. Does that work, chaps?"

"Suits me," Roger replied. "Everything's an unexpected bonus today."

They reached the den with welcome swiftness, before any second thoughts they might entertain could put a dampener on anyone's enthusiasm. They paid off the driver, who'd clearly recognised them and whose face was a picture of curiosity, and then headed along the Brooks's garden path.

Alasdair rang the doorbell, then waited hat in hand, feeling like a small boy whose ball had gone into the back garden and who wanted it back. If Miss Brook was surprised at finding four men on her step when she opened the door, she was too well mannered to show it.

"Sorry to arrive like a pack of forwards at a ruck, Miss Brook, but there's a good reason, I promise you."

"I should hope so." Her tones reinforced the naughty schoolboy sensation. "I'll have to get out all my best teacups."

"Oh, don't bother just for us." Toby gave her his most heartbreaking smile, often employed in the Landseer cause. "We're happy with everyday ware. Seeing that Alasdair's forgotten the introductions, this is Roger Henley, who'll be making sure we behave ourselves and *this* is Jonny Stewart, who's helping us with our investigation. I thought your mother might like to meet him as he's related to Dr Stewart whom I portray in *Death Stalks the College*."

"Oh." Miss Brook beamed. "She'll be delighted. Come in, all of you, before the neighbours start twitching their curtains. I've no idea what to tell them if they've realised who you are and start asking questions."

"That's easy," Toby said as they entered the hallway. "Say that you won a Landseer competition and the prize was for us to visit you. "All part of the publicity tied in to the latest film. Jonny and Roger here are our bodyguards."

"I can see you're going to get on with mother like a house on fire, Mr Bowe. She's very excited at the prospect. Any bit of fun to break up the routine." Miss Brook closed the door with evident relief. A deeply private person, Alasdair guessed. "Mother's insisted I helped doll her up although you'll be pleased to know I stopped her wearing a hat."

A nicely modulated female voice sounded from a room at the back of the house. "You won't stop me wearing one when we go to watch the coronation on Carrie Brown's

233

television." This had to be old Mrs Brook, given the similarity in accent.

Vera grinned. "Come along all of you and meet Mother."

She steered them along the hallway to a well-lit and well-proportioned bedroom with large windows looking out on a nicely tended garden. Mrs Brook, sitting regally in a high-backed chair and as immaculately dressed as she might be for a garden party, showed no surprise at the arrival of four visitors. Introductions were effected all round, with Toby and Jonny being ushered into seats either side of the old lady's. Mother and daughter made a handsome pair, both sporting jewellery and a hint of subtle makeup: no wonder Fred seemed to have taken a shine to them.

"I've got the kettle ready to boil so I'll bring everyone tea in a moment," Miss Brook said, backing out of the room.

"Please let me help you," Alasdair offered. "I'm quite domesticated."

She threw up her hands. "I couldn't have that, Mr Hamilton. What would my neighbours say if they saw you in my kitchen working like a maid? I can't excuse that with winning a competition."

"They wouldn't recognise me, Miss Brook," Roger said. "So let me lend a hand instead."

"While they're busy and before Vera drags you off, I'm going to ask you a question, Mr Hamilton. Is Fiona Marsden as nice as she's cracked up to be? I never believe half of what's said in the newspapers and magazines."

"Very wise, Mrs Brook, although in this case, it's all true. She's an absolute treasure." Alasdair regaled their hostess with the tale of Fiona dealing with a murderer and how she always displayed both common sense and notable courage, until Miss Brook returned with a tray of tea and biscuits.

"This is for you three," she said, laying it on a low table, "and Roger's taken the other one into the sitting room. Come along now, before the pot gets cold."

Alasdair followed her to the front of the house, where a large bow window let in the afternoon sun. Roger had already poured the tea, so once they were all three settled with their cups and a biscuit, Miss Brook asked, "Now gentlemen, how can I help you?"

"We're currently investigating what we believe is a suspicious death and trying to prevent a future atrocity. Not that we realised a couple of weeks ago that we'd be involved in such things, because the case we initially took on has changed considerably." Alasdair outlined the story of how Toby had been introduced to a strange group of people, who wanted help locating a missing person. How the person turned out not to be missing at all, yet the trail had led into other, more serious areas.

When he'd finished, his hostess—who'd appeared not overly surprised at anything that had been mentioned said, "Where do I come into this, Mr Hamilton? And please call me Vera, because Miss Brook feels so formal."

"Then you must call me Alasdair, for the same reason." He took a very welcome sip of tea. "In terms of where you come in, anything you can tell us that means we're not barking up the wrong tree, would be a useful place to start. We know from our enquiries that you accidentally walked in on a conversation between Chapman and another man about an act of violence. Was that man Robert Archer and can you give us any detail about what this act was intended to be?"

"It was him. At least that's what he calls himself: one can never be sure in our line of work. People come and go out of hours, they use aliases…" she shrugged. "I'm not proud of working for *Herbert and Chapman*, nevertheless I have little choice. It's easy for a pretty young thing like

235

Alexandra to flit from job to job, but I'm hardly in the first flush of youth and I can't afford to not be in employment. They pay me well and expect me to exercise my discretion."

Was there a hint of resentment, not only at her situation but at Alexandra?

Vera continued. "Robert Archer handles some of the more sordid parts of our work. In the past that's included rooting out information about people who might be giving evidence against our clients in court. Information that would help discredit these folk's testimony. However, on this occasion, Mr Chapman was asking him to help get rid of somebody who was causing trouble. I think that might have been Mr Carstone, because the meeting took place before his death. If you hadn't mentioned him I might have had to keep his name secret, but you already have your suspicions on that count."

"Why should they want him dead?" Roger asked, evidently fully briefed by Jonny. "He was a client and, as we understand it, an old associate of theirs."

"That's true, although this links to something else. I was asked to stay late one evening, to greet a client and make him feel at ease. It happens sometimes, especially if it's someone of note and they want a discrete record kept of discussions, because they know I'll keep my mouth shut. At least I always have done." She knitted her brows. "The client was Carstone, and he was agitated. Nervous or worried, perhaps. When I'd gone into the kitchenette to make a drink for them, he started to confront Chapman, saying he'd heard from James Salt what they'd got planned. How Chapman had gone too far and that—because he was an old friend—Carstone was willing to give him a week to change his mind about what he meant to do. Otherwise Carstone would go to the police himself. He must have left then, because I heard the office door slam and when I emerged, Mr Chapman apologised that I had to witness such boorish behaviour."

"He didn't explain what it was about?" Alasdair asked.

"No and he wouldn't expect me to ask. He simply said I could get home earlier than expected. A few days later, I read about Carstone's death in the paper. I know it's cowardly, but I didn't report what I'd heard, because I didn't want to be next." Vera clutched her cup, although she didn't drink from it. "I used to come home via Chancery Lane but now I walk to either Bank or Holborn stations."

"We understand that Carstone had been a Mosley supporter, like your employers, and only gave up when his career began to blossom," Alasdair said. "Do you know why was he suddenly at odds with them?"

"He'd seen the light, apparently. Your chap at Landseer—Sir Ian Cunningham I believe—had a long conversation with him, which Carstone described as being like scales falling from his eyes. He told me all about it on one of the occasions he was trying to chat me up, although to be frank he usually chatted up anyone female." Vera rolled her eyes. "It was as if he couldn't help himself, which is, I guess, why he ended up in such a stew. The biggest chance of his film career coming up and every chance it would come crashing down. He knew that his old pals dealt with tricky cases and apparently saw them as his only hope in sorting out the divorce cases he'd been embroiled in. Keep him out of the dock and the newspapers."

Alasdair gave a sympathetic twitch of his eyebrow. "The threat he made to Chapman about having a week to change his mind. When was this in relation the visit Archer made?"

"The day before. It's firmly lodged in my memory, because it felt like I kept hearing what I shouldn't. They say things happen in threes, so I was waiting for the third time, although that never came. Which perhaps is just as well,

237

given what happened to Carstone. I'm not saying for certain that he was deliberately killed, but it's all a bit too coincidental for my liking. I wouldn't want the firm thinking they should get rid of me, too."

"I suspect you'd have been safe. You've clearly proved your worth." And anyway, would Chapman have risked two suspicious deaths too close to each other? "Do you know what Carstone was referring to when he expressed his horror at what Chapman meant to do?"

"Getting rid of *that woman*, whoever *that woman* is. Knowing Billy Chapman, it doesn't narrow the field much, as he's firmly of the opinion that women should know their place. Fine as shop assistants or in an administrative role, like mine, but God forbid they exercise any authority over the male of the species."

"How does he feel about Her Majesty?" Roger asked. "A queen on the throne after fifty years of kings."

Vera shook her head, with a rueful smile. "That's different. Queen Elizabeth had a God-given, anointed right to rule. Via a male prime minister, of course, because my employers and their pals would never countenance a woman at Number Ten."

"What about other female monarchs?" Roger said.

"Oh, I think that would depend on the colour of their skin. Ah." Vera, clearly having had a road to Damascus moment, laid down the cup from which she'd hardly drunk. "Were you thinking of someone invited to the coronation? To be disposed of in the way that Carstone was, although not under a train? Surely anyone of note would have protection although I suppose that in itself isn't infallible. Archduke Franz Ferdinand, for example."

"Exactly," Alasdair said. "We're hypothesizing that's the type of act intended, whether by firearm or an explosive device, so anything you can say to help prevent such an outrage by narrowing down the means or location would be invaluable to the police."

Vera pursed her lips in thought. "Mr Chapman's watching the procession and I know where from, which is somewhere near the Theatre Royal on Haymarket. He's rented a place at an extortionate price, because I've seen the invoice. He's got catering, as well, so it's a real slap up do for those invited. On those grounds, it doesn't sound like he's planning any hanky panky."

"No, but equally that could be constructing a good front. He invites close associates—like Archer—who aren't afraid of being involved in a rough house and who'll support his overall intention." Alasdair glanced at Roger, who was clearly bursting to say his piece.

"Maybe he'll create another kind of front, while he's at it," Roger said. "If Archer and Salt managed to kill Carstone yet make it look like an accident, and have the coroner's court believe them, then they could have the skills to help stage an attack on the procession make it look like the Haymarket party were themselves victims. Afterwards they swear that an armed stranger came gatecrashing their slap up do, threatened those present with his gun, lobbed explosive devices into the procession and then scarpered before they could do more than give him a flesh wound with the bread knife. Blood at the scene, shock all round, heroics from those who'd allegedly tried to prevent the attack but were themselves wounded in the process. Maybe a bullet or two sprayed about and some so-called evidence left."

Alasdair nodded, appreciative of the intelligent thinking Roger displayed. *He'd* assumed that the other weapons Archer sought to buy were simply to back up the foreign potentate story, who'd surely not be wanting to buy hand-thrown missiles, but what if they played—as Roger had concluded—a bigger role?

Vera, who'd been taking her time to mull over this new suggestion, said, "In any other circumstances, and with any other people, I'd laugh and say such an idea was nonsense. I won't though, because it feels horribly in line with Mr Herbert's and Mr Chapman's characters and the way they've conducted business in the past. The lengths they go to when mounting a defence beggar belief, to the extent that sometimes the defendant themselves begins to believe the alternative version was what really happened."

"That's probably why they're so successful," Roger replied.

"Yes. And I've always suspected that's what happened to Mr Carstone. A beautifully—if that's not an awful use of the word—staged accident." Their hostess's cheeks had turned ashen at the thought. "I was one of the chosen few invited to the Haymarket to see the big parade, but I had to decline, because I can't leave Mother. Mr Chapman tried to persuade me, but I was adamant. Now I see there's a chance I would have ended up 'accidentally' killed as part of their plot. Collateral damage, you might say, because if I'd been allowed to witness the event I could have put two and two together."

Possibly that's why Chapman had tolerated her overhearing what she shouldn't. Not only because he knew she wouldn't blab—she could be a useful part of his plan on the day.

"Would you give a statement to the police outlining what you've told us?" Alasdair asked. "Our contact is a man of great charm and discretion and he would speak to you over the telephone if you feel that a police visit here would be too obvious."

"If I could be sure that none of this would get back to my employers, yes. Although if this went as far as a court of law, I'd have no chance of them not knowing."

240

"We'll have to cross that bridge if and when we come to it, making the passage as safe as possible."

Vera didn't seem entirely convinced and Alasdair didn't want to point out that if both her bosses ended up in the dock there might be no firm to employ her. She composed herself and said, "May I ask you some questions?"

"Certainly. If we can answer, we will." Although not if it touched on the two pairs of men's relationships.

"This odd group you mentioned earlier. Lloyd Conway's, is it? They meet at our offices every other Monday."

Alasdair nodded. "I guess you've met him."

"Oh yes," she said. "Once met never forgotten, because he told me he could detect I had special powers. I said that I did: managing to juggle work and looking after mother and not going crazy in the process. I can see that special powers thing is no surprise."

"He's always at it." Alasdair snorted. "He tried it on Toby, who gave him equally short shrift. Chapman's one of his victims, too."

"Mr Chapman is nobody's victim." Vera made a moue of distaste. "Are you referring to his influencing the weather nonsense? Conway told me identifying that power was the first time he realised he could tell if other people possessed special abilities. It happened just at the start of the war and it wouldn't surprise me if Chapman put the idea in his head."

"Is that why he drops in out of hours," Alasdair asked, "so he can have his ego boosted? Which he probably needs, given that he got short shrift during the war when he tried to persuade the authorities that he had this ability and because since then sensible folk like you and Toby have him where he can stick his ideas?"

"He might have that motive but I don't think Chapman would bother about massaging Conway's vanity, unless it suited his own ends."

Roger raised his hand. "Could Conway be tied up in either Carstone's death or and the possible upcoming attack?"

Vera paused, then said, "I hadn't thought of that. Yes, maybe. Not the coronation thing: whatever else he is, Conway's patriotic. To the extent I've heard James Salt ridicule him about it behind his back. He's mocked Conway's sense of chivalry, too. He puts women on pedestals, wanting to ride out and be their champion, despite the fact that no woman would have him in such a role. Those are Salt's words, not mine and spoken in the context of his own success with women. I also recall him mocking Carstone, saying that it was amazing how many women fell for the actor, despite his lack of looks or other obvious charms. Salt was definitely envious of *him*."

"How could Conway have been involved in Carstone's death?" Roger asked. "Telling *him* he possessed an amazing ability, like being able to survive falling under the wheels of a train?"

"I don't think Carstone would have fallen for anything so outlandish, although Conway might have told him he was irresistible to women, although that wouldn't have been any news to Carstone. He was full of himself, anyway. I was simply wondering if he'd been used to lure the actor to Chancery Lane so that the accident could be staged. More likely that Carstone would have trusted him than anyone employed by *Herbert and Chapman*." She shrugged, as elegantly as Fiona might.

"We wondered if Alexandra had been used to get Carstone there," Alasdair said, "Although I suppose it's possible Conway helped persuade her to do so." Which

242

might be why she no longer attended his meetings. The sooner they could talked to Alexandra and got her perspective, the better.

"Alexandra?" Vera narrowed her eyes. "It's possible she was used as a lure, because Carstone would have gone for such a bait hook, line and sinker. But believe me, that young lady couldn't be persuaded to do anything that wouldn't work to her advantage."

"Really?"

"Yes. Which is all I have to say on that subject."

Alasdair shared a glance with Roger, who gave a helpless gesture in response. "In that case, we must thank you again for all the help you've given us and now we should go and rescue Toby and Jonny."

When the party reached the back bedroom, it was plain that neither Toby nor Jonny seemed like they needed rescuing. Mrs Brook had apparently produced an album of photos and clippings featuring stage productions from the turn of the century, with which she was regaling her visitors. That and a bottle of sherry, appeared to have been making the time pass most pleasantly.

"Hello, each! We've been having a lovely chat." A gleam in Toby's eye seemed highly suggestive of discoveries made, although perhaps that was only the excellence of the sherry at work. "Thank you for your hospitality all round, ladies. It's been a most entertaining and fruitful afternoon."

"I'm glad it's been useful." Vera was looking increasingly uncomfortable, maybe still torn between what she'd said and left unsaid. Or perhaps having second thoughts, which would explain why she'd clammed up about Alexandra.

"Now," Mrs Brook said, "I've had a lovely time, but what if my Vera gets to the office on Monday and somehow word of your visit has got around. It's not like you two have faces that could be mistaken for anyone else, especially in combination. You've a reputation, too, for sleuthing and that Billy Chapman has a way of snooping stuff out."

"Mother's right. I think I've got a bit carried away this afternoon, getting stuff off my chest, yet the nub remains that I can't afford to lose my job. You've assured me that all will be well but fine words butter no parsnips."

"Then don't turn up at the office," Toby said. "Call in sick or whatever your conscience will allow you to do in the way of bending the truth. Instead, get yourself to the Landseer site on Monday morning at ten o'clock, go to the reception desk and ask for Sir Ian Sheringham's secretary, Miss Duckworth. She'll be expecting you at some point. Do you need anything for expenses?"

"I don't think so." Vera, evidently bewildered, glanced at her mother, who seemed equally perplexed. "The studio's only a short walk from Woodford Station, I believe. But why am I to see her?"

"Because there's a job interview lined up, for a position Landseer would love to offer you. Miss Duckworth's assistant is about to leave and they've not been able to find an acceptable candidate to fill the role. It would save her lot of work to have someone highly capable ready to ease into place, especially if you could work a handover period with the existing assistant. Sir Ian says they'll need references, of course, although they can take them up from folks other than your present employers."

"Oh. Thank you." Vera burst into tears.

"You don't know how happy this makes me, young Toby." Mrs Brook produced a voluminous hankie to blow her nose. "I hate what *Herbert and Chapman* do, but because of me, Vera's had no choice except to stick it for so long. Thanks for giving her an option."

"It's the least we can do." Toby bowed over Mrs Brook's hand, then over Vera's, a moving gesture that made Alasdair's heart leap as wildly as it had when they first met.

"It'll probably be safer for you away from Eagle Street, as well," he said. "We'll leave you two to share what's been said in our conversations, while the four of us do the same. I daresay we've all got something to learn."

***

They decided not to go in search of a taxi immediately, given how much they had to discuss. Instead, they took themselves off in the direction of some green areas they'd passed en route and which seemed ideal for having a private conversation while on the hoof.

As soon as they were out of earshot of Vera's house, Alasdair said, "Why didn't you tell us about Sir Ian's offer of a job?"

Toby snorted. "I felt like taking a leaf from Jonny's book, and maintain a bit of mystery. I also didn't want any hint getting out until after we'd spoken to Vera. No chance of tainting the evidence because of her wanting to make a good impression."

"How did you wangle it?" Roger asked.

"We've kept Sir Ian informed at all points," Toby said, "so when I picked his brains about making a reluctant yet possibly vital witness tell all, he and Miss Duckworth cobbled the plan together. There really is a vacancy, by the way, and a reliable employee who can keep her mouth shut when she needs to would be ideal to fill it. If the Carstone business gets to a public court it'll impact on Landseer, although no doubt Sir Ian will ensure the studio comes out of it smelling of roses."

"From what you've said about Sir Ian, everything will be turned into good publicity," Jonny observed. "Mind you, given what old Mrs Brook was saying, I do wonder how many people are taken in by the nonsense your publicity department spouts."

"Plenty, I believe," Alasdair said. "Not everyone will be as shrewd as those women we met today."

Roger brought them to a halt. "Hold on. Why *if* it comes to court rather than *when*?"

Toby shrugged. "I had in mind the intertwined nature of the cases. If an attack on the coronation can be both prevented and kept quiet, any case against the plotters may be heard behind closed doors, so as not to panic the public. If Carstone's death was occasioned to stop him shopping them, that too may be heard in private so no publicity would accrue."

"I see." Roger walked on. "Of course, if Chapman, Salt and Archer are found guilty of high treason, they won't be around to stand trial for Carstone's murder. You can only be hanged once."

Alasdair, with a shudder, turned the subject to what they'd learned today, giving Toby and Jonny a report of what Vera had told them, all bar the final bit about Alexandra, which he hadn't made a decision on. That remark could have arisen through pure jealousy, for example because of how much Fred was supposed to be smitten with the girl.

"It's clear Vera doesn't like her employers," Roger added, when Alasdair had finished, "and I don't think it was an exaggeration when she said she doesn't want to end up under a train like Carstone. I suspect she won't be going into the office again. Fred will have to pick up anything she's left there."

Alasdair nodded. "I hope she comes up with a good enough excuse for them not to smell a rat. A convenient illness, maybe. Not life threatening but highly contagious and lasting long enough for Matthew to do whatever he needs to."

"He's going to be pleased with what we've rooted out, on top of anything Neil provides." Toby itemised the points on his fingers. "A possible venue for skullduggery, a witness willing to give a statement who sounds like she'd be highly credible in court, and another person for him to grill, meaning Lloyd. Unless Matthew's already hauled him in, which is another interview I'd like to be part of but won't have the chance. Let's hope the net is tightening sufficiently that none of them can slip through to wreak havoc."

"So I should jolly well hope." Alasdair slowed the pace and awaited a revelation he felt sure was about to come from Toby. Knowing the man too long and too well had made him alert to subtleties of face and tone.

He didn't have to wait long. "Well, *we* have something to report, too, concerning another one of the characters in this fandango. Mrs Brook isn't one to mince words and as soon as you'd gone, she had plenty to say about Alexandra, who was also presented at their bungalow for that 'do' Fred attended."

"No love lost there," Jonny said. "Mrs Brook thinks she's a scheming minx, an habitual flirt and a nasty little liar, in no particular order. None of those are to do with her being pregnant, by the way—we dropped that into the conversation and it both came as no surprise and produced no opprobrium. She has quite modern views, Mrs Brook."

"What led her to those opinions, then?" Roger asked.

"What she'd heard from Vera and what she saw with her own eyes both at the party and an another occasion when they happened to be at the same cinema for a film. Mrs

Brook said Alexandra went all doe eyed and 'Oh, look at little helpless me' any time a man was in the offing, Fred included. The old lady can't abide that sort of behaviour at the best of times and when a girl has a chap of her own—she knew about Nicholas from the office—then said girl shouldn't be trying to inveigle herself with any other males."

"That takes care of 'flirt'," Alasdair said, "although Alexandra wouldn't be alone in that behaviour. You should see some of the starlets at Landseer. What about 'scheming minx' and 'liar'?"

"Partly based on what she'd heard from Vera, because one of the chaps Alexandra flirted with was Carstone and yes, it was reciprocated. Mrs Brook reckons that we should ask Vera about how Carstone ended up on that platform at that time because she's convinced Alexandra got him there and not under coercion." Toby paused. "Why doesn't that seem to be the bombshell I expected?"

Alasdair patted his shoulder. "Because we'd already got a hint of it. Vera said that Alexandra was nobody's victim and when we discussed Carstone being lured, she said that Alexandra wouldn't be pressured into doing anything she didn't want to. I hadn't mentioned that because I wondered if the remark was simply bitchiness."

"I doubt it," Jonny said. "I trust Mrs Brook's judgement and if she reckons Alexandra left the firm because of what she'd done—a case of conscience catching up with her—I'd give that theory due consideration."

"So would I." Toby nodded. "I'm glad we've heard all this before we meet her. Puts a different slant on things."

"Do you know, the aged relative once told me that there often comes a point in a case where it feels like you've been holding a picture the wrong way up or need to see it in a mirror." Jonny made a turning gesture with his hands.

"Suddenly what you thought was one thing turns out to be quite another. If that makes sense."

"It does indeed," Alasdair said. "We've seen it already in this case, for example with the false claims of special powers, so why not with Alexandra? The victim who is anything but."

"Wait a minute." Toby bounced on his toes. "Somebody said something."

"I think people say things all the time, Toby," Alasdair sniggered.

"Ha bloody ha. I mean—no, I've got it. Richard." Toby snapped his fingers. "Richard, who can't predict the length of a sermon but who seems to have a sharp eye for women. He said that Alexandra was glowing at that last meeting. He assumed it was about her new job, *I* assumed it was her being pregnant, but what if it was about Carstone and her feeling pleased at her success in luring him?"

"Lorelei. Of course." Alasdair made the sound he'd successfully used in films to express extreme annoyance.

"Lorelei?" Roger asked.

"Yes," Jonny said. "Richard said that Alexandra had a touch of Lorelei about her and because he'd been saying she would have liked to be in the movies, Moira connected it to something that Marilyn Monroe is making."

"An adaptation of a stage show. *Gentlemen Prefer Blondes*." Alasdair quite fancied seeing the film, given the quality of the two female leads. "The original hasn't made it to the West End yet, alas, so it's probably unlikely Richard would have been referring to it, unless he's a screen buff."

"Moira closed that part of the conversation down, perhaps not wanting to dwell on any resemblance Alexandra might have had to gorgeous actresses," Toby said. "Since then, any thoughts about the Monday Evening trio have focussed on Moira and Jeff and poor old Richard's been edged out."

"It's an interesting idea, but none of this is proof of her involvement, though," Roger pointed out. "You'll have to hope she's had a crisis of conscience and tells all if you get to meet her."

"I'm not sure I'm ready to believe anything she says, frankly. In fact, I'm sceptical about anyone having told us the truth. Let's find a cab." Alasdair turned them in the direction of the tube station.

"What next, then, for the investigation?" Jonny asked as they walked.

"Report to Matthew with everything Vera and her mother told us. I'll do that," Toby offered, "given that Alasdair's become a doubting Thomas. Then we hope Morgan's arranged us an interview with Alexandra and that it's as enlightening as the last few hours have been."

"You two will want to follow up with Neil," Alasdair suggested. "In fact, Toby should really hold fire on his report until we know whether Archer's proved a damp squib."

Roger nodded. "I'll get onto it this evening."

"Which just leaves playing cupid," Toby said, "but that can wait until these cases are wrapped up. A nice reward for a job well done."

"Playing cupid?" Alasdair's eyebrow, which he'd kept relatively quiet, leaped into action. "Jeff and Moira?"

"With poor old Richard playing gooseberry?" Toby chuckled. "Yes, although I also had in mind Fred and Vera. I'd not insult any independent woman by saying that she needs a man in her life but everyone can do with a bit of romance and I think they'd make a lovely couple."

"Perhaps she doesn't like men that way," Jonny said. "Look at us four. We shouldn't assume."

"I'll be the soul of discretion," Toby said. "Irrespective of any romance, I think we should suggest the mesdames Brook as companions for the premiere of *The Heart That Wears the Crown*. Although I'm not going to suggest that until Vera's made all the statements Matthew might need from her."

"You don't want that lure being snapped up via perjury committed in the cause of furthering one's fortunes?" Roger said. "Very sensible."

Particularly so in this case, which had seen a mass of deceptions and downright lies. Almost as many as in a Landseer press release concerning Alasdair and Toby.

As they neared the station—happy to take the tube this time, should there be no cabs in the offing, and having agreed to travel in separate carriages—Toby said, "I've had an awful thought. It's so awful, and so scantily grounded, that I'm not sure I should share it."

"You can't leave things like that. You've had your share of mysteries today." Alasdair contemplated shaking the secret out of him, but that would be unseemly.

"As long you understand this has merely been prompted by Jonny's thing about turning the evidence the other way up and your being a doubting Thomas." Toby sniffed. "What if everything's part of the same deception? Lloyd asks me along to his meeting because he knows that Moira and pals will want to ask me to look into Alexandra's disappearance. Maybe he's planted the idea in their heads. She's in it, too, dropping hints all around about this and that before she makes herself scarce. Hints that people know we'll follow up on, building up a bank of circumstantial evidence about Carstone's death and a planned act of terror that we're bound to pass on to the authorities, given our track record. Only this evidence has been planted, to make us—and police—look in the wrong direction."

Alasdair opened his mouth to reassure him that couldn't be so, but the words wouldn't come. What if Toby was right and they'd been led by the nose?

"I refuse to believe that," Jonny said. "It would mean Vera and her mother were in on it, too, and they'd have to be better actresses than even Fiona Marsden to bring that off. Faking those tears of gratitude for a start."

"Unless they'd also been duped," Toby pointed out. "Like Moira and Jeff and Richard will have been."

"No, I can't see that." Roger said, with a note of authority. "I'm not saying these things don't happen. The deceptions that went on during the war, their scale and complexity, would make your eyes roll out of anyone's head. But one of the reasons these deceits worked was our enemies being persuaded to believe what they wanted to believe. Proper scrutiny wasn't employed on their part, or not at a high enough level to make a difference. That's not the case here."

"Because we keep an open mind about what we hear and are willing to flip our theories on their heads?" Toby, who'd been sounding quite desperate, had a note of hopefulness returning to his voice.

"Not only that. It would be blinkered to say that Matthew and this Bruce chap and all their cronies can't be taken in, but the more eyes the better and they'll be used to sifting false alarms from real. If you need reassurance, mention your qualms to them and see if they've been getting a whiff of good red herring."

"We will, Roger. Thanks for the encouragement." Alasdair gave Toby his best smile, saved only for his light of love. "You might say that not everything can turn out to be as artificial as a Landseer set and surely if Lloyd and Chapman wanted to dupe us they'd have chosen something more believable than secret powers as part of the story?"

"Very true, oh great mind." Toby grinned. "Apologies for the wobble, chaps."

"No apology needed," Roger said. "You can also remember that the more people you have involved in one of these deception schemes, the more likely it is that things leak out. I'm not going to discuss anything in detail here, but I've got a good example. If you've heard of the eighth crew member onboard for some of the Lancaster operations, you'll know what I'm referring to. Several of those planes went down due to what's termed 'security failures', which meant somebody—probably one of the other eighth men—snitched to the enemy about what was going on. Either because of pressure exerted by the enemy or going with where their loyalties ultimately lay."

"I have no idea what you're talking about," Alasdair said, "so maybe we'll have to arrange a full briefing on the subject at a more convenient occasion. I take the point, though. If the authorities put enough pressure on enough people, one of them might crack and reveal the plan, whatever it is."

"Or you appeal to their decency." Roger spread his hands. "Lloyd's or Alexandra's. Because Chapman, Archer and Salt are probably too far gone."

Chapter Nineteen

Saturday evening, at the very point where Toby was thinking about heading off to bed with his very own living and breathing hot water bottle, his telephone rang. North had been given the weekend off in order to visit Norwich, where he'd be standing Godfather to his sister's child, so answering the call was another domestic duty to be fulfilled by the master of the house.

"Toby?" Jonny's distinctive voice sounded down the line. "Jonny here. I tried Alasdair's number but Morgan said he was out gallivanting and I guessed he'd gallivanted to yours. Don't need to be Sherlock Holmes to deduce that."

"Cheek. Do you have Neil related news to convey?" Toby mouthed "Jonny" at a sleepy-looking Alasdair who'd just emerged from the sitting room.

"Naturally. Neil found Archer as fishy as a bream that's lain too long on the Macfisheries slab. He's arranged another meeting tomorrow, ostensibly to sign contracts, not that any contract will be there. Your pal the dreaded Bruce will be, though."

"Bruce? How did he get involved?"

"Bad timing on the part of our side. When Neil rang Scotland Yard after his chat with Archer, Bruce was with Matthew having some sort of council of war, I guess. They're both aware of Archer and are looking forward to being able to pin something on him, because he's as slippery as an eel in terms of evading the law. If nothing else, Chapman and co will have to look elsewhere for their armaments. Any luck with Alexandra?"

"Yes. Alasdair can tell you." Toby held the receiver so that they could both use the instrument. "Update on Alexandra required, please."

"Hello. Morgan's worked his usual magic, so we're seeing Alexandra tomorrow afternoon. His pal Dennis says she's tickled pink about it, as she's such a huge fan of ours, but I'd be inclined to think she's getting ready to deliver her version of the story."

"He's not going to believe a word she says," Toby barked. "Especially after I put the cat among the pigeons with my doubts, earlier today."

"Ignore him, Jonny. I'm simply approaching the interview with the correct degree of scepticism."

"Nobody would blame you." A sound like a stifled yawn from Jonny. "Sorry about that. It's late. Probably too late to contact Matthew with what we learned from Vera."

"Yes. We'd reached that conclusion, and it's endorsed by not wanting to risk Bruce still being around. I'll update Matthew in the morning and your good self after we've seen Alexandra."

"Wish us happy hunting," Toby said.

Jonny snorted. "The very best of British luck from Roger and me to the pair of you."

"We'll need it," Alasdair said, then made his goodbyes before Toby put down the handpiece. "Telling truth from lies. I thought we were getting adept at sorting them out but now, like you, Toby, I'm having second thoughts."

"Let's sleep on it, then. My brain feels quite a muddle." He took Alasdair's hand. "We've a bed awaiting us, which isn't solely for slumbering in. Love, sleep and a good breakfast: if they don't bring clarity of mind in the morning, I don't know what will."

***

Toby had been ordered to Matins by his mother on Sunday morning, on the grounds that it would not only benefit his soul, it would also be good publicity, because one of the columnists for the *Telegraph* was a regular member of the congregation and she was bound to regard his attendance favourably. So, Alasdair was left to lounge in bed while he preened himself to as near perfect as he could achieve without benefit of his dresser.

"I suppose," Alasdair said, from his nest among the sheets, "that you'll be particularly charming to the lady of the press."

"Of course. To the vicar, as well, so that I hedge my bets on the making a good impression front. Will you be staying in that there bed all morning?"

"No. I'm off home to get myself spruced up and enjoy one of Morgan's sandwiches for lunch."

"Need to get your strength back up after last night?" Toby gave his tie a final tweak. "There's rolls and jam for breakfast here. I've already indulged while you were purring in here."

"Purring?" Alasdair flung a pillow in Toby's direction.

"It's how you snore. Rather endearing, really. Anyway, there's plenty left for you, so make sure you get a decent meal before you go. Mother would never forgive me if you don't. Will you ring Matthew?"

"I thought I might delay that until after we've seen Alexandra. One hopes there'll be more to give him by then, either in amount or quality of information."

"Probably wise, or else he'll be sick of our little gang." Toby brought the pillow back, then leaned down to give his lover a kiss. "See you at Manor House."

"You will indeed. Two sets of eyes and ears to make sure she doesn't get anything past us."

"I was tempted to see if I could drag mother along, because nothing gets past her when the female of the species is involved, but she's got a luncheon party on. All I'll have to see me through is a cold collation in the scullery." With a tousle of his lover's hair, Toby headed off.

By the time he was on the way to a small hotel at Manor House where they were meeting Alexandra over afternoon tea, he felt ready for the fray. A pep talk from his mother hadn't gone amiss, either, especially when she'd made a few helpful suggestions about getting at the truth. Perhaps Toby should suggest to Matthew that he employ her as a special constable to help get to the bottom of whatever Chapman was doing.

Alexandra was waiting in the foyer of the hotel when Toby arrived. She was dressed in a demure, dark blue dress and sported a wedding ring, which he suspected was merely for show, or surely Dennis would have been toasting that event with Morgan, too. She didn't appear noticeably pregnant, although not every woman carried their baby like a galleon's sail billowing in the wind. One of Toby's cousins had been a good seven months down the line before her bump was obvious.

"Mr Bowe," she said, rising from a chair and thrusting out her hand. "I'm so pleased to meet you. Is Mr Hamilton not coming?"

"I'm sure he'll be here soon. Let's order some tea and find a corner where we can talk." Best to concentrate on the practicalities of refreshments rather than discussion of Alasdair's diary and how familiar Toby was with it.

By the time they'd found an acceptable place and placed their orders with a waiter, Toby had decided that he couldn't warm to Alexandra and probably wouldn't have been able to warm to her even without the doubts about her honesty. He knew he shouldn't form an opinion before they got down to business, but the first impression he'd formed was so strong it couldn't be overcome. She came across as highly flirtatious, despite the wedding ring, yet horribly coy as well. Mrs Brook had described her as the "Oh, look at little helpless me," type and that was being amply born out with every word and glance, including her interaction with the waiter.

It was therefore with great relief that Toby spotted Alasdair entering the hotel lounge. He rose to meet him, shot him a "This is awful" glance and made the introductions.

Alasdair, who'd clearly decided not to shilly-shally, took his seat and said, "Thank you for seeing us. We won't take up much of your time."

"Oh, that's all right." Alexandra appeared disappointed at the prospect of only a short interview.

"Could we start with asking who you were arguing with outside *Fortnum and Masons*?" Alasdair asked.

"What's that got to do with anything?" The question, clearly wrong-footing her, had caused the veil of helplessness to slip momentarily.

Alasdair's uninsured eyebrow took on a severe angle. "Because people are concerned for your welfare. Before you took yourself off without telling them where you were going, you were seen in a heated disagreement. No wonder they were worried."

"By *they*, you must mean Richard and the others. I think I saw him nearby when I was arguing with Nicholas." She shook her head, smiling patronisingly. "They did get themselves into a muddle with all this powers nonsense. Mind you, I suppose I was silly, too, to let myself get embroiled in such a tangle of deceit just so we could keep old Lloyd happy and meet up with each other."

"You knew the others were pretending to have powers?" Toby asked.

"I guessed. I mean, it couldn't possibly be true, could it? Lloyd laps it up, of course: he does like to be the centre of attention, the silly goose."

Toby felt a pang of pity for Lloyd, pity tempered with a reminder that he might also be the centre of the web of intrigue, goose or not. "You said you argued with Nicholas. Is that your fiancé?" Toby cast a quick yet intentionally noticeable glance at the wedding ring.

Alexandra twisted the item under scrutiny. "I put this on because I didn't want to embarrass you, given my condition. Yes, Nicholas is my chap. He wanted me to go to police and I wouldn't because I was scared they'd come after me."

"Go to the police about what and who are *they*?" Toby asked, am optimistic gleam having appeared over the horizon.

"Going to the police about what they made me do regarding Mr Carstone." She dabbed at her eyes with a handkerchief she'd got from her bag. "How I'd helped get him to the station where he was killed."

"But Alexandra," Toby said, "Charles Carstone was still alive then. The argument was in January."

Sheer terror passed across her face before she recomposed herself. "Oh, I do get so muddled. Of course you're right. I was thinking of a different argument. The first one was about the baby. I'd not long discovered I was expecting and Nicholas wanted to get married straight away before it became too obvious. I'm afraid I dug my heels in and said it would still be terribly obvious in retrospect, when the baby arrived well within nine months since the ceremony. I wanted to have my head clear rather than being rushed into something I might later regret."

There appeared to be some truth in that answer, given a slight change in her tone of voice, although there was also an air of a lady who protested too much. Something had rattled her badly.

"Miss Munsey, Alexandra," Alasdair said in a dulcet voice that was every bit as artificial to Toby's ear as Alexandra's had mostly been. "What do you mean by saying you helped get Charles Carstone to the station?"

"James Salt asked me to. I worked with him at *Herbert and Chapman*. He said that Mr Carstone could use his Landseer connection to arrange for me to meet you. It's stupid, I know, behaving like a schoolgirl with a crush, but I believed Salt was telling me the truth. I had no idea they were going to tip him onto the tracks." She stopped, clearly having spotted a tray-laden waiter and waitress heading in their direction.

While she fussed over the teapot and flirted with the chap who'd brought it, signalling ignoring the waitress, Alasdair flashed Toby a glance signalling doubt at what they were hearing.

"Thank you." Alasdair received his cup and took a sip while he watched the waiting staff depart. "Weren't you suspicious about being asked to arrange a meeting with Carstone at Chancery Lane station rather than elsewhere?"

"Oh, not at all, at the time." Alexandra stirred her tea. "They said Carstone had a bit of a reputation, so it would be safer for me to meet him in a public place rather than in a secluded bar or anywhere else he might suggest. It would also look less suspicious, given that he was in a delicate situation with his private life, which is why he'd come to the firm in the first place."

A gold star for Fred's theory on how they might explain luring a victim to such a public place. "You said *they* made you do it. James Salt is only one person." Toby said.

"Mr Chapman, who owns the firm, and Mr Salt. They were in the planning together, although another chap took part, on the day. Of course, they'd been lying to me. I shouldn't have been so stupid." She cast about for her handkerchief, which appeared to be a better prop for suggesting contrition than a teacup. "And I've carried on being stupid. After Mr Carstone went under the train, I took the opportunity of getting away from the scene as quickly as possible. I didn't want to be called to an inquest and I couldn't have stood in court and told the lies the others did. Other people acted in the same way, you know, getting away."

"Some folk like to evade responsibility." Toby waited to see if the barb hit home, but Alexandra merely smiled. "How did they actually do the deed, though? Knock him onto the line without everyone else present realising what had really happened?"

"I don't know. Not entirely." She looked helplessly from one man to the other.

It would depend how many women are on the jury, dear.

Toby's mother's words from earlier in the day seemed particularly apt. She'd been saying that some women could be highly persuasive in the witness box, when the listening ears were male, whereas any woman would see straight through them. Whether that summing up was universally true, Toby wouldn't have liked to say, but from what they'd been told about Alexandra from the two sexes, she appeared to fit the bill.

"Go on," Alasdair said.

She nodded, as though giving herself a pep talk. "I can tell you what happened right up to the bit where the train hit him, because I can still see it in my mind, like a film running in slow motion. After that is a blur because I edged back and then I got away—not running, I thought that would look suspicious—just walking purposefully."

261

"I'm sure you can remember more than that. A smart young woman like yourself." The insincere words almost stuck in Toby's throat. "Start from when you arrived at Chancery Lane station."

"I'll try. I was a bit nervous when I got there, but I bucked myself up and went straight to the platform. Mr Carstone was there and he seemed so delighted to see me. He gave me *that* look—the one he used in *Patrick in Paris* when he tried to pick up that gendarme who was disguised as a woman."

Toby hadn't seen the film, but he remembered the stir it had caused because of how near the knuckle it had got, and he could well imagine the famed Carstone leer. The actor would surely have used a similar, toned down, version in *Naughty Nelly* when eyeing up the voluptuous Miss Gwyn. "He was clearly delighted at your keeping the assignation. What then?"

"Salt and Archer—he's someone *Herbert and Chapman* use for certain jobs—arrived. I remember thinking they seemed intent on something, and wondered if they might have been there to protect me, so I wasn't suspicious when they made a beeline for us. Carstone spotted them and moved away, only we were already close to the platform edge and that movement took him nearer. He looked a bit panicky. Then everything happened very quickly." She wrung her hankie again. "There was that rush of air that tells you the train is approaching, and then Salt said, 'Steady on!'. He grabbed for Carstone, only he didn't really grab him, he must have pushed him. But it looked like a grab."

Again, a note of truthfulness had appeared. The description reminded Toby of being taught how to act a strangling scene. The attacker pulled their hands back while the attacked pulled those same hands towards their neck and the resulting tension onscreen appeared authentic.

"I'll never forget the looks on those two men's faces. It wasn't shock, not at first. That came later and it seemed false. Previously they'd been almost smug, just for a moment." She shuddered, theatrically, clearly presenting herself as one of the wronged parties in this. Perhaps she was the manipulated and perhaps she was the manipulator. Best to let her chatter on and hopefully reveal herself one way or the other. "What they mouthed to each other, as well. *Job well done* or something like that. Afterwards, and when I tried to explain to Nicholas what had happened, I wondered if I was reading things into the situation that weren't there. But I can picture it so clearly."

"So clearly that you'll stand up in court if need be and swear to it?" Alasdair's suggestion didn't seem to come as a surprise. "We have a close contact within Scotland Yard, and he would no doubt look at your situation with sympathy, especially if you were to give King's—I must get out of the habit of saying that, but it's been a lifelong thing—*Queen's* evidence. Against Salt and Archer and anyone else involved in killing an innocent man."

"I don't know." The air of pretence had returned, with Alexandra's poor handkerchief almost being turned in knots. "Couldn't you stand up and say what I've told you? You'd be so much more convincing."

Alasdair shook his head. "Hearsay evidence can be easily thrown out or pulled to pieces. Why can't you do it yourself?"

"I'm sure I'd get it all wrong. I'd not be a credible witness."

What would Toby's mother have said on hearing that? She'd probably have left off finding words, taken Alexandra by the shoulders and shaken some sense into her. Toby glanced at Alasdair, whose hands were almost imperceptibly twitching, as though he was tempted to give Alexandra a shaking up himself.

"We can't do your work for you, I'm afraid," Toby said. "What we *can* do is reassure Moira, Jeff and Richard that you're safe and well, because they've been worried about you. I'm sure they'll be fascinated to hear everything you've said about what happened at Chancery Lane. Moira especially, given that she witnessed your purported funny turn there."

"Oh, yes. It was all the memories flooding back. Please tell them I'm sorry, but I'm trying to put all associations with Clanfield House behind me, which includes Lloyd's group."

"I'll certainly make it clear that you want nothing more to do with them." That may have been harsh, but Toby had little sympathy for her. He wished he could turn on his heels and make the kind of exit which would have caused a sensation on stage, but there was still work to do.

"And *I'll* make it clear to our contact at Scotland Yard that you'll be pleased to help him with his enquiries," Alasdair said. "He'll want to reach you through your poste restante address, so no changing that, please."

"No, of course not. I realise now that I have to do my duty." She sat up straighter in her chair. "I'm sure he'll be sympathetic towards my situation. It's awful to be made to do something and be frightened about the consequences of not doing it."

"Hold on." Toby laid down his cup. "You said that Salt suggested you met Carstone because it would enable you to meet us. Where do coercion and consequences come into things?"

Briefly, Alexandra's eyes registered feeling wrong-footed at being caught out, but she soon recovered her apparent calm. "I wasn't entirely honest earlier. I just didn't want to get people into trouble. James Salt said I had to get Carstone to meet me on the platform and if I didn't, it would work out badly for me. It might still work out badly if they knew what I was telling you, so I'm trusting your policeman friend to protect me if need be."

Were Toby and Alasdair being too harsh in their reactions to this young woman? Was she simply a person who was easy to manipulate into doing things she later regretted and unwilling to face the consequences? Maybe time to try another tack. "Talking of our police contact, there's the other matter. The party at Haymarket."

Alexandra pouted. "I'm afraid I'm no longer going to that. I was invited and it would have been lovely to watch the procession from there but when I left my position, Nicholas said I should leave that opportunity behind, too. He said I shouldn't have anything to do with the firm."

"But you knew what was planned to happen at that party? While people were supposedly watching the coronation," Alasdair added.

"I don't follow you…"

"Did you or did you not overhear a conversation regarding people planning an attack of some sort on the event?" Alasdair had never portrayed a barrister, but he'd be most convincing in the role.

"Ah." Colour spread across Alexandra's cheeks. "You've caught me out in a lie. I spun Moira that yarn because I wanted to create a bit of a smokescreen about why I was leaving my job. I didn't want her to know about either Carstone or the baby."

"So, there wasn't any telephone call?" Toby didn't often get a sinking feeling, but now his stomach had hit his boots. Surely his qualms couldn't have come to fruition and they'd sent Matthew and Bruce on a wild goose chase?

"There might have been, for all I know, but I didn't overhear it. I'm sorry."

"Let me get this perfectly straight." Alasdair's eyebrow demonstrated every guinea of its insured value in a portrayal of disapproval. "Did you ever hear anyone discussing the coronation and how they wanted to disrupt it?"

"No. Mind you, Nicholas definitely heard something similar, as did other people I worked with, so it wasn't completely a fairy tale." A note of defiance had appeared. "Anyway, it's exactly the kind of thing Mr Chapman and his black shirt pals *would* indulge in."

"Do you realise that you might have been instrumental in sending the authorities off chasing shadows when they've more important things to be doing with their time?" Toby asked, livid. "You'd better not have lied to us about Carstone, or you'll find our police contact won't be any friend to you. Does Nicholas know what lies you've been spreading? Will you tell your baby how many deceptions its mother's been party to?"

His comment about Matthew lacking sympathy appeared to have been water off a duck's back, but the mention of the unborn child worked the oracle. Just as Toby's mother had predicted it might, when she'd suggested it earlier. The flush had gone from Alexandra's cheeks, to be replaced by an ashen hue. She opened her mouth, gulped and then burst into tears.

"I'm sorry. I know I've said it before but I really mean it this time," she gasped, between bouts of crying. "It's all such a mess. Nicholas doesn't know half of it, so please don't tell him."

"We won't, but you should. Whatever this mess is about." Toby waited for her to speak again, sharing the odd glance with Alasdair, ones that screamed, "This is all a bit of a turn up."

266

"Would you like a brandy?" Alasdair said, once the sobbing stopped.

"No thank you. I've this little one to think of." Alexandra smiled, as she touched her stomach. "Another pot of tea would be lovely, though."

Alasdair called over the waitress, said that their guest had received a shock and asked for more tea to be brought as soon as possible.

"Thank you," she said, once the waitress had gone. "I promise I've now told you the truth about the phone call and the story I made up about it. I also told you exactly what happened on the platform."

"You've lied about something, though. That's plain. Best to put things right now." Alasdair smiled encouragingly.

"I'm not making excuses for myself, but I've always wanted to be the centre of attention. Like you are. Nobody really notices me although everyone looks at you, and people like that waitress have been watching me talking to you. Maybe they envy me."

Which would in part explain the flirting and the obsession with film stars; basking in their glory and getting herself noticed. The confession also smacked horribly of self-centredness.

"You might say I've gone down the line of what you'd call make believe if I were still a child," Alexandra continued. "The claim I made about predicting the weather. Lloyd was very impressed with me and so were the others. Or pretended to be. It was such fun."

Being teacher's pet? And with the added bonus of Jeff hanging around her like a puppy. Toby could imagine her lapping up the attention.

"How else have you lied about what you did with *Herbert and Chapman*? Apart from the lie about the

267

telephone call." Alasdair, evidently struggling to be civil, kept his words clipped.

"I told you it was their idea, when it was actually mine. Not to get rid of Mr Carstone—that really did come as a shock when it happened—but using myself as a lure. It started when I was taking coffee in for Mr Chapman while he was chatting to James Salt. They asked me what I would do if someone wanted to get someone else to be at a certain place at a certain time, perhaps when they were wary. I'm sure they were taking the mickey out of me, because I don't think normally they'd have any regard for my opinion, but I thought I should show them I wasn't dumb. I asked if this person was a man and they said he was, so I suggested they get a nice young woman to arrange to meet him. They said that was a good idea, although what if the chap was highly suspicious and might not agree to going to a secluded location?" She paused, eyes on the waitress who was returning with a fresh pot.

"Thank you. We can help ourselves." Toby poured Alexandra a cup, handed it to her and when they were alone again, said, "What happened next?"

"I said the woman could put his mind at rest by arranging to meet in a public place, at least to start with. Somewhere like a train or underground station where there are lots of people milling around and you can bump into people by chance. Then she could perhaps persuade him to go on to a more secluded location if that's where he needed to be brought." She sipped her tea. "They seemed genuinely pleased at the idea. Mr Chapman said something to Salt like, 'An underground station would be even better, if you could bring it off,' and Salt said, 'It's a challenge, but give me and Robert a couple of days and we could work it out.' Words to that effect. Then they asked me if I'd like to be the young woman concerned. How it would be a good for my career, to take on an active role."

"And you agreed?" Alasdair asked.

"Of course I did. It made me feel so important. It was only at the point when Carstone was killed that I realised how stupid I'd been and how the tube station part had all been my idea." More tears, although they seemed to be for her, rather than the victim.

"If it hadn't been there, the murder would no doubt have been carried out elsewhere," Toby said with grudging reassurance. "Is there any more to tell?"

She shook her head. "No. That's it."

They finished their tea in silence, Toby wanting to be out in the fresh air where he could shake the dust from his boots of all this dissembling. Eventually, Alexandra said, "I should be going. This afternoon has taken it out of me."

"Would you like us to call you a taxi?" Alasdair suggested, before offering his arm to help her from the seat. "Or would you prefer if we accompanied you home?"

Alexandra started, the idea evidently unsettling her. "No, I shall be fine. Nicholas is coming to get me in his father's car as soon as I ring through to the pub for him. I'll have time to compose myself first." She forced a smile. "I'm so pleased I met you. You're not at all like film stars. You're more like Holmes and Watson."

They'd have to take that as a compliment.

"Well, what do you make of that?" Toby said to Alasdair, as they left the hotel.

"I'm not sure where to start. I think we got somewhere near the truth in the end, although I bet it's not the whole truth and nothing but. Matthew will have to wheedle that out. I wonder what Nicholas will have to say when she comes out with her story?"

269

"If she tells him. I can't trust her at all." Toby sighed. "Let's walk for a while. I need the air." They crossed the road and meandered along the pavement, which was Sunday afternoon quiet. "That confession she made about the phone call felt like having an opposing forward flatten me in a tackle."

"Quite. Shades of *your* Doubting Thomas moment." Alasdair swished the air with his hand. "I kept asking myself how we'd ever explain to Matthew and Bruce that we'd sent them on a wild goose chase. Then I remembered that we had other circumstantial evidence, including this business of Neil's, and didn't feel quite as bad."

"I've been wondering what would have happened if we'd learned earlier that Alexandra had told Moira a whopper. We'd never have gone digging any further and Neil might be signing contracts for small arms supply this very moment, enabling Chapman and his pals to unleash who knows what." Toby shivered, despite the warmth of the day, then lowered his voice on hearing footsteps behind them. "The chosen few. That's who Vera said had been invited to that Haymarket do. Not necessarily the great and good, though. If she and Alexandra were both invited, what was the intention? Two lives—no, three if you include the baby—sacrificed to make the thing look realistic and in the process get rid of people who knew too much?"

"It feels horribly like that. I can imagine a mass of headlines revolving around their needless sacrifice as well as that of the intended victim. Who'd have been the man with the gun, though?"

"I suspect," a voice sounded behind them, "that might be me."

Chapter Twenty

Alasdair spun on his heels to see a handsome young man behind them, one whom he was certain he'd seen somewhere before but couldn't place. There was, however, a more important and more urgent call on his attention than working out where that could have been. The small matter of the man's hand in his coat pocket and the outline of what seemed to be a handgun he was holding there. A brief partial exposure of the weapon confirmed Alasdair's worst fears but snapped his wits into action: this was the man from the tube, whom Alasdair thought had tailed him on part of the journey to *St Bride's Tavern*.

"Mr Archer. Or is it Mr Salt?" Toby surely couldn't be as calm as he sounded. "I'm certain your picture was in the newspaper reports of Charles Carstone's inquest but I don't recall which of the pair you are."

"Well remembered. James Salt, at your service." He had the nerve to tip his hat, using his free hand. "I'm here to ask the pair of you to make your way to Manor House tube station. I'll be right behind you, so don't get any ideas, because I'll use this." He slipped the weapon partly from his pocket again, before hiding it. "Nice and quiet around here on a Sunday so I'll easily get away if I have to shoot. Come along. Chop chop."

As they set off, Alasdair had a strange feeling of consolation, in that Salt's actions were proving that the cases they'd been investigating were unlikely to be wild goose chases. He tried to catch Toby's eye, but Salt growled, "None of that, you two Brylcreem boys. No sending secret messages to coordinate an attack. That's your only and final warning about funny business."

"Have you followed us all the way here?" Alasdair asked.

"Not bloody likely. A certain young lady tipped me the wink about where you'd be because I can't watch both houses and get any kip."

"A young lady called Alexandra?"

"That's her. She's very convincing, isn't she? Carstone fell for her nonsense, as did young Nicholas."

Vera and her mother appeared to have got it spot on with their judgement on the woman.

"Oh, for goodness shake," Toby groaned. "You're her baby's father, aren't you?"

"Yep. I wanted her to get rid of it but she insisted on keeping it so we had to find someone to keep her honest. Luckily she'd already given Nicholas cause to think it was his. I can tell you all this now because you won't have the chance to repeat it."

"What exactly have you got planned for us?" Toby asked.

"A touch of what Carstone got. It's worked once so we'll try it again, only this time I've another person helping this time as Robert Archer's in an important meeting. Oh, how tragic it will be." Salt ladled on the melodrama. "More Landseer actors throwing themselves under a train."

"Won't that look suspicious?" Alasdair said, all the while trying to slow their progress without Salt realising.

"Not necessarily. The public will wonder what the studio can be doing to its assets to make them so unhappy or they'll speculate that there was a nasty secret about to emerge. Assignations with starlets in the dressing rooms and the like." Salt sniggered, although the more he got caught up in his own cleverness, the better.

"The newspapers would have a field day," Alasdair said, again strangely relieved that Salt hadn't suggested any secret was connected to their relationship. If the worst happened, he wouldn't want the families Bowe and

Hamilton to be dealing with public revelations about their sons' lives or obituaries carrying loaded phrases such as "he never married".

"They will." Salt emphasised the certainty of the word will, as opposed to would. "The whole business would make an interesting case for an amateur sleuth to investigate, but alas, you won't be there to do it. Just as well, considering what a pain you've been in this instance. Why couldn't you have left things alone?"

"Because that's not in our nature," Toby said. If he'd been this apparently nonchalant and valiant in the face of the airborne enemy, no wonder he'd proved such a feared opponent. "Once we're on the trail, we follow it to the bitter end."

"Well, you're right about this end being bitter." Salt gave a nasty chuckle. "What you've discovered will go to the grave with you, under that train."

Toby snorted. "You must take us for idiots if you think we haven't told other people what we've uncovered."

"Your pal from the house of Stewart and his po-face friend? They're next on my list. Shame you won't be able to get word out to warn them that they're marked men."

"Not only them," Alasdair said, sensing an opportunity to wrong-foot their assailant. "The police know and so do those involved in security for the coronation. We've told them about Carstone's murder, too. If they don't manage to hang you for one, they'll hang you for the other."

While he couldn't see their assailant, Alasdair picked up the tension in Salt's voice when he replied. "They'll have to catch me first and find anyone with the guts to stand up and testify. A man's still innocent until proven guilty in this once great country of ours, no matter how much people are trying to drive it to the dogs."

273

"I'm sure your mother's very proud of you," Toby said. "Assuming she knows what you get up to."

"Leave my mother out of this." The tension in Salt was unmistakable now. Maybe if Toby riled him some more, he'd lose enough concentration that they could turn and overpower him.

Before they could make any such move, Alasdair caught sight of another young man on the other side of the road. A second one with a familiar face—this time the chap who'd waved to Toby on Eagle Street. Was this the person Salt had referred to as his partner? Two against one might have been reasonable odds, even if the one were armed, but two against two felt insurmountable.

The Monday morning newspaper headlines flashed onto the Pathe newsreel of Alasdair's mind.

Tragedy at Manor House station.

He stole a glance at Toby, who appeared to have tensed, perhaps having also noticed the new threat. At least they were facing death together, even if they couldn't make any last avowal of their affection: they knew what they meant to each other.

"Keep up the pace, you two. No funny business."

"Wouldn't dream of it," Toby said. "We'll leave that to when we get to the platform, as we've already planned."

"What are you talking about?"

"You'll have to wait and see, Mr Salt."

So would Alasdair, who couldn't decide if this was simply trying to distract the man or a cunning plan Toby had just hatched and was trying to subtly convey to *him*. He hoped if it was the latter then the second man had also been taken into account.

"Maybe I shouldn't take the risk of waiting until we get to the station," Salt muttered. "I could shoot you two now and scarper, taking my chances."

"Afraid not, old bean." A different voice, this one accompanied by two loud whacks and followed by a groan and a thud.

On turning, Alasdair saw Salt lying at his feet, apparently out for the count, with his right arm at an angle, while the other chap—grinning—cradled a hefty truncheon.

"A well struck blow, there," Toby said. "Luck or judgement?"

"The latter, I'd hope. Skills learned at Beaulieu ten years ago and never forgotten." The man kneeled, removed the handgun from Salt's pocket and then gave him a cursory check over. "He'll be fine, although he'll wake with a headache and maybe a broken arm."

"Are you a policeman?" Alasdair asked, still befuddled at what was going on.

"Technically no, although if anyone else asks, then yes. I'm one of Bruce's men. Here." He produced a piece of paper. "This is from Matthew Firestone, confirming it. He said that if I had to intervene, you'd be sceptical, given what this case has been like."

The note, in Matthew's unmistakeable handwriting, began by referring to a lunch the three had shared after Christmas.

That should prove who I am, if my scrawl doesn't. This is Mr Brown, although I doubt that's his real name. He's been detailed to keep an eye on you over the last few days. Bruce says he knew you'd be a bloody nuisance and keep digging.

"Oh of course," Toby said. "I saw you in Eagle Street. Twice over."

"Yes. I did try to hint that I was friend not foe with my greetings, but I couldn't say more in case this chap—he nudged Salt with his toe—or his mates were watching. I think they picked you up at the pub, yesterday."

275

"Why didn't Bruce let us know we had a nursemaid?" Alasdair enquired.

"Because he wanted to see what you were up to. Your track record means you're either efficient or lucky and whichever applies, he wanted to take advantage of it. Some relation of his called Geraldine told him you'd plough your own furrow, no matter what you told him." The laughter this remark evoked eased the tension.

Aware that people were starting to stop and stare, Alasdair asked, "What do we with *him*?"

"That should be in hand. My partner's been keeping an eye on us and once he saw Salt go down, he'd have gone for his car, where he'll no doubt have used the radio to ensure we have a doctor waiting at Scotland Yard. He's very thorough. As am I." Brown produced a pair of handcuffs from his coat pocket. "We'd better get these on Salt as he's as slippery as an eel."

The action of applying the cuffs seemed to rouse the man and—like a drunk might—he awoke in fighting mood, clawing at his pocket.

"Don't bother," Brown said. "I've got your gun and these two are handy with their fists, so it's pretty hopeless. And here's Mr Wilson to take you on a trip to see the police doctor." A car had pulled up beside them, with what must be Wilson at the wheel.

"You bastards." Salt squirmed on the pavement. "You won't win. There are plenty of us who still believe in fighting for what's right."

"Oh, do shut up. Can you give him the once over, Wilson?" Brown asked the driver as he emerged from the car.

Wilson knelt down to inspect the casualty, while Brown flashed some kind of card at the small crowd which had formed. He told them he was a police officer and insisted that they please move along.

"Touch of concussion and a badly bruised arm, I'd guess," Wilson said. "He'll live until we reach Scotland Yard, although I'll put his arm in a sling and make him comfy."

"Thank you very much," Salt replied, tartly.

"It's more than you deserve. Now shut up or I'll gag you with that sling when I've fetched it."

While Wilson retrieved his first aid kit to patch up the casualty, Toby said, "I feel rather flattered at your diligence, Mr Brown. Isn't it an awful waste of official manpower?"

Brown grinned. "Act of genius, I'd say. Irrespective of what happens regarding the murder and the attack, we can remand this chap in custody solely for this incident. You'll make a statement about it, of course?"

"Absolutely. Do you want us to drop into a police station now? Or talk to this chap?" Alasdair had spotted a real police officer approaching the scene.

"Is everything under control here?" The sergeant asked. "We were told to keep an eye out but we've all been down at Manor House underground, dealing with someone who was making a nuisance of himself."

Hopefully that would be Salt's partner in crime rather than a drunk or a flasher.

"Nasty." Brown grinned again. "No, we're about to cart this chap off to the Yard where they're expecting him. His two victims here need to make statements about what happened but could that wait until tomorrow, when the shock's worn off?"

"I don't see why not. Unless the Yard want to handle it, given it's a bit delicate?" Clearly the sergeant wouldn't be upset if the matter got shifted off his patch.

"That sounds a good idea." Brown turned his attention to Wilson, while the policeman busied himself with dispersing any onlookers.

"Need a hand to get matey in the car?" Toby asked.

"No, but thanks for the offer." Together, with several comical, "Oops a daisy" type comments, Brown and Wilson bundled Salt into the vehicle.

Before Brown could get in, Alasdair said, "Could you get the word to Matthew that Alexandra Munsey is embroiled in this, including letting Salt know where we were. He'll want to talk to her. To Lloyd Conway, as well."

"Noted." Brown nodded. "I'll also ask him to arrange for someone to take those statements of yours. Are you in the studio tomorrow? Maybe he could send someone there: imagine the publicity Landseer could drum up. The nation's favourites held at gunpoint in a plot to foil their current acts of detection."

"Would they be allowed to use the story in such a way?"

Brown shrugged. "I'm sure Matthew and Bruce could advise you on that but there have been enough people about to spread the tale, so hushing it up would be counterproductive, probably. You have such easily recognisable faces." He closed the car door, presumably so that Salt couldn't hear. "One of the other reasons Bruce wanted you kept an eye on was that he didn't want to risk you being killed or badly injured. The effect on national morale would be terrible and Bruce's cousin would apparently make his life intolerable." He saluted, got into the car and then drove away.

Alasdair and Toby stood for a moment dumbstruck. "What do you make of that?"

Toby jerked his thumb in the direction of where the car had gone. "That Brown's not the silly ass he portrays himself as. I'm glad he's on our side."

"Quite. Did you really have a plan to put into action when we got to the station?"

"As our old flight mechanic used to say, did I heck as like. I wanted to get him riled."

"I thought as much." Alasdair realised his hands were trembling. "Do you fancy a drink?"

"No. Well yes, although only in my own home. Or yours. Although first, I'd like to find a box and ring through to Matthew. I trust Brown to pass on the message as we gave it to him but we forgot all about Vera Brook. I'd hate her to get tarred with any brush that's applied to the rest of the employees. Then we'll get a cab, because I don't fancy the underground."

"Will a cab be safe, or should we go and find that sergeant and get a ride in a police car?"

"We'll be fine." Toby edged what looked like another handgun from his pocket. "Here's a little present sneaked in by Mr Brown with a silent 'Shh!' while you were reading Matthew's note. It must be intended to keep us away from harm, maybe in case Salt's colleague at Manor House is still in the offing. I don't think the gun's Salt's because they slung that in a bag for evidence."

"Brown's clearly got it all covered." For which Alasdair was most grateful.

***

They'd barely started their brandies, sitting feet up on Alasdair's sofa, when the telephone sounded. Morgan—still shaken from hearing their account of the afternoon—answered, then announced it was Mr Stewart.

Alasdair took the call, to hear a gleeful Jonny booming down the line that Archer had been arrested and there was likely more to follow.

"Word is they're intending to have all employees of Herbert and Chapman—Vera excepted—rounded up by the end of the day and the offices are going to be raided, too. Probably not in that order. How did your meeting go?"

"You'd better sit down, because it's been quite an afternoon." Helped by Toby, who had come to join him, Alasdair described what had happened. He gave it strictly in chronological order, so that Jonny—and by implication Roger—would experience the same twists and turns they had. He finished with, "So we're now waiting to hear arrangements for making our statements and wondering how long we'll need to keep the handgun for. Although that at least would give us a reason for having to go around together."

"Every cloud has a silver lining and all that, I suppose. I don't envy you the day you've had, though."

"Don't envy us the next bit, either," Toby said, as they shared the handpiece. "We're waiting to see if Alexandra's arrested. Accessory before the fact and all that."

"Morgan's beside himself." Alasdair added. "How's he going to be able to face Dennis if she ends up in custody and we were responsible?"

"I'd say *she* was entirely responsible for her own actions and has to live by them," Jonny said. "Is the baby Salt's, do you think?"

Toby nodded. "I've been wondering the same thing. What if *he* was arguing with her outside Fortnum and Mason? No wonder she got confused in her cover story, if it was. I bet she'll still dob him in, though, when she gets in the interview room with Matthew. Safest thing for her to turn King's evidence."

"Any idea, if Salt had a gun, why they should need all Neil's stuff?" Jonny asked.

"I guess because—if we've worked this out correctly—one little gun wouldn't fit the bill of the scenario they were trying to create. It's not impossible to tackle a man with one weapon if there are enough people at the Haymarket to overpower him, so people might smell a rat. And. anyway, a few shots into that procession wouldn't be enough to make big statement. They needed more." That was the best theory Alasdair had at present.

"I must pass on thanks from Neil, who's been rather chuffed at taking part in such an adventure. Not as much of an adventure as yours has been, of course. Keep us informed of any further developments, please."

They ended the call and managed another couple of sips of brandy before the telephone rang again. A tired yet satisfied sounding Matthew had called to thank them for their help and say that much needed evidence was already turning up at the Clanfield House offices. Evidence which would help clarify the plans for the attack and who was supposed to be involved in its execution.

"I got your message about Miss Brook and I've merely sent an officer out to get her statement at present, rather than arrest her, as I'm doing with the other employees. Some of them will no doubt turn out to be innocent but I'm not taking any risks until I can eliminate them from consideration. None of this would have been possible, of course, if you hadn't followed up on those early leads," he added.

Alasdair exchanged a glance with Toby, then took a deep breath. "Not sure if you're aware of this yet, but the crucial lead we had at the start—the phone call Alexandra Munsey allegedly overheard—was a story she made up."

Matthew gave a loud whistle. "Just as well you fell for it, then. On such small quirks of fate big outcomes depend. We're going to quietly ensure the Haymarket premises are

281

out of bounds for the big day, which will no doubt put the owner's nose out of joint, but these things have to happen."

"They do. When do you want our statements about today's events to add to your evidence, by the way?"

"I'll send a couple of chaps to the studio tomorrow, as per Brown's suggestion. Good bloke, that. Useful in a tight corner. Quite a war record, Bruce tells me, although one can't ask for details." Matthew chuckled.

"I'd have been pleased to have him as my wingman," Alasdair said. He ended the call and they returned to their drinks.

"Perhaps you should leave that thing off the hook," Toby suggested, "or I'll never get this brandy down me."

"I'm tempted to, but I worry that someone might need to get in contact." Alasdair eyed the handgun, which lay on the table. "Do you suppose one of Bruce's chaps is still watching us?"

Toby rose, went to the window and did a scan of the street. "If they are, they're well hidden, which is likely, given that we'd not spotted them before. Mind you, if we've been having an eye kept on us, those eyes can't solely belong to Messrs Brown and Wilson, surely. Which means, depending upon how long we've been being nurse-maided, that several people will know about who sleeps at whose house."

"I hope they keep that fact buried among the other secrets they harbour." Alasdair wouldn't let himself be overly concerned. They were alive and well, thanks to Bruce's boys. "It'll be a while before I stop glancing over my shoulder, though. Whether I'm looking for friend or foe."

"We're well used to that." Toby joined him on the settee. "When we were in the air or now when leaving each other's house. We've been leading charmed lives and long may that continue. Now, what next for us, case wise, apart from taking a secret pleasure in our success?"

"I'd like to tell Moira that Alexandra's safe and I'll maybe drop an unsubtle hint that she's not to be trusted. I won't go as far as warning against all contact with the scheming hussy."

"Will you warn Moira that they might see Alexandra in the dock one day? Or at least in the witness box."

"I think so. She should also be told that the overheard conversation was a lie, although a productive one as it transpired. If for nothing else than the satisfaction she'll take in passing that titbit on to Jeff." Alasdair could picture Moira's restrained glee at the prospect.

"Then I will forgo the pleasure of doing that myself. It'll make his pep talk easier if he knows already, so I'll time that for after you've given Moira the good news."

"Pep talk?"

"Yes." Toby draped his arm around Alasdair's shoulder. "The 'stop being bloody blind, forget about Alexandra and see what's on your doorstep' one. I know I have to do it and I've dreaded the prospect."

Alasdair snorted, but he also took Toby's hand to rub. "That bad?"

"Let's say that facing the Luftwaffe seemed a doddle in comparison. Anyway, I'd decided simply to tell Jeff that Moira fancies him something rotten and then inspiration struck. I remembered some lines I had to speak, although the film or play escapes me. 'Sometimes we're so focussed on the brightest and most distant star in the constellation that we miss the equally beautiful star that's closer. And when we focus on that, instead, we find that it was the one we should have been looking at all the time.' What do you think?"

"It sounds perfect." Alasdair drew his lover's face towards him, for a kiss. "You'll always be both my brightest star and my safe harbour. Only let's keep that gun of Bruce's close to hand for a few days."

Epilogue

The morning after the great Manor House excitement, Toby and Alasdair made their statements to a nice young detective sergeant who was thrilled at being told to go to the studio, because he was besotted with Fiona. As Toby observed, it would be a miracle if the statements themselves weren't covered in hearts and Cupid's arrows when they arrived back at the station.

Meanwhile, the publicity department leaped into action, so that by the time the evening editions of the newspapers hit the streets, the story of what had happened in the environs of Manor House—suitably adjusted to cover up the name of the assailant and the true role of Messrs Brown and Wilson—was featured in their pages. A representative from the *Daily Telegraph* had been invited to the studios on Tuesday to interview the two heroes before he dashed off to a planned press conference on the matter to be given by the police. Sir Ian had also arranged a rota of bodyguards to accompany each of the two actors about their business until they could be sure all threat had passed.

To crown a satisfying day, Toby returned home to find a message from Matthew that Alexandra was indeed going to turn King's evidence, and was already singing her little heart out, although how many of the lyrics she warbled were true only time would tell. Vera had agreed to reveal everything she knew, as had two other employees of the company. While the authorities couldn't be sure that any chance of an attack had been foiled, they were confident this one wouldn't happen and were on high alert for any other disruptions. Alasdair also got in touch to say Morgan had been to see Dennis and reported that he was heartbroken. As was Nicholas, who was threatening to eschew women for life and join a monastery. Which might seem appropriate if your most recent experience of ladies had been Alexandra.

"They're supposed to be meeting, tonight. The *Monday Evening Association*," Toby said. "I wonder if they'll turn up to find the offices locked and Lloyd nowhere to be found?"

"No. I realised the date and forestalled it by ringing Moira this afternoon. I told her about Alexandra and said not to turn up at Eagle Street tonight as events had run on at a lick and maybe grabbing one of the evening papers might be an idea. I think they'll all go to the *Swan* instead, to mull over the news. I got Jeff's telephone number for you, too," Alasdair added, with a cackle. "After what he hears tonight and whatever the newspapers report over the next few days, he should be ripe for his pep talk."

"I hope so. With any luck, he'll have seen the error of his ways and asked Moira out by the end of this evening so my job will be done. Then there's just Fred and Vera to nudge."

***

The following Tuesday, Toby met Jeff—at *St Bride's Tavern*, because the location felt like it brought him luck—and delivered his distant star line, with great success. Jeff confessed complete ignorance about how Moira felt, but that surprise soon turned to optimism at the thought that she might like him as he was, rather than wanting him to change, as his ex-wife had. The meeting had proved so effective that Toby decided to craft a final knot in the loose ends of the case on his way home.

He took a cab the short distance to Eagle Street and asked the driver to wait, clock running, while he nipped in and left a message for his pal at Clanfield House. He entered the building to be greeted by Fred's cheery cry of, "Mr Bowe! I've been reading about your adventures in the paper. It's all been going on here, as well. Coppers up and down the stairs like yo-yos."

"So I hear. Augean stables job, I think."

"I'm not sure what you mean by that, but if it's clearing out a load of old junk, you're right." Fred thrust out his hand to shake Toby's. "I want to thank you all for what you did for Vera. She's like a dog with two tails over her new job."

"A pleasure, Fred. She's a lovely woman, as is her mother. Even if her sherry's on the strong side."

"*She's* made up, too. Hasn't stopped talking about your visit and how she wonders if she played a small part in getting this mob sorted." Fred jerked his thumb towards the door Toby had taken when he'd come to that first Monday meeting. "I guess the full story will come out in the news, because it's a bit of a mystery at present."

"As much as can come out," Toby said. "I can't tell you anything at present, I'm afraid, except that we hope it's a job well done. Two jobs, really. You played your part and so did Vera, for both of them."

"More to come for her, too. Reckons it'll be an Old Bailey job."

"She'll have to wear her best black frock in the witness box, then." Toby leaned closer, like he always did onscreen when giving Alasdair advice. "See if Ted can cover those days, if it's your turn on the rota, because she'll need a good friend at her side."

"She will that." Fred rubbed his forehead. "Maybe that'll be my chance. I've been like you are in your films, Mr Bowe, if you follow me. Always the one admiring Fiona and getting nowhere cos she's got her eye on Mr Hamilton."

"I follow you indeed, Fred. But this isn't the films, and I don't think you've got an Alasdair as a rival." He saluted the

287

doorman and grinned. "Once more into the breach, my friend. You'd make a lovely pair."

***

The second of June seemed to come round in a flash. Toby and Alasdair enjoyed every minute of their glorious party watching the magnificent coronation parade, despite the hideous British weather's attempts to throw a soggy blanket over the event. They'd then settled down to watch the coronation itself via a small screen with fuzzy monochrome images. While everyone present enjoyed the novelty of the device, most of them felt it would never replace the experience of watching a film in the cinema.

As the drizzle fell, Toby imagined Chapman sitting in his cell somewhere, maybe looking out of a window at the rain and convincing himself that *he* was responsible for bringing a damp touch to the proceedings, rather than blaming a typically unpredictable English summer day. Chapman would no doubt be furious if he discovered the precipitation hadn't dampened the spirits of Queen Salote, who'd been smiling and waving in the rain and generally winning hearts all round. Hopefully somebody would give him a full account or he'd be allowed to read the story in a newspaper. Some poetic justice to add to the all too real justice he'd be facing.

"Isn't she beautiful?" Alasdair said, referring to the newly crowned Elizabeth the Second.

"She is. Solomon in all his glory couldn't match her." Toby raised his umpteenth glass of champagne. "Here's a health unto her majesty."

"A toast to our small part in making the day a success, as well." Alasdair chinked his glass against Toby's, then mouthed, "To the king of my heart, too."

"Hear hear." Toby would take a vow of allegiance on that count any time it was required.